COME TO THE CAPE

EMI HILTON

5 PRINCE PUBLISHING
5PRINCEBOOKS.COM

Published by:

5 Prince Publishing and Books, LLC

DBA 5 Prince Publishing

PO Box 865

Arvada, Colorado 80001

Digital ISBN: 978-1-63112-425-9

Print ISBN: 978-1-63112-426-6

Cover design by Marianne Nowicki

Interior design by 5 Prince Publishing

First Edition F09162025

For more information about this title, visit: www.5princebooks.com

To those beautiful years I lived in Boston.

ACKNOWLEDGMENTS

First, a huge heartfelt thank you to my readers. Thank you for following me on this writing journey, sharing my novels with friends and family, leaving me five-star reviews, and interacting with me on social media. With every book of mine that you share with a friend, my readership grows, so thank you.

A big thank you to the editing students at BYU, Raquel Wilson, Kaylee Ann Ashby, and Alyssa Knutti. Thank you for reading this novel in its most raw form and helping me to shape it on its journey to what it has become. I truly appreciate your kind and thoughtful feedback. And I am grateful for the time and energy you spent helping to turn this story into something truly special.

To my editor, Cate Byers, as always it was a pleasure working with you. I appreciate your constant nudges to help me grow and develop in my craft. Thank you for championing my work and helping make this story shine brightly.

To my publisher, 5 Prince Publishing, thank you for finding the beauty and merit in this story. I am forever grateful that so many of my stories have found a home at your publishing house. I'm thankful to the entire 5 Prince team who grant me a mountain of support and guidance. A thousand thanks.

As always, I am nothing without my better half, Tyler. Thank you for believing in me, especially when I don't always believe in myself. I know every dream is possible with you by my side. I cherish the years we have shared together, and I hope for many more. I love you always and forever.

To my friends and family, thank you for sharing my books with your friends. Thank you for listening to me talk about deadlines and storylines. I know without your network of support championing me and my work, I would be lost. So, thank you.

Finally, I thank God, my faithful Father in Heaven. I know I am nothing without thee. I am grateful for thy never-ending grace and love. I thank thee for giving me the gift to write and for opening doors for me beyond my own doing. In all things, I humbly devote the glory and honor to thee.

ALSO BY EMI HILTON

COME TO THE CAPE

CHAPTER ONE

Without hesitation, Melissa shoved her hand into the half-eaten bag of Hershey's kisses. "There you go, kiddo." She tossed one over her shoulder to her five-year-old daughter, Ellie, in the back seat of her sensible sedan.

Sure, she'd pay for it later, but for a few seconds, she basked in the beauty of silence. Then she grabbed a few for herself, unwrapping and popping them into her mouth in rapid succession. Afterward, she balled up the foil wrappers into a tidy little pile in her cupholder. She wished she could blame the half-eaten bag on Ellie, but the kisses were her personal kryptonite—they had been since she was a kid. She used to eat them on the back porch with her brother, Andrew and his best friend, Luke.

Luke used to buy a bag big enough to share from the corner convenience store when they got a hankering for a treat. Andrew was always good about letting her stick around and hang out with them, even though she was two years younger. It became their thing: Hershey's kisses and late-night summer chats. The night that Melissa's boyfriend dumped her in ninth grade, Andrew and Luke bought her a bag and they all ate the chocolates together while she cried. The boys managed to cheer her up by slingshotting the foil wrappers across the porch, trying to hit the lights along the railing. Even now, she couldn't eat one without smiling from the memory.

As she peered out the passenger side window, she watched the mile markers fade into a sea of green behind her. Ellie hollered from the back seat for another Hershey's kiss, and Melissa catapulted one to her in a swift movement any baseball player would be proud of. Ellie captured it in her tiny fist. Her blue eyes matched Melissa's own, but Ellie's blonde hair differed from her light brown locks. Years prior, she used to spend a fortune on highlights. She tried not to dwell on yet one more thing she'd had to give up after her ex-husband cheated on her.

It's best not to focus on the past.

Today they had Hershey's kisses.

Melissa cheered when Ellie caught the piece of chocolate.

She caught her smile through the rearview mirror.

Winning.

By now the crowded streets of Boston were far away, and they inched their way closer to the calm, meandering roads of Cape Cod. In the few minutes of quiet, her mind wandered to the conversation she'd had with her mom two months prior.

"Come here, to the Cape," her mom had said over speakerphone as Melissa munched on a chip during her lunch break.

Lunch break—more like a few short minutes where she attempted to shovel food into her mouth while answering emails.

"The Cape?" Melissa repeated. "I don't know …"

She'd mulled over the idea. It wasn't the worst way to spend her upcoming three-month sabbatical. Cape Cod had always held a special place in her heart; she'd grown up on the Cape.

Located only an hour-and-a-half drive from Boston, where she lived and worked, it could be the perfect way to spend her break.

Lack of time and energy to plan an extravagant three-month trip made the Cape a viable option. Also, where else would she take a five-year-old who preferred parks and beaches to cathedrals and museums? But one thing held true: she needed this sabbatical, more than anything. The past five years had been one long, hazy fog as a single mom. Every midnight feeding, every cold and flu, every tantrum—she had handled it on her own. And boy, was she tired. The bone-dead, can-you-die-from-lack-of-sleep type of tired. You probably can't, by the way. She'd googled it.

The sandy beaches of her childhood called her name. Sand between her toes with nowhere to go sounded like a dream. Then she'd remembered the bike rides, the saltwater taffy, and the clam chowder. Most of all, she'd thought of Luke.

"Yes, come!" her mom had continued. "Ellie could play with Cole. You'd get a break. Plus, Dad and I are headed on that European cruise all summer. We'd feel better not leaving the house empty. You can house-sit for us."

"Well ..." She'd ripped off the foil top of her yogurt and shoved a spoonful into her mouth. A bit dribbled down her chin and splattered onto her shirt. Melissa had desperately glanced around for something to wipe it off, and spotting the box of tissues, had yanked one out. "When you phrase it like that—" She swiped the yogurt off her chin and then dabbed at her shirt. Useless, the stain remained.

"You can't refuse it," stated her mom matter-of-factly. "So, come to the Cape. You know everything is more magical here in the summer. And it's about time Ellie saw where you grew up. She's five, and she's only spent a few weekends here."

It was true. Traveling with a newborn and toddler, even for

a relatively short drive, had been intimidating for her. Most of the time, Melissa's parents traveled to her to lessen her stress. With Ellie a little older now, she hoped for her daughter to spend more time on the Cape.

She crumpled the tissue and tossed it into the trash. "Right."

"You have nowhere else to go. Unless you've piled up cash that I don't know about. I know you make decent money, but I also know it all gets eaten up with rent and childcare."

"Yikes." Melissa winced. "Way to go straight for the jugular."

"You know I'm right."

Melissa contemplated finishing her yogurt but decided against it. "Um," She tossed the half-eaten carton into the trash can. "It's true that living in Boston isn't cheap. And I should probably put my extra money toward my retirement and not some lavish vacation Ellie won't even appreciate at this age." She pondered her mom's proposal for a moment, then continued, "I thinking coming to the Cape is a nice idea. We'll watch the house, you'll go on your trip of a lifetime, and I'll get a much-needed break from work."

Her job as a software engineer offered a sabbatical every four years as part of their benefits package, a nice perk Melissa needed to cash in on. Especially since her ex had yet to pay a dime of child support.

So, the Cape it was.

Melissa had ended the call and spent the next few weeks making the necessary preparations for her sabbatical. Then when she'd packed up her car with their suitcases, she'd practically hummed to herself. Three months with nothing to do.

Come to the Cape, the sea breeze whispered to her.

"How much longer, Mommy?" Ellie asked, interrupting her thoughts.

Melissa flashed her gaze to the rearview mirror. Ellie stared out the passenger side window and ran her finger down it, leaving long, chocolatey streaks.

"Not too much longer." Melissa readjusted her grip on the steering wheel. "We're almost to the Cape."

"What's the cape?" Ellie removed her chocolate-coated, sticky fingers from the window. She promptly stuck them into her mouth and licked some stray chocolate off, but somehow it only smeared further across her face. How in the world had Ellie managed to make such a mess with only two Hershey's kisses? They weren't even big.

"The Cape is short for Cape Cod, where Nana and Papa live. Remember, I told you we are going to stay there for summer while Mom takes some time off work. Nana and Papa are gallivanting around Europe, so it'll just be us at their house. We'll go to the beach every day, take bike rides, and walk to town for ice cream. It is going to be awesome! Uncle Andrew and Aunt Olivia live in Cape Cod too, so you'll get to play with Cole."

Ellie snapped her head forward at the mention of her cousin. "Promise?" she asked earnestly.

"Promise." Melissa made an *x* motion over her heart.

Then she caught the wide smile on Ellie's face. Her heart melted a little. Cole and Ellie were only a few months apart, and they loved playing together. Luckily, Andrew and his wife Olivia were good about coming up to Boston to visit, but it had still been a while since the kids had seen each other.

The tension between her shoulder blades loosened. She rolled the windows down a few inches, letting the tangy breeze drifting off the ocean filter through the cab of the car. With each mile away from Boston, her stress dissipated a bit more. They would be okay, she knew. This sabbatical came at the perfect time. Melissa had three whole months to relax, regroup, and revitalize herself, and spend time with Ellie before she went to kindergarten in the fall. She hoped it would give her the break she needed; she enjoyed her work but had spent the past years torn in a million different directions.

Andrew, who was the local dentist, promised to bring over Cole a bunch and even offered Melissa and Ellie free dental cleanings. Which didn't sound like much, but she hadn't had the time to visit the dentist in at least a year, and a crown on her back molar was giving her trouble.

Twenty minutes later, Melissa pulled into her parents' driveway. From the back porch, you could see the Atlantic Ocean and a sandy trail of beach ran from one side of the home out to the water. Picturesque, absolutely, but come winter, this place was colder than cold. Just thinking about all those winters here as a child made her shiver. Today, though, it was a breezy seventy. *Yeah, come to the Cape, but only in the summer*, she thought.

As soon as she parked the car, Ellie unbuckled herself, scrambled out of her booster seat, and shot out of the car. She bounded up the front steps.

Melissa opened her own door and shouted, "Ellie, come back, honey. Remember, Nana and Papa aren't home, and I have the key. Plus, you need to help carry things inside. I can't do it all on my own."

An audible groan was followed by the dragging of light-up sneakers across the creaky wood of the porch and back down the stairs. It made her smile. Parenting alone wasn't easy. Her ex-husband, Grant, left her when she was pregnant. He'd never even laid eyes on Ellie, which meant every parenting decision was on her. Many times, she wondered if she was doing anything right. Then every so often, Melissa felt a pinch of confirmation that Ellie was going to turn out fine.

She wished she could give Ellie a dad, but the dating pool of single men in their thirties was pretty limited. After a few very rocky dates, she gave up, years ago. Her life consisted of work and Ellie. Dating—yeah, that wasn't happening. A future husband for her and stepdad for Ellie wasn't likely in the cards for them, not when Melissa's weekends were spent in sweatpants taking her daughter to places she couldn't during the week.

Melissa rounded the car and popped open the trunk. Ellie arrived beside her as she unloaded a few of the roller suitcases onto the driveway. One attempted to roll away, and she stopped it with her foot and gently pushed it toward the front lawn, where it stopped in place.

Ellie peered up at her with wide blue eyes and chocolate-smeared cheeks. "Can we go to the beach today?"

"Umm," Melissa reached into her purse and retrieved a wipe. She motioned for Ellie to come closer.

She wiped her face with it.

"Ouch," Ellie whined.

"Oh, you'll live." Once her face was clean enough to be passable, Melissa wadded up the wipe and shoved it back into her purse. "There, much better." She refocused on unloading the trunk.

"So can we go to the beach today?" Ellie clasped her hands together in a plea. "Please?"

"Yes, we can go once we get unpacked." Melissa unloaded the last suitcase and closed the trunk. "And we're here for three months. We'll get to go to the beach every day."

"Woohoo!" Ellie pumped her little fist then used her fingers to swipe messy blonde hair from her eyes.

Dang it, she'd forgotten to wipe her hands off. Mother of the year, everyone.

"Melissa?" A voice came from behind her. "Hold on there, girl."

Melissa swiveled around. Her eyes widened as they landed on a man crouched down, rubbing the back of his mini poodle. Luke. As in her brother's best friend from high school. Luke, as in the guy who she'd loved so fiercely for so long that very sight of him made her pulse simmer and heart gallop. Yep, that Luke. And he looked good. He still had his full head of messy, dark locks. His shoulders somehow looked broader than she remembered, like maybe he had started going to CrossFit. And somehow the wrinkles around his eyes made him look wiser and more distinguished rather than older.

"Luke?" Melissa instinctively smoothed out the top of her hair. "Is that you?"

Why, oh, *why* had she worn this tattered t-shirt today? She couldn't remember the last time she'd washed her hair, and it showed. Of all those times she had dreamed of seeing him again in the flesh, this was not how she pictured it. In her daydreams, she was wearing her sexiest outfit and a full face of makeup that made the dark circles under her eyes disappear. This couldn't be happening. She already had an imaginary strike against her in a game she only played with herself.

"It's me, alright." He flashed her a smile and continued to pet his dog between the ears.

Ellie tugged on Melissa's hand. "Mom, you promised we'd go to the beach."

Melissa's eyes stayed glued to Luke. She almost felt that if she looked away, he wouldn't be real. "We will, sweetie. Give me a second." Melissa squeezed Ellie's hand. "Luke—it's good to see you again."

Luke gave his dog one last pat and stood. "Likewise." His six-foot-three frame towered over Melissa's average height and slender build.

Why did it look like his skin glistened? Had his jaw always been that sharp? What type of hair product did he use to get that perfect messy-but-trying look? The questions came in rapid succession, and she tried her best to shut them off and concentrate on holding the conversation.

He scratched at the scruff along his jaw. "Andrew mentioned you were coming to town for the summer." His dog barked and he made a motion with his free hand. The dog obediently sat back on its hind legs. "This can't be Ellie? I can't believe how much she's grown since the last time I saw her!"

Melissa glanced down at Ellie, giving her a crooked smile. "I know, right? Kids do that to you. But she's five now." Then, feeling brave, she met his dazzling hazel eyes.

"Yes!" Ellie smiled shyly and held up her hand with fingers spread widely. "I'm five. I'm going into kindergarten."

"My, my, you don't say!" Luke said, winking at Melissa.

Heat grew in her middle. So, nothing had changed. Melissa still had the hots for Luke. And it seemed she was still nothing more than Andrew's sister. A girl he maybe flirted with but never asked out. *Geez, she sounded like she was back in high school.*

"We just arrived, but you heard right. I'm here for the summer." Melissa bit her bottom lip, then awkwardly shoved her free hand into the pocket of her sweatpants. "I'd love to get together with you sometime to catch up."

It wasn't like Melissa didn't know every little detail of his life. She always asked Andrew about him in a sly, casual way. She knew way too many details about him breaking off his engagement to his college girlfriend a while back. She had even found out before Andrew that Luke's parents had left him their bed and breakfast in Cape Cod, causing him to leave his corporate law job in Boston. She doubted he had tracked her life as closely as she had followed his.

Luke pulled back on his dog's leash, patting the dog

between the ears. "I'd love that. How long has it been since I've seen you?"

Two years. Funny how Melissa knew that immediately. It was two years ago that she thought they'd shared a moment together after his mom's funeral wake. Her parents had taken Ellie back to their house and Melissa had stayed back with Andrew and Olivia to help serve food and clean up. After the guests left, Olivia and Andrew loaded the folding chairs and tables into the garage while Luke and Melissa washed the dishes in the kitchen.

Melissa scrubbed pots and pans and handed them to Luke to dry. When she was up to her elbows in soapy water, Luke whispered, "I can't believe they're both gone."

Melissa pivoted to face him, swiping at the loose strands of her hair with the back of her wrist. Earlier, she had curled her hair into beachy waves, something she did often in her pre-kid years but not now. Since Ellie was born, she had mainly worn it up.

"Losing both of your parents in less than a year—that's rough. I'm so sorry." She met his gaze and held it. "For what it's worth, I think you're holding it together incredibly well."

He leaned his back against the counter. "What am I going to do now?" His voice cracked, making her stomach twist. "I'm probably going to have to move back here, take over Bayberry House. I don't know how to do that. Where do I even begin?" He looked away from her. Tears tickled the corners of his eyes, but he blinked them away before they spilled over.

Melissa placed the pot she'd been washing back in the sink and shut off the water. She wiped her wet hands on the front of her dress. "Hey," she said softly, lightly touching his forearm. "You're Luke. There isn't anything you can't do." She moved her hand to his shoulder. "If anyone can figure this thing out, if anyone is strong enough to face this—it's you."

"I don't feel strong." Luke's gaze bored into hers. "Will it ever be any easier?"

"I don't know." Melissa squeezed his shoulder. "But little by little, with each day that passes, things will get better." Then she tugged him into a tight embrace.

He melted against her. "Thanks, Melon," Luke whispered, his breath tickling her neck.

Hearing him use her childhood nickname made her smile against his chest.

Then Olivia and Andrew barreled into the kitchen. Melissa and Luke jumped away from one another. The moment was whisked away, leaving as quickly as it came. She knew Luke was grieving, and she wanted nothing more than to be able to take some of his pain away.

Once everything was clean, the leftover food packed away into the fridge, Luke walked the three of them out to their cars to drive home. Luke hugged Andrew and Olivia first and thanked them again for coming. They drove home, leaving Melissa alone with Luke for the first time since that moment in the kitchen. In silence, they shuffled the few feet to where Melissa had parked.

"Thanks for coming." Luke went in for the hug first. Melissa sank into the curves of his arms, wrapping her arms around his trim waist. He whispered into her ear, "I'm so glad you were here, Melon."

There it was again, the name that moved her back into a never-ending childlike state in his mind.

"I'm glad I could make it back," Melissa whispered back.

Before he broke their embrace, Luke kissed her gently on her temple. "I hope you know you'll always feel like family to me, even more so now with mine gone."

The feeling of his lips had lingered long after she left Cape Cod that night. For the next two years, she would replay the moment over and over again in her mind. She'd memorized the feeling of his chest pressed against hers, and the tender graze of his lips on her skin. It meant everything to her and most likely nothing to him.

"I think it was your mom's funeral," offered Melissa.

"Really?" He furrowed his brow. "I think you're right. Thanks again for coming to that. It really meant a lot that you were—"

Interrupting them, Ellie loosened her hand from Melissa's. "Can I pet your dog?" She inched closer to him and his dog.

"Absolutely. Gigi here loves kids." Luke crouched back down, wrapping the leash a few times around his hand to tighten his grip. "Pet her right here." He ran a hand again between Gigi's ears then patted her back end. She sat obediently on the sidewalk.

Ellie rubbed her hand back and forth between Gigi's ears.

Luke smiled first at Ellie. "You're doing an excellent job." Then he peered up at Melissa and smiled again. "She's a natural with her. Do you have a dog at home?"

"No way," Ellie piped up. She ran a hand along Gigi's back. "Mom says we can't have one."

Melissa nodded. "Our apartment complex doesn't allow pets."

"Ahh. I see." Luke nodded. "You're welcome to come over anytime to Bayberry House if you want to pet Gigi. I don't mind sharing her. If it's okay with your mom, of course." He stood back up, slowly unrolling the leash so it hung loosely by his side.

"Really?" Ellie gave the dog one last pat then scampered to her feet. "Can we, Mom? Please?"

"I—" Melissa bit her bottom lip. Her heart rate ticked up. "I don't see why not." She brushed a hand over the top of Ellie's hair to smooth it out.

Seeing Luke act so naturally with Ellie was doing all sorts of things to her insides. Growing up, Luke always treated Melissa kindly. She remembered that when she got her braces off, he was the first person to compliment her on her new smile.

"Yippee!" Ellie cheered and did a little half jump, half jig.

They both laughed at Ellie's dance. For a moment, Luke and Melissa stared back at each other.

Luke spoke first. "I guess I'd better be going." He stepped past her. "It really is great seeing you. Don't be a stranger! I hope you'll come by Bayberry House."

"Okay," she mustered. "I will. I'll bring Ellie by to see Gigi sometime."

Luke grinned, making his eyes dance. "Bye, Ellie." He moved to leave with Gigi tugging at the leash.

"Bye." Ellie bounded back up the porch steps.

Once Luke was out of sight, Melissa stared down at her winkled college tee and sweatpants. They weren't even chic athleisure sweats. She cringed and pinched the bridge of her nose. Since they'd been teenagers, Luke had managed to get hotter while she looked like a train wreck. She guessed that was what being a single mom could do to a person. The thing was, she hadn't really cared until today.

CHAPTER TWO

Melissa made quick work of dragging their suitcases up the stairs and into the bedrooms they were staying in. They needed to unpack and get groceries, but Ellie begged her to go to the beach. And she decided those things could wait.

She reached into the pocket of her sweatpants to retrieve her phone. "I'm going to text Uncle Andrew to see if he and Cole can come join us too."

Andrew had instructed her to text him when they arrived. He planned on taking the afternoon off.

"I hope he can come," Ellie said.

A minute later, her phone dinged. It was Andrew agreeing to bring Cole to the beach in a little while. She shoved it back into her pocket then clapped her hands together.

"It looks like they can come." Melissa motioned Ellie to follow her to her bedroom. She unzipped the suitcase that contained their swimsuits. Once she located Ellie's, she tossed it to her. "Get dressed. I will too. Then we need to get the sand toys out of the garage."

They both changed, then Ellie obediently followed her out to the garage. Melissa dug out the sand toys, putting them in a mesh bag for Ellie to carry. After she strapped a beach chair to her back and grabbed an umbrella, they scuttled out of the garage, rounded the side of the house, and followed the sandy path down to the beach.

The minute the ocean came into view, the tension in Melissa's shoulder blades loosened. The cool sea breeze played with her hair, blowing some in front of her face. Sunshine tickled her arms. Salty air filled her lungs. She forgot about the heavy load she had been carrying around for the past five years. *Come to the Cape.* Her mom had been right—this place was magic in the summer. Sand squished between her toes with each step she took toward the water's edge.

With only a few yards to go until they reached the hard-packed wet sand, Ellie sprinted toward the water, tossing the mesh bag of sand toys at the edge of the dry sand. Soon, the water nipped at Ellie's ankles. She shrieked with delight, making Melissa smile to herself.

Melissa cupped her mouth with one hand as she set down her chair and umbrella next to the forgotten sand toys. "Remember to not go past your waist!"

Ellie giggled as a wave rushed past her knees. She had been in swimming lessons practically since birth and was a strong swimmer for her age, but still Melissa worried about the dangers of the ocean and unpredictable riptides.

Ellie held both her thumbs up. "I won't!"

The water rose around her little body as she edged further and further out. Soon it came to her waist.

Melissa's heart rate racketed. "That's far enough."

Ellie stopped as directed. Then she dipped her hands in the water, splashing it around. Melissa kept her eye on her daughter as she unfolded her chair and set up her umbrella. Then she sat and relaxed in the shade. They rarely went to the beach though Ellie loved it, which meant Ellie was happy to play by herself.

Melissa knew not every day would be like this, but for the first time in nearly five years, she relaxed.

Ellie played. Melissa watched. Summer sun warmed her skin, and she stretched her legs out in front of herself. About an hour later, Andrew arrived with Cole in tow.

On their arrival, Melissa jumped out of her chair. "Hey!" She held her arms out to him in an embrace, "it's so good to see you."

"You too, sis," Andrew replied as they hugged.

Letting go of Andrew, she crouched down and gave Cole a hug. But he quickly scampered out of her embrace and raced toward the water to join Ellie.

"I see how it is," Melissa laughed. "I've been outranked by my daughter."

"Don't take it personally." Andrew set up his chair next to hers and settled into his seat. "I've been outranked by pretty much everything else too."

They watched the two cousins play together in the water. It made Melissa smile. She wished she could've given Ellie a sibling, but a cousin was the next best thing.

"Do you think you're going to miss working this summer?" Andrew asked. "I know how much your job feeds your soul."

"Hmm ..." Melissa wondered the same thing. At work, she thrived and felt competent and capable, a feeling that she didn't always get as a mother. "I was ready for a break. If anything, I felt like I needed some time to focus on just Ellie. I know my job will be waiting for me when I get back, and I'll be thrown right back into the chaos of it all. I'm hoping this summer will be good for me, and for Ellie too. How about you? How is the dental practice doing these days?"

"Really well," Andrew said. "We've been so busy that I had to hire another hygienist."

"I'm glad to hear it. I hope you can pencil Ellie and me in for some cleanings," Melissa said.

"Of course. Just call the office and we'll get it set up."

They watched the kids play for a minute.

Then she remarked, "I saw Luke today when I arrived. He was out on a walk with Gigi when I was unloading my car."

"That's nice," he said casually. "I went golfing with him last week, but I probably need to text him again to see when he can meet up. He's a busy guy—I mean, I am too."

Melissa rubbed her hands back and forth on her thighs. "Right." She didn't want to reveal how much she wanted to know about every little detail about him, like when he'd transformed from cute to downright hot. "I'll bet Bayberry House keeps him busy."

She itched to ask about his personal life, but she didn't want Andrew to suspect she was interested in Luke. For all these years, she had kept her never-ending crush tightly packed away. The last thing she wanted was for Andrew to tease her about it.

Andrew stretched his legs out and crossed them at the ankles. "Yeah—" He abruptly pointed toward the kids. "Do you think they've gone out too far?"

Melissa shouted out at the water, "You're out too far!" She scampered to her feet and grabbed the bag of sand toys, edging closer to the waves. "Why don't you both come play in the sand for a while?"

Ellie and Cole exchanged glances then dashed toward her. She dumped the contents of the mesh bag onto the sand. The kids busied themselves with the toys, and she returned to her chair.

Once she settled back into her seat, Andrew remarked, "Luke's been dating one of my dental hygienists, Ashley, for a few months. I set them up. You'd like her. She's sweet, and they seem good together. We've gone on a few double dates with them, but it's still pretty new."

A sinking feeling spread through Melissa's gut. She kept her gaze on the kids. She hated how much she cared; how much she wished Luke would look her way just once. Then she reminded herself it was a childhood crush, and those tended to be the hardest to shake, no matter how much time had passed.

"That's great to hear." Melissa tried her best to sound enthusiastic. "I'm glad he's happy. From what you told me, his broken engagement was tough on him, and I'm sure he really misses his parents. I'm glad to hear he's found someone."

"It's the happiest I've seen him in a long time."

"Fantastic," Melissa added with a tad too much gusto.

Andrew furrowed his brows, probably noticing that she was acting strange. She added hurriedly, "Good for him—dating past thirty can be challenging, to put it mildly."

Andrew nodded, his earlier suspicion vanishing. "Yeah. Speaking of which, I know you don't have many opportunities to date in Boston, being a single mom and all. But I want to set you up with someone while you're here."

"What? Have you lost your mind?" Melissa shoved him. "What have you done?"

"So," Andrew continued without a bit of hesitation, "there's Jake, Cole's pediatrician. He's a really nice guy, never married. I ran into him the other day at the grocery store and mentioned you would be in town for the summer. He seemed more than interested after I showed him your picture."

Her eyes widened. "You're kidding." She tilted her head. "Tell me you're kidding."

"Nope."

She groaned, then asked, "What picture did you show him?" Melissa waved a hand. "Wait—I don't want to know."

Andrew yanked his cell phone out of the pocket of his

shorts. He tapped the screen a few times then pulled up a photo. He held the phone up for her to see. "This one."

"When was this?" Melissa snatched the phone out of his hands. It was a decent photo of her, one from last summer when Andrew and his family came up to visit them for the weekend. "At least you picked a recent one." She handed the phone back to Andrew.

He shoved it back into his pocket. "I know a photo goes a long way. After I showed him, he seemed excited to meet you. This is a small town, not a lot of new women move here, and most walking around are tourists. You can't blame him for being interested."

"I—I—" Melissa pinched the bridge of her nose. "I'm so mad at you right now. Regardless, I'm not looking to date anyone. I don't have time." Melissa peered out at the ocean. Cole and Ellie knelt side by side and dug with their bare hands for sand crabs. The toys were scattered everywhere and a half-built sandcastle had been abandoned. "Plus, I have Ellie."

"So?"

"So," Melissa shifted in her seat, "that makes me someone who most men run *from*, not *to*."

Andrew tsked. "Hey, not every guy is going to treat you like Grant did. Cheating on you then abandoning you when you're pregnant is not a normal thing."

"Doesn't exactly encourage me to try again," Melissa muttered.

A tinge of hurt clenched her heart. Years later, she still carried the sting of such callous betrayal. But she tried to remind herself that her life was full and busy with Ellie and work. Sure, a husband would be nice—someone to share the highs and lows with—but sometimes it was easier when one person did everything.

Yet every so often, she would catch Ellie watching dads at

the park or when they went out to eat. She'd started asking questions about her own father, which was usually followed by a firm declaration that Melissa needed to find her a new dad. Melissa wished that was something she could give Ellie. Maybe someday, when the time was right, she could. But then fear overtook her, and she worried she'd just pick wrong again.

For a long time, she and Andrew stared out at their kids playing together at the edge of the water. Hearing Ellie's laughter made Melissa glow with happiness. A peace settled over her. This summer, she could give Ellie something different, something special. Maybe not a dad, but at least her undivided attention.

"It wasn't your fault." Andrew's voice broke through her thoughts. "I just want to see you happy and with a guy who treats you right. Isn't that what every good brother wants for their sister?"

She knew deep down that Andrew cared and meant well.

"I know you want to see me happy and with someone. But I don't know if that's in the cards for me. I don't see myself ever remarrying."

"Do you mind me asking why not?"

"Honestly?"

Andrew nodded.

She exhaled and geared up to reveal her deepest, darkest secret. "I don't have it in me to get hurt again. It would kill me."

"Melissa—" His voice was so full of compassion it made her stomach swim.

She cut him off. "Drop it, Andrew." She shifted to face him and gave him her most challenging stare. "I have Ellie. It's enough for now. It took me so long to recover after that dirtbag left me pregnant and alone. I can't do it again. I just can't."

"Okay." Andrew sounded defeated, like he regretted bringing any of it up.

"I'm not complicating my life with someone new."

"Noted." He pursed his lips.

Ellie screeched and scurried away from a big wave in time to avoid being clobbered. Cole chased after her. Melissa and Andrew quieted, which allowed them to listen as the sea breeze mingled with the kids' joyous cries. A seagull swooped in front of them, then landed on a cluster of rocks poking out of the water. After a few minutes of silence, Andrew announced, "I need to get back." He scooted out of his beach chair.

Melissa checked her watch and realized how late it was getting. "Me too." She started to form a mental list of everything she needed to do before bedtime.

They called the kids to come in from the water.

"We're having a cookout tonight." He strapped his folded chair to his back. "You and Ellie should come."

"Thanks." Melissa tugged the umbrella out of the stand and closed it. "That sounds perfect. I haven't had a chance to run to the grocery store. We'll be there."

"Luke's coming with Ashley." Andrew waved at Cole for him to come. "It'll be a good time for you to meet her. We go out with them a lot, and I think you'll see how good they are together."

Melissa hated how her stomach twisted and her heart fell at his words. Luke deserved to be with someone he liked. She only wished it could be her.

"Perfect." Melissa yanked the umbrella stand out of the sand. Then she gathered it up with the umbrella and shoved it into the bag. "What time?"

"Come by around six-thirty."

Ellie and Cole arrived, wet and shivering. Melissa and Andrew wrapped towels around their shoulders.

Ellie's lips were blue and her teeth were chattering, but she wore a bright smile. "I love it here."

"I'm so glad." Melissa rubbed the top of her towel-covered arms to warm her up. "I love it here too. I'm glad I can share this place with you."

Andrew and Cole said goodbye and walked in the opposite direction toward their car.

"Come on." Melissa gathered up their belongings. Ellie picked up the sand toys. "We need to get you showered and changed before we head to Cole's house for dinner."

"I get to play with Cole again?" Ellie's eyes sparkled.

"Yep, kiddo. Get used to it." They trekked across the sand back to the house. "You're going to be playing with Cole all summer long."

CHAPTER THREE

Luke double-checked his watch as Gigi took her sweet time relieving herself on the front lawn of Bayberry House. He needed to leave in five minutes to pick up Ashley. His extensive list of to-dos rattled off in his head. Though he loved being back in Cape Cod, sometimes he missed the bustling city of Boston. When both his parents passed about two years ago, he had had no choice but to leave his corporate law job there to take over the B&B. At first, he'd enjoyed the change of pace, but now he found most tasks around the B&B cumbersome.

He'd tossed around the idea of selling it, but he wasn't quite ready to say goodbye. Carol, the longtime manager of Bayberry House, helped relieve some of the burden, but it wasn't enough for him to return to law. And recently, things had grown more serious with Ashley, which meant any of the ideas he'd entertained of leaving came to an abrupt halt. Perhaps he'd stay in the Cape forever. But the thought made him just the tiniest bit queasy.

Finally, Gigi finished. Luke bent down and bagged up the remains. "Come on, girl." He patted his thigh. Gigi rushed to his heels, wagging her adorable tail. "We have a cookout to get to."

Cole loved Gigi and liked to play with her, so Andrew and Olivia had encouraged him to bring her along too.

Luke jogged back up the big steps to the full wraparound porch. In the front, there were two porch swings guests enjoyed using. Luke himself spent summer nights sitting out on one of the swings, watching the tourists walk on by. Tonight was no different—the small town was abuzz with the out-of-towners. People passed by in a steady stream on the sidewalk that weaved past Bayberry House and down the street toward Main Street.

Summertime at the B&B bustled with excitement. Every room was filled, weekends were full of weddings, and family reunions often packed the place. In fall, things slowed down. Fewer and fewer tourists came with each passing week. By winter, the town only contained locals. Bayberry House depended on the summer season to carry it through the bleak winter months.

When he swung the front door open and entered the foyer with the check-in desk, Luke unhooked Gigi's leash. She promptly trotted over to her little dog bed behind the front reception desk. She plopped herself down and made herself comfortable.

Carol, who was in her sixties, was stationed behind the desk.

"So Carol," Luke hung the leash on the appropriate hook. "I'm headed out for dinner."

"Okay." Carol whacked him with a stack of opened bills. "You need to pay those bills by tomorrow or we won't have electricity come Monday."

He gathered the bills from her, leafing through them. "I'll do this first thing when I get back." He double-checked on Gigi then continued through the stack. "Ashley's coming with me to Andrew and Olivia's for a cookout." He paused on the water bill and groaned inwardly. A pipe in the basement busted last month. It had been a nightmare to get it shut off and fixed, and the extra water use had doubled the bill for the month.

"That sounds nice." Carol wiggled the mouse of the reception computer and pointed to a reservation on the screen. "Also don't forget—we have that wedding party checking in tomorrow. We'll need all hands on deck."

"Yes, of course." He placed the stack of bills into the drawer where he kept his ledger and checkbook. "Melissa's in town. Remember, Andrew's sister? Andrew mentioned he invited her to dinner too."

Seeing Melissa earlier had been a pleasant surprise. She'd grown up following him and Andrew around, since she was only a few years younger than them. He smiled as he remembered her from long ago, because almost every memory with his best friend was peppered with memories of her too.

"Melissa." Carol typed something into the computer. "I haven't seen her since your mom's funeral. I still remember how she and Andrew would come to Bayberry House all the time. That girl had the brightest blue eyes and cheekbones to die for."

Cheekbones? Was that a girl thing? He couldn't remember even once thinking about a woman's cheekbones. Luke had never seen Melissa as anything more than his friend's kid sister, but he imagined many guys did find her attractive, especially now.

"What's she up to?" Carol continued. "I still can't believe her husband left her. Melissa was always such a sweet girl. I hope things are going better for her now."

Carol had been the hotel manager for as long as Luke could remember. She was practically his second mom. When his mother passed, she stepped in and helped him with all of the funeral arrangements. She ordered the flowers, set up the service at the church, even called the newspaper to list his mom's obituary. Carol never questioned how to help—she simply saw what needed to be done and did it.

"Is she here for the summer?"

"Um, something like that." Luke leaned his back against the reception desk and crossed his arms. "Andrew said she's taking a sabbatical. Her daughter is with her, Ellie."

"So, I'm assuming if she's only here with Ellie that she never remarried?"

"Yeah, she hasn't remarried." Luke picked a piece of lint off his shirt. "From what Andrew has said, she hasn't really dated since her husband divorced her."

"Ahh, I see." Carol made a funny expression that he couldn't quite decipher.

He shifted closer. "What was that look about?"

"What look?" Carol opened a drawer and removed a stapler, feigning innocence. "I always thought she had a thing for you when you guys were kids. She used to follow you and Andrew around like a little puppy dog."

"I mean, she did follow us around." Luke scratched his head. "But it was mainly because there weren't any kids her age in the neighborhood. And I think she was more following her big brother around than me."

Luke had always cared for Melissa, but his feelings toward her were always platonic. They were friends. It meant so much that she had come to the funeral, and he enjoyed the familiarity she brought when she was around.

Carol shrugged. "Maybe I am wrong." She shuffled a stack of papers together, then stapled them in the corner. "There is a first for everything."

Luke chuckled. "True." He bent down and gathered up Gigi. She snuggled against his chest. "Well, I'm off."

Carol raised an eyebrow. "Are you taking Gigi?" She tossed the stapled papers into a bin. "I thought Ashley hated her."

"Ashley doesn't hate her. She's just ..." His voice trailed off as he tried to think up a comeback. "... not a dog person."

Carol paused, then opened a drawer and placed the stapler back inside. "But you are."

"I am." Luke hugged Gigi against his chest. He had adopted her after his broken engagement several years back. She'd filled the big gap in his heart and comforted him through one of the hardest times in his life. Gosh, he loved his dog. He wished Ashley did too, but he figured that sometimes you can't have it all. "Cole loves Gigi. Melissa's daughter, Ellie, met her this afternoon when I ran into them, so I thought she'd enjoy seeing Gigi too."

Carol shook her head. "Ashley is not going to like it."

"It's not a big deal." He smiled down at his fluffy, golden furball. "I'm sure Ashley will understand I'm bringing her for the kids."

Apparently, Ashley had had an incident back when she was kid. A dog nipped her hand, and since then she had avoided all dogs. But he wanted to believe that once she was around Gigi a bit more, she'd learn to love her like he did. Gigi would never bite anyone. Maybe this experience with Gigi and the kids could help Ashley see she was safe around her.

Carol muttered something under her breath that he couldn't make out.

"Why don't you say that a little louder so I can hear?"

"Nope." She pursed her lips together. "I'm keeping my mouth shut."

"Well, that would be a first," he teased.

She jutted her chin. "I can't help it if people need to be told where they are going wrong."

"Oh, is that what you tell yourself?"

Playfully, she whacked him on the arm. "I hope you have a

great dinner." Carol shooed him away. "Now, get out of here before I ask for another raise."

He traipsed to the door and before he left, he caught her worried expression.

There was a pit in his stomach as he drove to pick Ashley up. Her apartment was in a house that had been converted into four apartments. When he arrived, Luke bounded up the front steps and buzzed the intercom for her apartment.

"Coming," Ashley answered.

Luke waited outside. A minute later, Ashley emerged, looking gorgeous in a white summer sundress. Her tan made her skin glow against the crisp fabric. Luke greeted her with a kiss, and they walked hand in hand down to his car.

When Luke opened her car door, Gigi's head popped out and barked a hello. Ashley stumbled back. Her gaze whipped to him.

"Why did you bring your dog?" She tightened the grip on her clutch.

"Andrew invited his sister Melissa. I thought her daughter Ellie and Cole would enjoy playing with Gigi during the cookout."

Ashley grimaced. Her jaw tightened. "I told you, I'm not a dog person." She took another step back away from the car when Gigi barked again.

Luke grasped the corner of the door then leaned in and petted her between her ears to calm her down. "I didn't think you'd mind. Gigi is friendly, and she's a mini poodle. Everyone loves a poodle."

Ashley's fingers turned white as they dug into her clutch. "I don't."

Luke had underestimated Ashley's fear and dislike of dogs. She *really* didn't like them. He hated that Carol was right and that he'd ignored her warning. He regretted his choice to bring Gigi along.

He checked his watch. "Should I drop Gigi back off at Bayberry House?"

A trip back to the B&B would make them late, but Ashley's comfort mattered more. She was, after all, his girlfriend, and he shouldn't have pushed Gigi on her.

"No—" Ashley bit her bottom lip. "Could you at least tie her up or something? I don't want her jumping onto my lap in the car."

"Gigi is an obedient dog. She'll leave you alone." Luke leaned in and scooped her up, then opened the back passenger door. He set her back down on the seat. "Sit, Gigi," he instructed. Gigi lowered her hind legs, then her front legs. "Stay, girl." Luke rubbed her with a few long sweeping strokes. She relaxed her head against the seat. "See?" He smiled at Ashley. "Gigi will stay."

"Fine." His girlfriend's voice held no warmth. Her rigid posture made his stomach clench. She then whipped her head over her shoulder and narrowed her gaze at Gigi. "I don't know about this," Ashley muttered as she turned to look forward again.

She tugged down the hem of her dress. Luke prayed Gigi stayed as instructed, because the evening already had a weird vibe to it. He hoped the rest of it would go better. He shut Ashley's door and rounded the car.

When he climbed into the driver's seat, Ashley said, "You mentioned kids. I know Cole well but who else will be there?"

Luke started the engine. "Ellie, Melissa's five-year-old daughter." Then he peered over his shoulder to see if he could merge onto the road. A car passed. He waited.

"Melissa, Andrew's sister?" Ashley glanced over her

shoulder to the back seat, checking on Gigi. Only when she confirmed Gigi hadn't moved, she shifted forward again.

"Yep, the very one." With the road clear, he nudged the car away from the curb and merged onto the road. Their town was small—it would only be a short drive to Andrew and Olivia's.

"I remember Andrew mentioning she was headed into town, but I don't remember for how long."

"I guess her work gave her a sabbatical, so she'll be here the entire summer."

"That's nice." Ashley peered out her window. "She's a single mom, right?"

"Yeah."

"Well, it isn't easy being a single mom." Ashley's demeanor softened a bit. "I know how my mom struggled to raise me and my sister on her own."

"From what Andrew has mentioned, I think things were really rough for her when Ellie was a baby, but they've gotten easier for her as her daughter has grown."

"You're probably right." Ashley patted him on the forearm. "I look forward to meeting them. Andrew has spoken highly about his sister, and it will be nice to finally meet her in person."

They rounded the corner onto Andrew and Olivia's street. As soon as Luke parked the car in front of the house, Gigi leaped from the back seat into his arms.

"Oh no!" Ashley yelped, leaning away from him and Gigi. "Get that dog away from me!"

Luke flinched and snuggled Gigi tightly against his chest. "I'll keep her away from you, but I hope you can give Gigi a chance. I really think she'll convert you to being a dog lover. Gigi has won over many hearts." He picked Gigi up and brought her adorable face close to his. "I mean, look at this face."

Then with a tad too much hope, he shifted Gigi to face Ashley.

"Nah." Ashley flipped down the visor, revealing the little mirror. She rubbed her lips together then tilted her face this way and that way, checking out her image. "Some people aren't meant to have pets, and I'm definitely one of them." She opened her clutch and retrieved her lipstick. She reapplied it to her lips then slammed the visor shut.

He wondered where that left them, because he refused to get rid of Gigi. Maybe this was a red flag? If Ashley wasn't going to be flexible about her, then this relationship could be doomed to fail. He shook the thought away. They were only dating, and there was plenty of time to work out these slight differences.

"Okay." He unbuckled his seatbelt. "Let me grab your door."

With Gigi in one arm, Luke clambered out of the car and went around the front to her side. He opened her door, and Ashley climbed out. But when he reached for her hand, she sidestepped him and maintained a wide distance between them. Chatter and laughter drifted toward them from the backyard.

"Come on." He jerked his head toward the house. "We can go through the side gate. Then I can set Gigi down to run around in the back, and she'll have plenty of space to not go near you. I hope that will make you feel a little more comfortable."

They strode across the lawn to the gate. He opened it with his free hand while juggling Gigi in the other. Ashley passed through, and Luke latched it closed behind them. A concrete path wrapped around the house leading to a large grass area in the back. Andrew and Olivia's home wasn't on the beach, but a few blocks away from it. Even though they couldn't see the water, they could hear the waves crashing on the shore.

Luke loved their backyard, and through the years Andrew and Olivia had hosted him many times for cookouts and dinners. It almost felt like a second home to him. In the summer, the grass was green and inviting. Come wintertime, the grass would be covered in a foot of snow that never seemed to melt until late spring. It often left the grass brown and dead, but after a few months it regained its glory.

When they reached the back, they found Andrew grilling chicken and hot dogs on his barbecue. Cole and Ellie played a game of tag. Olivia and Melissa sat at the back patio table, chatting.

When Ellie spotted Luke and Ashley, she bolted toward them and yelled, "Gigi!" A huge smile was spread across her face.

Despite Ashley's prickly attitude toward Gigi, Luke was reassured he had made the right decision in bringing her.

"Hey, what about 'hey Luke'?"

Andrew chuckled.

"Ellie, make sure you say hi to Luke too," Melissa called from the patio.

"Hi!" Ellie raced the rest of the way to him and Ashley.

Sweaty and out of breath, Ellie landed in front of them. Ten seconds later, Cole collided to a stop at Ellie's heels.

"Can we play fetch with Gigi?" Cole asked. His eyes shone with childlike wonder. "We have some tennis balls."

"Sure." Luke smiled. "She loves to play catch."

Ashley stood stiffly by his side. She glanced around the yard at Andrew then up to the porch where Melissa and Olivia sat. Without another word, Cole bolted around the side of the house toward the garage, disappearing out of sight.

Ellie inched closer. "Can I hold her?" She didn't hesitate to run a hand down Gigi's back.

"Absolutely." Luke handed Ellie his dog. Once she was safely in her arms, he stepped back. "But as a warning, the minute she sees a ball, she'll leap out of your arms."

Ellie snuggled her face against her. "Okay."

Cole came back from the garage with a canister of tennis

balls. "I found them." He shook the canister, making them clank inside.

Gigi shimmied out of Ellie's arms and bolted across the yard to Cole. Ellie sped off behind her. Cole peeled the top off the canister and dropped it on the grass, abandoning it.

Luke interlaced his fingers with Ashley's, leaning in closer to her. "See." He nudged her with his shoulder. "Gigi will be distracted by the kids, so she shouldn't come near you all night."

"I suppose."

"Come on." Luke gave Ashley's hand a reassuring squeeze. "Let me introduce you to Melissa after we say hello to Andrew."

"I'd love that," Ashley said.

Then, she leaned in and kissed Luke on the cheek.

CHAPTER FOUR

From the back porch, Melissa stared at Ashley and Luke as they chatted with Andrew in front of the grill. Ashley looked beautiful in her white sundress, her dark hair standing out against it. Melissa glanced down at her pathetic attempt to dress nicely and instinctively ran a hand over her lackluster hair. Maybe some summer highlights would brighten her face? Highlights or not, dress or no dress, Melissa would never look half as good as Ashley.

Ashley wrapped an arm around Luke's waist and leaned into him. He laughed at something she said, then brushed her hair over her shoulder.

Melissa wondered how good he smelled or how his skin would feel against hers. She'd never know, and it was high time she accepted it.

"I definitely want to take the kids on a day trip to Martha's Vineyard sometime this summer," Olivia said.

"Great." Melissa half listened as she stared at the happy couple. Why couldn't she look away? Because they seemed perfect together, and Luke looked happy.

Olivia said something else, but it didn't register. Then she snapped in front of Melissa's face. "Earth to Melissa."

Caught red-handed, Melissa's cheeks warmed. "Say that again." She came out of her daze and met Olivia's eyes.

"Are you up for a day trip to Martha's Vineyard this summer?"

"Sure." Melissa fidgeted with the hem of her dress. "Anytime, just name the day."

Olivia craned her neck and peered over Melissa's head to where she had been staring earlier. "What were you looking at? Ahh ..." Smirking, she settled back into her chair.

"Luke looks good tonight."

"What?" Melissa's heart rate pounded. "I ... wouldn't know," she stammered.

Olivia rolled her eyes. "Yeah, you would. You've been checking him out since he arrived."

"No way." Melissa pointed at herself. "Who, me? Nah."

"Yes." Olivia leaned her elbows on the table, cradling her chin. "I don't know why I never saw it before. Andrew never mentioned you had a thing for Luke, but I should've put the pieces together. Do you remember the one time we saw you both when Andrew and I came to Boston for that dental convention? Luke was still working at the law firm downtown, and we met at The Thirsty Scholar. Ellie must've only been two or three. Andrew and I had to duck out early, and you told me later that Luke rode the subway with you all the way home even though he lived in the opposite direction. The way you talked about him, I should've known."

"I don't have a thing for him."

Melissa fanned her face. Why was it so hot out here?

Olivia cleared her throat. "Uh-huh." Then she waved her off. "You keep telling yourself that. But they're coming this way."

Melissa stopped talking and froze. She hoped they hadn't heard their conversation. But she convinced herself they weren't close enough to hear anything. Their feet hit the stairs leading up to the porch. After a moment, Luke and Ashley arrived beside them.

"Hey, you two." Luke gripped the chair in front of Melissa with his hands. "Do you mind if Ashley and I join? Andrew said we were crowding in on his grilling."

"Sure." Olivia motioned to the open chairs at the table. "Hey, Ashley." She smiled. "It's good to see you again. Thanks for coming."

Ashley slid into the chair Luke pulled out for her. "Thanks for having me."

Luke sat down next to Ashley and across from Melissa. Their eyes met for the first time since he'd arrived. "Melissa, this is my girlfriend, Ashley." He wrapped an arm around Ashley's shoulders.

Melissa and Ashley introduced themselves to each other. With introductions out of the way, Melissa wondered what they could possibly talk about. She racked her brain for an interesting topic but was too nervous to think of one in time.

Olivia filled the silence. "Thanks for bringing Gigi." She nodded toward the kids on the lawn. Ellie tossed a tennis ball across the lawn. Gigi ran to fetch it then turned around and darted back. When she reached them, Cole wiggled the ball from her mouth and threw it to the far corner of the yard, near the tall maple trees. Gigi dashed toward it. "You're giving Melissa and me a much-needed break."

"True." Melissa gave a crooked smile.

"Happy to help." Luke watched the kids for a minute. "Gigi loves it too. I like seeing her happy."

Ashley stiffened, straightening her posture. A palpable

tension drifted between them. Then again, maybe Melissa had imagined it.

"So ..." Melissa tucked her hair behind her ear. "Andrew said he introduced you two to each other."

Luke smiled and Ashley's demeanor softened. They shared a tender glance.

"He did." Ashley grinned and squeezed Luke's thigh. "Andrew purposely had me clean Luke's teeth. Then later, he had me assist him when Luke needed some fillings."

"I swear I brush and floss every night," Luke added.

Ashley leaned into him, and he cupped her shoulder. "He has great dental hygiene, and the fillings weren't due to lack of care. Sometimes they are unavoidable."

"See," Luke pointed out.

"But after the fillings, Luke was a bit out of it. Andrew made him wait until the numbing medicine wore off, so we chatted while I cleaned up the instruments. Once he was ready to leave, Luke surprised me by asking me out."

"That's right." Luke smiled. "Andrew definitely had his hand in it, but I saw a good thing and jumped at the chance to ask out such a great woman."

"What a lovely story." Melissa pulled her gaze away from the happy couple, afraid she might hurl from their picture-perfect happiness. On the lawn, Ellie played with Gigi on the grass. Cole laid flat on his back with his arms stretched wide. "Did you grow up around here, Ashley?" She kept her attention on the kids.

"No, I grew up in Boston." Ashley caught Luke's glance. A twinge of jealousy ran down Melissa's spine. "I needed a change, and the dentist I worked for was retiring and closing his office. I applied for the job Andrew posted. I guess it was meant to be, because I met Luke."

Luke and Ashley smiled at one another. This looked like the

beginning of something new and great. Melissa wanted Luke to be happy. Surely, she couldn't blame him for falling for a gorgeous woman her brother handpicked for him. They looked good together, and Melissa would have to give up whatever was brewing inside her. She would most likely be seeing this happy couple frequently over the summer.

"I guess so." Melissa managed.

"Dinner's ready." Andrew climbed the stairs to the porch with a platter of grilled meat. "Let's eat."

Melissa welcomed the distraction and jumped out of her chair. "Let me help," she said, holding her arms out.

"I've got this, sis." He set the platter in the center of the table. "Why don't you see what Olivia needs brought out from the kitchen."

Olivia rose. "Come on." She waved for Melissa to follow.

Melissa walked with her into the kitchen. They quickly gathered the salad, baked potatoes, and corn on the cob to accompany the grilled chicken and hot dogs.

"Ashley seems great." Melissa hoped her voice sounded sincere. "Luke seems happy."

"She is great," Olivia grabbed the salad and handed it to her, "But it's okay to be jealous. I won't tell."

"I'm not jealous." Melissa snatched serving tongs for the baked potatoes out of a drawer. "I'm not."

A lie. A total lie.

"Ahh, honey." Olivia shook her head. "You're not fooling anyone."

"Is it that obvious?"

"Only to me. I don't think Luke has the slightest idea you find him hot."

"Geez." Melissa's cheeks splashed with heat. She set the tongs on top of the platter of baked potatoes. "I—uh—"

Luke suddenly popped into the kitchen. "Anything I can help carry?"

Melissa's eyes widened. She wondered if he'd heard their conversation.

Olivia cleared her throat. "Can you handle those potatoes?" She pointed at the platter. "Then Melissa can take the corn."

"Sure." Luke moved in closer as Melissa pushed the platter toward him.

Ellie darted in from outside completely out of breath. "Mom, are we eating now?" Sweat glistened on her brow, dampening her temples.

"Yep." Melissa gathered up the corn. "Can you go wash your hands? They must be filthy from playing outside."

Ellie grinned and held up her brown-stained hands. "They sure are, but don't you always say that's a sign you've had a great day?"

Luke chuckled. "I love that." He shimmied around them toward the patio. Over his shoulder he added, "If that's the case, I had plenty of good days as a kid."

Ellie disappeared into the bathroom.

Melissa followed behind Luke with the corn. "I remember you as a kid." She set the corn on the table. Ashley had remained seated. "You did love to play outside, especially at the beach."

He set the potatoes down. "And I remember when you—" Luke gripped the back of Ashley's seat, "ate so much watermelon you threw up all over the beach when we went to play in the waves." Then he quickly tapped the middle of her forehead with his pointer finger. "I used to tease you and call you Melon."

Olivia set her platter of food on the table and said, "Melon? Really, Andrew never mentioned that nickname before."

"Melon. I haven't thought about that in years." Melissa

glanced at him and smiled from the memory. Even when Melissa pretended to hate the nickname, deep down she loved that Luke noticed something about her. "I haven't eaten watermelon since then."

"Honestly, I haven't either."

"Sorry, I ruined an entire food for you."

He shrugged. "I don't mind, Melon."

Ashley cleared her throat. Melissa pressed her lips together. Luke rubbed the back of his neck and averted his gaze.

Olivia's eyes went wide, and she half coughed, half choked. "Excuse me," Olivia pounded her chest with a fist as she peered out across the yard, "I need Cole to wash up too," but Cole was nowhere in sight.

"Andrew already took him to the bathroom to wash his hands," Ashley remarked.

"Perfect." Olivia glanced at the preset table. "I think that means I can take a seat."

An odd feeling settled over the table.

Andrew and Cole returned from the bathroom and joined them on the patio.

"I'll go check on Ellie," Melissa said.

She wandered into the house and found Ellie alone on the living room floor playing with some building blocks.

"Come on." Melissa crouched in front of her. "You were just asking about dinner. It's ready now." She grasped Ellie's hand and led her to the bathroom.

By the time they washed their hands and returned to the patio, everyone else was seated. Only two spots remained, directly across the table from Luke and Ashley. She slowed her walk and gave herself a quick pep talk. Even though it made her jealous to see them cuddled up next to one another, she needed to get over it. Luke had done nothing wrong, neither had

Ashley. Luke didn't know about her long-buried crush on him. It was time she allowed herself to finally get over him.

She squared her shoulders as she scooted around the table to their seats. Sure, she was the odd man out, but five years as a single mom had taught her to not dwell on it. If she made the choice to not feel out of place, then she wouldn't. This wasn't uncharted territory for her. She'd attended every holiday party for work alone and handled it fine. Still, this time felt ... different. For a split second, Melissa realized she wanted someone next to her too.

When Melissa and Ellie settled into their seats, Andrew announced they should eat. Plates began to be passed around family style until everyone had everything on their plates.

After Ashley took a few bites of her chicken, she commented, "Great job at the grilling, Andrew."

Everyone at the table wholeheartedly agreed. Ashley seemed like a pleasant enough person.

"He didn't always know how to grill." Melissa picked up her corn on the cob. Her gaze darted to Luke. "Remember when he almost set the backyard on fire?"

Luke nearly spit out of his mouth full of water. "I'd completely forgot about that." He set his cup down. "Andrew doused the charcoal in so much lighter fluid it incinerated his eyebrows right off his face."

"Mom says playing with fire is bad," Cole piped up.

"That's right, honey," Olivia agreed.

"Hey." Andrew shook his fork in their direction. "I was trying to impress a girl."

"Julia," Luke and Melissa said in unison.

Then they burst out laughing. Andrew grumbled something to himself.

"I still don't know why you liked Julia," Olivia added.

"I hadn't noticed you yet." Andrew smiled at her. "Once I did, there was no turning back."

"They never hung out again. Julia couldn't get past the no eyebrows thing."

Luke keeled over laughing.

Ashley sweetly added, "I'd still date you, Luke, even if you had no eyebrows."

Luke kissed her on the cheek. "I love that about you."

"I know we have pictures somewhere." Melissa set her corn on the cob on her plate and took a drink of water. "Of Andrew with no eyebrows."

Olivia patted Andrew on his arm. "It's okay, you learned your lesson. But I'm glad you tried to date me after your eyebrows had grown back," she smirked.

They spent the rest of dinner with Ashley and Andrew talking about dental procedures. Luke listened intently when Ashley spoke and even wrapped his arm around her shoulders once he finished eating. The guy looked like he was in love.

The kids became restless and went back to playing on the grass with Gigi, leaving the adults alone. After a short lull, Andrew leaned his elbows on the table and pressed his hands together. "We all need to do this again sometime, without the kids."

Luke glanced at Ashley and they exchanged a look. Then he said, "We'd love that."

Melissa knew she'd bow out of a double date scenario where she was the tagalong. It was one thing to come to a cookout with Ellie, but there was no chance she'd spend a kid free evening watching the little lovebirds make eyes at each other. *No thank you.*

Andrew smoothly added, "Friday night. I already have a babysitter lined up for Cole and Ellie."

"Oh." She snapped her head in his direction. "I don't think

I'll be joining, so I can watch Cole and Ellie. Then you four can have a nice double date."

"You need a night off too." Olivia's gaze softened. "You probably more than anyone. Our babysitter is excellent. Honestly, with Ellie there, it will be easier for the sitter because the kids will play together."

Dang, these two had thought of everything.

"I appreciate the offer," Melissa rubbed her hands over her thighs, "but I think I'd feel too much like a third wheel. So, thanks, but no thanks."

"You won't be." Andrew crumpled up his napkin and tossed it on his plate. "Jake agreed to come. He's excited to meet you."

"What? Who is Jake?" Melissa nearly toppled out of her chair from her exaggerated hand gestures. "I don't know any Jakes."

Luke furrowed his brow. "Sounds like a set up to me."

Melissa couldn't read his masked expression. "Uh—"

"Jake is Cole's pediatrician," Olivia chimed in. "Andrew and Jake also golf together sometimes."

"Umm ..." Melissa rolled her eyes. "I never asked to be set up. Did you somehow forget the entire conversation we had on the beach, Andrew? When did you even have time to set this up?"

"A doctor, that sounds promising," Ashley added.

Instinctively, Melissa's jaw clenched. A steady throb pulsed behind her ears.

"I remember the conversation, but I'm your big brother, and I think Jake is a nice guy. And what can I say, I work fast." Andrew took a sip of his drink. "I knew you were less likely to shoot it down if I told you in front of everyone."

"I really don't appreciate that." Melissa clasped her hands together, making her knuckles turn white. "If I don't want to go,

I won't. I don't want Jake to come out of pity or just to do his friend a favor."

"Hey," Luke piped in. Their eyes met across the table, and her cheeks instantly warmed from the power of his gaze. "Any guy would be lucky to go out with you. It wouldn't be a pity date, not even close."

His words hit her with a punch. *Any guy? But just not him, right?* She wanted to dwell on his words, but she knew better than to think they were anything but a way to ease her awkwardness.

"And," Ashley said. Everyone shifted their attention to her. She continued, "You shouldn't be turning down available men, especially a doctor. It's hard to find a decent guy out there. Why do you think I jumped at the chance to go out with Luke?" Ashley shifted a tad in her seat.

"Trust me, I'm aware of what a dating wasteland it is out there."

"I'll bet," Ashley replied. "My mom was a single mom for a long time. She'd often go out with guys who, once they learned she had kids, they would dump her. They thought she had too much baggage."

"Do you think I have baggage?" Melissa hissed. "That Ellie is baggage?"

"No, no. That isn't what I'm saying at all." Ashley looked to Luke for help. "I was trying to sympathize with you, but I can see that came out wrong. I'm sorry."

Luke chimed in. "I think Ashley just wanted to encourage you to give that Jake guy a chance."

"Yeah, come on," Andrew said. "Go on this triple date with us."

Abruptly, Melissa pushed out her chair. "I'm officially done with this conversation. I think I need to head home and get Ellie to bed."

CHAPTER FIVE

They all watched Melissa leave. Luke wondered if maybe they had all pushed her a bit too much on the dating thing. Andrew was the most at fault—he was the one who had started it.

"Yikes," Luke commented. "I don't think she's very happy with us."

Andrew shrugged. "She'll get over it. Plus, Jake was the one asking about when I could set them up after he saw her photo."

"I should've just kept my mouth shut." Ashley straightened her back and pulled her shoulders back. "But it's true that being a single mom makes things complicated. I saw it time and time again with all the guys my mom dated when I was a kid." A tad of defensiveness inched into her voice.

"I think she thought we were ganging up on her," Olivia added. "I wish I'd talked to her about it privately first." She shot Andrew a pointed look. "You know I'm better at buttering her up than you are."

"True." Andrew clasped his hands together on the table. "I'll smooth things over with her. I know I can convince her to go out with Jake once I show her a picture of him."

"Why? Does the guy moonlight as an Old Navy model or something?" Luke asked.

Andrew tugged his phone out of his pocket, tapped it a few times, then flipped it around to show Jake's social media profile.

Olivia snatched the phone from his hands. "Oh, he does look good in these." She scanned a few pictures on his profile. "I thought he might be Melissa's type but these photos of him on the beach confirm it."

"See," Andrew said knowingly.

"Are they shirtless photos?" Luke questioned.

"Let me see." Ashley took the phone from Olivia and scrolled through Jake's profile. Luke peered over her shoulder as she looked. He appeared to him to be your run-of-the-mill guy. "Oh, yeah, he's cute. He has a nice face and beautiful eyes too."

"Hey, I'm right here," he said only half kidding.

"It doesn't mean anything. I'm only making an observation." Ashley handed the phone back to Olivia.

Cole ran up the stairs with Gigi at his heels, interrupting them. "Why did Ellie leave?"

"Oh, it was getting late." Olivia stood, pushing back her chair. "But can you help me serve dessert?"

Cole beamed. "Dessert?" His eyes sparkled, helping replace Luke's suddenly sour mood.

"Yep." Olivia gathered some of the empty plates. "I made Luke's favorite, peach cobbler."

"Thanks." Luke smiled. "I love your peach cobbler."

"Let me help you." Andrew stood and took the large stack of plates from Olivia. "You both stay here."

Andrew and Olivia strolled into the house, leaving Luke and Ashley alone. When Gigi jumped onto his lap, Ashley leaned away from him, but Luke didn't care. Gigi relaxed and promptly fell asleep after she wiggled her head between his legs.

Luke stroked her fur. The kids had run her ragged, which made Luke very happy.

One thing itched at the back of his mind.

"Do you think you could ever learn to like Gigi?" Luke kept his gaze on Gigi.

"What?" Ashley paused. "I don't know. I want to like her, I really do. But I had that incident with a dog way back when, and I've just decided I don't ever want a dog."

Luke wondered where that left them. He loved Gigi. "Could you try? For me?"

"I don't know." Ashley exhaled. "Let's not focus on it right now. I would rather keep getting to know you and worry about Gigi further down the road."

His stomach twisted. He knew he'd never give Gigi up, but he liked dating Ashley too.

"I know this might be coming out of left field, but did you and Melissa ever date?" Ashley asked.

He froze, then turned toward her. "What?" He raised an eyebrow. "Melissa and me?"

"Yeah, Melissa. The one you nicknamed Melon." She scratched her wrist. "You two never even kissed?"

"No." Luke shook his head. "I don't see her like that."

"Okay." Ashley pressed her lips together. "Forget I brought it up."

Luke paused, his hand mid-stroke on Gigi's back. "I'm not interested in Melissa."

"I just wanted to check." Ashley added, "I think she has a thing for you. She lit up when you called her Melon."

"We're friends," Luke explained, feeling overly defensive. "We've known each other forever. She was Andrew's sister. I liked teasing her when we were younger because it made her so mad."

Melissa didn't have a thing for him. Ashley was reading it all wrong. She didn't understand their shared history. Luke had only ever seen Melissa as a cute little tagalong who laughed at his jokes and boosted his ego. *Busted.* Luke paused, letting the realization settle in. He loved the way she lit up when she saw him, and how when they were teenagers, she listened to him talk about all the girls he liked and kissed. Melissa even helped him come up with a creative way to ask a girl to his junior prom. But even if Melissa did have a thing for him back then, she didn't now. No way. Not a chance.

"Okay," Ashley replied.

Olivia, Andrew, and Cole interrupted their conversation with the arrival of dessert. Luke hoped to never talk about Melissa liking him with Ashley again.

Friday night, Luke spoke with Andrew on the phone. "I'm picking up Ashley, then we'll be there in ten minutes."

"Sounds great," Andrew replied. "If you arrive before us, let the host know the reservation is under my name. I've got Olivia and Melissa with me. We're picking up Jake, and then we'll be there."

"You bet."

Luke ended the call and went to pick up Ashley.

On the way to the restaurant, Ashley flipped down the visor and opened the mirror. "What restaurant is it again?" She dabbed on lip gloss and smacked her lips together.

"Skipper's Chowder House. Melissa said if she was being set up, she at least got to pick the restaurant."

"Oh, that place." Ashley scrunched her nose and snapped the visor back up to the roof. "You know I'm not a big fan of seafood."

"I know," Luke slowed down and stopped at a red light. "But Melissa picked the place."

Ashley tossed her lip gloss into her purse. "I guess I'm going hungry tonight."

Luke rubbed the back of his neck with one hand while he gripped the steering wheel with the other. "I'm sure they'll have more on the menu than seafood." The light changed to green, and he continued through the intersection.

"Doubt it." Ashley set her purse by her feet and gazed out the passenger window.

The past few days had been a bit tense with Ashley. Things at Bayberry House had been very chaotic. He had canceled a date Wednesday night when the water heater broke. Ashley hadn't handled the last-minute cancellation well. It wasn't like Luke planned on it, but running a business meant unexpected issues came up. As much as he wished he had another manager, he didn't, which meant there were several things around the B&B only he could deal with. He hoped she'd learn that one had to be flexible when dating a business owner.

"Let's try to make the most of it. Andrew is my best friend. Melissa is his sister, and I'd love for her to find a nice guy. Maybe this Jake will end up being the one for her. The least we can do is sit through one dinner to ease her back into the world of dating."

"Fine." Though she sat only a few inches from him, she felt far away. "But you owe me a meal afterward if I can't find anything on the menu."

"Sure." He kept his response light, hoping to get their relationship back on good footing. "I can have the cook at Bayberry House whip you up something later if we need to."

Ashley didn't reply, which made Luke question himself for a second. He had apologized for canceling earlier in the week and had explained that he hadn't picked the restaurant. *Why wasn't that enough?* He hoped the beginning of their evening wouldn't ruin the rest of it. When they arrived, he helped her out of the car and interlocked his fingers with hers, giving them a reassuring squeeze. He hoped it would help, but she didn't lean into his arm like normal.

When they checked in, the host told them Andrew had already checked in and was seated on the outside patio overlooking the ocean. Luke led Ashley to the table outside where Olivia and Andrew sat across from each other. Melissa and Jake occupied the middle seats across from each other, leaving the two end seats for Ashley and Luke.

Quickly, Ashley selected the vacant seat next to Melissa, leaving Luke to sit next to Jake.

Before he sat, Luke held out a hand and introduced himself and Ashley to Jake. He seemed like a nice guy and had certainly dressed well for the occasion in slacks and a button-down. Luke glanced down at his jeans and polo shirt and regretted not dressing up more. Ashley had dressed up in a navy dress and white cardigan. Melissa wore a light floral dress with her hair curled down like she had worn it to his mom's funeral. His mind flashed to the moment in the kitchen where she'd comforted him, but he pushed the memory away and took his seat.

Once Luke sat, Jake engaged him in conversation. "They were telling me you own Bayberry House on Waterman Road."

Melissa took a sip of her water, her gaze dancing between the two men.

"I do." Luke picked up the menu in front of him. "It's a second career for me, I used to be in corporate law. I might go back to it in the future." He shrugged. "We'll see."

Ashley looked up from her menu. "I didn't know you wanted to go back to law. Would you move back to Boston?"

"Ahh, maybe." Luke flipped open the menu, scanning the selection. He already knew he was getting the lobster roll with a cup of clam chowder. "I haven't thought that far. It's just a possibility."

Ashley tossed her hair over her shoulder. "You might have wanted to tell that to the person you're dating." She snapped to the next page in her menu.

Melissa's eyes widened. She pressed her lips together and quickly turned the next page in her menu, pretending to study it. An awkward tension settled over them.

Leaning across the table, Luke lowered his voice, "I would never make a choice like that without letting you know. It's not even really a maybe, more like a probably never going to happen unless everything went to pot and I had to sell Bayberry House."

The tight line on Ashley's forehead loosened and she eased up slightly. "Okay." Ashley closed her menu and set it down. "I was beginning to wonder if you shared anything with me."

He winced internally, wondering why he had revealed his little itch to return to law. The words had tumbled out before he had time to think them through. Sometimes he spoke without thinking, and this was a prime example.

"I do." Luke reached for her hand and placed his on it. The others at the table carried on a conversation without them. "I do share things with you."

"Like what?"

"I told you about how Gigi got caught in the chain-link fence three weeks ago, and I had to take her to vet to get stitches." He tugged at the collar of his shirt with his other hand. "I tell you things."

"I'm not talking about your precious Gigi." The comment made his back stiffen. Ashley rolled her eyes. "I'm more interested in your plans and goals for the future."

"Bayberry House is my future."

Ashley shook her hand free from his. "Is it though? You just said you might go back to corporate law."

Luke pinched the bridge of his nose. "I ..." He wondered how to get them back on track.

Why was everything suddenly a challenge with Ashley? The past few weeks of getting to know one another and dating had been a breeze, but now things seemed to pop up left and right.

The server arrived, interrupting the tense exchange. As they placed their order, Ashley managed to find a grilled chicken sandwich. Luke breathed a sigh of relief, hoping that meant the evening would go better.

Once the server left, Andrew opened the conversation to everyone. "So, Jake, since you have two people here who grew up with Melissa, what are you itching to know about her?"

"Oh dear." Melissa exhaled. She held up a finger. "Remember to be nice."

Jake smiled across the table at her, his gaze full of wonder. The guy seemed smitten, and Luke didn't blame him. Melissa was fantastic in many ways. Maybe Jake would be smart enough to pursue her.

Luke rubbed his hands together like he was conspiring. "Let me think." His mind quickly ran through the countless memories he had of her as a child and teenager. But his mind landed on one. "Do you remember when we told her she could only go fishing with us if she carried both tackle boxes?"

Andrew nearly spit out the sip of his drink. Coughing, he wheezed and said, "Yes. I'm sorry we were such jerks about that."

"You should feel sorry." Melissa motioned with a thumb at Andrew. "You both were fourteen and had fifty pounds on me. I was only eleven, and I had to carry those heavy things from our house all the way to the ocean. By the time I arrived, my hands were covered with blisters." She rolled her eyes and muttered under her breath, "I can't believe I did that."

"Hey, you're tough." Jake winked at her from across the table. "I like tough women. It showed you had grit."

Red splashed Melissa's cheeks. "Thanks."

"I'm sorry." Luke crinkled his nose. "It was Andrew's idea. I told him I would carry them, but he insisted you do it."

"I believe it," Melissa said.

Olivia chimed in. "I promise Andrew is much nicer now. He might have been a jerk back then, but he isn't one now."

"You were my little sister, and Mom told me I had to let you come. I decided to punish you because of it. So, sorry."

"You did love following us around," Luke added.

"My only other option was hanging out with Mrs. Matherly and her seven cats," Melissa replied.

"I completely forgot about her. I wonder if she's still alive." They both shrugged. Luke continued, "That lady did have a ton of cats."

"Besides that one time," Melissa said, "you both were mostly good sports about letting me tag along."

His mind wandered as he remembered Melissa during their childhood. He remembered drinking lemonade with her and Andrew during the summertime, eating Hershey's kisses on the back porch, and his mom letting them raid the fridge after they'd hosted a wedding at Bayberry House. His heart ached a little for the past. They had all changed and grown up. He admired Andrew and the family he had created with Olivia. And he sat in awe of Melissa and her resilience. Many would have crumbled under the weight of her circumstances, instead she'd moved forward and managed to make the most of a challenging situation.

Ashley cleared her throat. He must have been staring at Melissa as she chatted with Jake. He vowed not to glance in her direction again for the rest of dinner. This proved to be much harder than he anticipated, because Jake and Melissa kept laughing together. Their date appeared to be going well.

Their food arrived, and the chatter quieted as they took their first bites. Luke ate a bit of his lobster roll before turning to his clam chowder.

"How's the chicken sandwich?" Luke asked Ashley as he blew on his chowder.

"Fine." She grimaced as she nipped at the sandwich.

If he had learned anything from past relationships, "fine" was girl code for "terrible."

"I'm sorry it isn't better." Luke ate a spoonful of clam chowder. His mind searched for something to talk about to improve their conversation. With Jake and Melissa engaged in conversation, and Olivia and Andrew out of ear shot, he was left with Ashley. And she wasn't making it easy for him. "Anything interesting happen at work today?"

"Umm." Ashley set the sandwich back on her plate, wiping a napkin across her chin. "I had to clean a person's teeth today who hadn't been to the dentist in a decade. You know, real riveting stuff."

"Gross." Luke's appetite soured. "Could you tell they hadn't been to the dentist in forever?"

"Oh yeah, the minute I used my first scaler, their gums wouldn't stop bleeding."

A mental image popped into his mind and he cringed. "How do you stand putting your hands into someone else's mouth?"

Ashley shrugged. "I'm used to it." She picked up a fry and bit into it. "Blood doesn't bother me either."

It bothered him. The sight of blood made him faint—even talking about it made him queasy.

He set down his spoon and took a deep breath. "I can't handle the sight of blood. I passed out when Andrew slammed his arm through a window in his backyard. He was trying to catch a ball I hit him. He split his arm right open and had to get twenty-four stitches. I remember looking at his arm covered in blood for a split second then splat, I was out."

"Well, it's a good thing you have me." Her demeanor softened and the tension in Luke's shoulders dissipated. "I promise to deal with any blood when it comes to us."

"Deal." Luke smiled at Ashley for the first time all night.

They ended up having an enjoyable conversation as they finished their meals, and the others seemed to as well.

With dinner over and the check paid, Andrew rose and came over to their side of the table and asked, "Luke, can you give Olivia and me a ride home?"

"Umm, sure." Luke peered over at Melissa and winked. "Do you two have plans?"

"Jake and I are taking Andrew's car for a drive," Melissa jutted her chin. "There's a lighthouse he wanted to show me."

Apparently, sparks had flown between them during dinner. And if Luke didn't know better, with the way his gut twisted, he could've sworn he was jealous. But then he reminded himself— this was Melissa, a woman he'd known forever.

He scratched his chin. "Great idea, I hope you both have a nice time."

"I'm sure we will." Jake stood, pushing back his chair.

Melissa slung her purse over her shoulder as everyone rose to their feet. Andrew yanked his keys from his pocket and handed them to Melissa.

"You two kids have fun." Andrew's voice was laced with innuendos.

If his tone bugged her, Melissa didn't show it.

She smiled and said, "Thanks. We won't be long."

"Take all the time you need," Andrew said.

Olivia wrapped a hand around Andrew's elbow. "We'll get

Ellie to bed. She and Cole can have a sleepover in the extra room. They'll love it."

"Oh." Melissa's face darkened to scarlet. "You don't need to do that. I'll pick her up."

Olivia winked. "Why don't you just see where the night takes you?"

Melissa straightened her back, then directed her attention to the group, "Thanks for a nice evening. I'll see you all later."

Then she tugged on Jake's sleeve, and they exited.

Andrew and Olivia lingered by the table.

Andrew commented, "I think Jake and Melissa really hit it off. They didn't stop talking the entire dinner."

"You don't say." Jake rubbed the back of his neck. "Good for Melissa." He motioned toward the exit. "Let's get you all home."

And for some odd reason, he wondered if Melissa and Jake would kiss at the end of the night. He shook off the thought and drove everyone home.

CHAPTER SIX

"I think I've been here before." Melissa peered out the window toward the lighthouse far off in the distance. She parked the car. "I mean, the Cape is covered with lighthouses, but I remember visiting this one when I was a kid."

Jake unbuckled his seatbelt. "Are you up to walking to the base of it?"

"Well ..." Melissa grinned. "I didn't come all this way for nothing."

"Attagirl." Jake opened his door.

Melissa climbed out while he rounded the car to join her.

The sun dipped a little lower, casting streaks of gold and yellow across the sky. "I love it here in the summertime." She breathed in the salty air and closed her door with her hip.

"Me too." Jake shoved a hand through his hair. It was brown and peppered with the beginnings of gray around his temples. It made him look distinguished rather than old. "I've only spent five summers here, but I always look forward to it after the long winter."

"That's right, you grew up in upstate New York." A light wind whipped her hair and made her shiver, so she tugged her cardigan out of her purse and put it on to fight against the slight chill. "Do you miss it?"

"Sometimes." Jake motioned toward the sandy path that wove through the dunes to the lighthouse. They started on the path. "But I'm grateful to be at the practice I'm at. I have plans to buy the other doctor out when he retires. And the Cape is close enough to my hometown that my mom manages to come down and visit me when she can fit it in, and I try and go back for the holidays."

Melissa's sandaled feet sank into sand as she walked. The grains wiggled between her toes, but she didn't mind. The evening was beautiful, and she enjoyed the change of pace from her normal working life.

"How about you? Will you be anxious to get back to your job when summer ends?" Jake asked.

"I think when my three months are up, I will be." Melissa tilted her face closer to him. "I enjoy the work. Being a software engineer is challenging and rewarding at the same time. And it provides for me and my daughter, which I'm grateful for. But I definitely needed this break. Being a single mom is the hardest thing I've ever done."

Their arms brushed, and Jake interlocked his hand with hers. "I can only imagine." He squeezed her hand.

They walked the remaining distance to the base of the lighthouse. When they reached it, the last bit of sunlight dipped below the water and the first inkling of stars smattered the sky.

"Why is the beach so beautiful after the sun disappears?" She stared out at the water and leaned her back against the lighthouse.

"It's peaceful, right?" Jake stepped closer, resting his back against the lighthouse too. Their bodies were close together, shoulders touching.

"Thanks for bringing me here." Melissa shifted, leaning on her shoulder against the wall.

Jake mirrored her movement, so they faced one another. "I hope we can go out again. I've enjoyed getting to know you."

"Me too."

A gust of wind whipped her hair in front of her face. Gingerly, Jake brushed the strands out of her eyes and tucked them back into place. His hand lingered, sliding a bit to cup the back of her neck. "Did I remember to tell you how beautiful you look tonight?"

Melissa smiled. "You did. But I don't mind hearing it again." Their eyes locked, making her breath hitch.

Then, ever so slowly, Jake leaned in and kissed her, soft as a whisper. Their lips only touched for a split second. "I'll try to remember that." He grinned at her.

Then he pulled away, and they watched as the sky grew darker and darker. They stayed until the moon shone brightly and the stars hung around it, giving them enough light to walk back.

Later that week, Melissa and Ellie enjoyed the leisurely walk from her parents' house to the small downtown. It was sprinkled with restaurants and shops. During the summer, every place was open, but by the time fall rolled around, most of them closed for the season. Salty air filled her lungs as Melissa reflected on the kiss she and Jake had shared a few nights ago under the glow of the lighthouse. It hadn't been a showstopping kiss, but it was sweet and tender. Enough was there that she'd agreed to a second date.

"Are you sure they have saltwater taffy that tastes like cotton candy?" Ellie asked, peering up at her, eyes stretched wide with wonder. It made her heart tug in her chest. Her little girl was so easy to love.

"Promise." Melissa made an *x* motion over her heart with her free hand. "It was my favorite flavor too when I was a kid, and the little candy shop still has the same flavors. Because that's one thing you can count on around here. Nothing changes."

Ellie's face split into a huge grin.

As a working mom, most of Melissa's days were busy and chaotic. She hated that she didn't have more of these relaxing, carefree days to spend with Ellie. In the thick of it, she barely could keep her head above water. The past five years were a blur, but this summer was one she knew she would remember. She'd recall the size of Ellie's hand in hers, how her hair grew blonder by the day, and how her cheeks became smeared with freckles from time in the sun. She imagined that someday, while looking back at this summer, she would remember it as the best one of her life. And she'd had some killer summers growing up.

The sidewalk curved a bit, giving way to Bayberry House, Luke's B&B. She remembered how much Ellie enjoyed playing with Gigi the other night.

The majestic Bayberry House, on its stately property, overlooked the beach. "This is where Luke lives with Gigi." She pointed to the place.

They halted on the sidewalk and stared. It had an impressive front lawn with a huge wraparound porch. The back of the house faced the beach, with another huge lawn that eventually gave way to the sand. It was the perfect wedding venue: the grassy area had enough room for tables and chairs, and even featured a gazebo for couples to exchange their vows.

"Is he rich?" Ellie peered at Bayberry House. "That's the biggest house *ever*."

Melissa laughed. "I don't know if he's rich or not, but this building is a bed and breakfast. A place where people can stay overnight, like a hotel." She pointed to a window on the highest story. "I think he lives in an apartment on the top floor."

She assumed that Luke had moved into the small apartment his family had occupied when he was a child. Melissa remembered it being tight but tidy. It had a small kitchen and living room with two bedrooms. She remembered the inside from the time when she was twelve and cut her hand on a rusty nail sticking out of a floorboard on the porch. Luke had nearly passed out from the sight of it. But he somehow had managed to find his mom, and they had taken her up to the apartment. His mom dressed and wrapped her wound while Luke kept his eyes firmly shut. He only reopened them once the wound was dressed. She remembered how he ran a finger down the length of her covered palm and asked her if it still hurt. Even now, years later, her skin tickled at the memory of his finger gliding down her palm. She forced the memory away.

"Do you think Gigi is inside?" Ellie used the heel of her hand to swipe hair out of her eyes. "Luke said I could come anytime to play with her."

"He did say that." Melissa gnawed on her bottom lip as she contemplated his earlier offer. People gave invitations all the time out of politeness, but it didn't mean they thought you'd take them up on the offer. Then again, this was Luke. At the time he extended the invitation, it had seemed sincere. "I don't know. I should probably call first and not stop by unannounced."

"No!" Ellie stomped her foot. "He told me to come play with Gigi. Grown-ups know lying is bad. Right?"

Well played, kid.

"Fine." Melissa held up a finger. "But when I say it's time to go, it's time to go. No arguing or asking to stay longer. Do you understand?"

"I promise," Ellie eagerly replied.

Melissa exhaled, hoping this wasn't a huge mistake. What if he and Ashley were hanging out together? She didn't want to interrupt them. But before she could rethink the entire thing, Ellie dropped her hand and dashed up the front steps, her blonde head disappearing inside before Melissa even finished climbing the stairs. Out of breath, she entered the Bayberry House lobby. Luckily Ellie had waited for her by the front door. The lobby bustled with guests coming and going. A line formed in front of the reception desk, so she grasped Ellie's hand and joined the end of the line.

Part of her hoped Luke might stroll on through the lobby, but she didn't spot him, or Gigi, for that matter. They shuffled forward as the line moved, and soon they were next. The woman from behind the counter motioned for them to come forward.

"Hi, Carol." She recognized the woman from so many years ago. Carol had always greeted her with a smile and a warm hello. Except for a few more wrinkles around her eyes, she appeared nearly the same. "I'm Melissa. I don't know if you remember me, but I recognized you the minute I walked in." She rested her forearm on the high counter. Ellie wrapped her arms around her legs.

"Melissa?" Carol's brow furrowed then eased. Excitedly, she clapped her hands together. "Melissa! You look fantastic. I'm glad you decided to stop by." She tipped her head toward Ellie. "And who do you have with you? Is that your daughter?"

"Yes." Melissa unwrapped Ellie from her leg. "This is Ellie."

Carol sidestepped around the front desk and crouched down in front of her. "Well." Carol scanned her face and smiled. "Aren't you just the cutest thing to walk in here in who knows how long?"

"Thanks." Ellie didn't waste time and asked, "Can I play with Gigi? Luke said it was okay."

"Oh, I see." Carol laughed, standing back up. "You're only here to see Gigi. I can't blame you—she's one cute dog."

Eyes wide, Ellie nodded.

"Come on over here, little lady." Carol motioned for her to walk around the reception desk. Ellie obeyed. Under the desk, hidden from the guests, Gigi was curled up on a dog bed, sound asleep. "She's sleeping, but you can pet her if you do it gently."

Ellie knelt next to Gigi. "She looks so peaceful," she whispered. Softly, she gave Gigi a long, slow stroke. The poodle didn't even stir.

"So," Carol said, reverting her full attention to Melissa. "Luke told me you were back in town. He's looking surprisingly good these days, isn't he?" She waggled her eyebrows.

"Umm." Melissa's gaze landed on a big bowl of Hershey's kisses sitting on the top of the reception desk. She snatched one out of the bowl, trying to think of an appropriate response. "I couldn't say. Because I'm—not checking him out or anything." She unwrapped the chocolate and popped it into her mouth.

A flash of memories of eating them with Luke flooded her mind. She wondered if he remembered too.

Carol's gaze flickered across her, scrutinizing her for a second. Melissa was sure that Carol thought she was lying.

"No need to worry." Carol waved off the idea. "You are too. Looking good, that is." Then she opened and closed a drawer of the desk. She leafed through the contents and commented, "I always thought you two would end up together. Come on, brother's best friend, how cute would that be?"

She wondered if Carol knew how her unrequited love had haunted her through her teen years and that she'd never managed to stop her infatuation. Either way, she wasn't having this conversation. She did have at least a shred of dignity left.

"Er ..." Melissa hoped her indifference would put the kibosh on the idea.

Out of nowhere, Luke barged into the lobby, stopping in front of Carol. His eyes were wild. His hair was messier than usual, like he'd run his hands through it multiple times. Melissa doubted he'd noticed her presence, because he didn't acknowledge her when he leaned in close to Carol and whispered, "Please tell me the order for more toilet paper has arrived."

Carol cleared her throat and tilted her head toward Melissa. Luke tracked her gaze. He flinched, then recovered so quickly that she wondered if she'd imagined it.

"Hey." Luke ran a hand down his face. "What are you doing here?"

Melissa cringed. Immediately, she regretted stopping by without a text. Luke had an entire B&B to deal with. He didn't need her or Ellie getting in the way.

Ellie popped her head around the side of the desk. "Shh." She placed her finger to her lips. "Gigi is sleeping. We don't want to wake her up."

Luke glanced at Gigi then returned his gaze to Melissa. "Sorry, I didn't mean to sound so harsh. It's been quite the day." His demeanor softened. The worry lines on his forehead smoothed out. He smiled and crouched down next to Ellie. "You are so right," he whispered. "I'll be quieter. I'm glad you stopped by to pet Gigi."

"You are?" Her eager face lit up. "Mom almost didn't let me come. Your house is so big. You must be really rich."

Luke chuckled and rose to his feet.

"Sorry." Melissa wrung her hands. "I tried to explain to her that this is a business, and it wasn't a house only for you. I mean, maybe you are rich. Maybe you're one of those fancy real estate tycoons. I don't know—" She noticed she was rambling and snapped her mouth shut.

His lips twitched mischievously. "I've never considered that I might appear to be a real estate tycoon, but I like the sound of it," he teased.

Melissa gnawed on her bottom lip.

"What's a real escape raccoon?" Ellie asked with a scrunched-up nose.

"It's real *estate tycoon*," Melissa replied, laughing. "And it's just someone who owns a lot of buildings."

Ellie shrugged then disappeared back behind the desk with Gigi.

"Regardless." Luke rubbed the back of his neck. "I'm glad you stopped by. It's nice to see you again so soon."

"Really?" Her voice sounded shocked, and she immediately wanted to grab the word back and try it again.

Carol smirked and shot Luke a look Melissa couldn't quite decipher.

He shifted closer, edging his body ridiculously close to hers. So close, her breath caught in her chest and her nostrils flared from the cologne wafting off him. He could be the poster boy for an outdoorsy catalog.

"Why are you so shocked?" His voice lowered. He studied her for a moment. "You're my best friend's sister. You can stop by anytime you'd like. Also, I love it when people love Gigi."

His words put her surfacing feelings of attraction and hope back into a tightly packed box. She reminded herself that he would forever see her as Andrew's little sister. *But his girlfriend doesn't seem to like Gigi,* her traitorous mind whispered. She shoved the thought away. *Their relationship is none of my business.*

"Right." Melissa straightened her back. "Gigi—Ellie does love her. I mean, I do too," she quickly added.

Luke stared at her. His attention made her skin itchy. She knew she tended to ramble when she was nervous. It was time she packed Ellie up and got the heck out of there.

"I'm going to go check on the toilet paper order." Carol looked between Luke and Melissa for a moment. She peered around the reception desk to Ellie. "Do you want to go on a tour with me? If that's okay with your mom, I can show you the special trick door."

Ellie popped up. "Sure. Mom, can I go?"

"Of course. Thanks Carol," Melissa said.

Luke didn't remove his attention from Melissa as Carol left the lobby and wandered down the hall to the back with Ellie in tow.

"How was the lighthouse?" He rounded the check-in desk and snagged a Hershey's kiss out of the bowl on the counter and peeled the wrapper off. "Did you and Jake have a nice time?" He tossed it into his mouth and chewed.

It took her a moment to process what he'd asked, because his shirt had hiked up an inch, revealing the tanned skin above his hip bone. Trim abs blinded her and made her head swim. Had Luke always been that buff?

Melissa twirled a piece of her hair around her finger, just for something to do to distract her from ... him. "Are you asking so you can tease me about it?" She raised an eyebrow. "Andrew already did, and I'm not up for more of it."

"No." Luke was still. He swallowed. "I wouldn't tease you. Jake seemed into you. I was curious if it was two-sided." Then he opened a drawer of the desk and tugged out a pack of sticky notes along with a pen. He jotted down a few things.

"I see." She peered around the lobby to make sure Ellie hadn't returned without her knowing. "I don't like to talk about men in front of my daughter, so try to keep that in mind next time you inquire about my colorful dating life."

"Oh." The tips of his ears went pink. "Duh. I'll make sure to remember that. But you didn't answer my question—did you and Jake make a love connection?"

"Why are you so interested?" Melissa teased, crossing her arms and raising her eyebrows.

He shrugged then glanced down at his sticky notes. He wrote something else down. "I care about you," Luke said without looking up. "I want to see you happy. Your ex was a jerk, and I'd hate to see your past to keep you from finding happiness with someone new."

"Thanks. I appreciate it." They stared at one another. Then for some odd reason, Melissa kept talking. "It's true I've haven't dated a lot since my divorce. Only a bunch of bad first dates—" She waved a hand, mostly to stop herself from jabbering on and on. "But the date with Jake gave me a bit of hope, like maybe I *could* find someone when the timing is right. It's hard being a single mom. Most days I handle it okay, but in the evenings after Ellie is asleep and I'm alone, that's when I wish the most that I had someone to share my day with. It would be nice to have someone to talk about the highs and lows of my job or to help handle the load of parenting."

"I hope—" Luke said.

They were interrupted by a guest inquiring about the water pressure in their room. Apparently, the water in the shower came out in spurts rather than a steady stream.

Luke calmly listened to their complaints and then reassured them he'd check on it right away.

"I should probably be going. You've got a lot to handle." Melissa walked to the edge of the hallway where Carol and Ellie had disappeared.

They emerged from one of the doors and spotted her. Melissa waved and said, "Ellie, we need to go. Remember, I promised you saltwater taffy?"

Ellie's face lit up, and she dashed down the hallway, rejoining her. Carol opened another door, gave them a little wave, and slipped inside.

Melissa and Ellie crossed the lobby back to where Luke stood. "Thanks for letting us stop by. It was nice seeing you again. Next time, I'll text beforehand." She stepped toward the door.

"Oh, that isn't necessary. Come by whenever you want." Then Luke crouched down in front of Ellie. "I'm sorry Gigi wasn't too much fun today and only slept. I might take her for a walk later to the tide pools. Would you want to come?" He tilted his face up toward Melissa. "That is, if it's okay with your mom."

Excitement danced across Ellie's face. "Can Mom come too?"

"Yes, absolutely. I assumed she would." Luke stood, readjusting his shirt, which had snagged on his belt. "What do you think? Does late afternoon work?"

His hypnotic stare made her forget to listen. Then she remembered something about tide pools, later today. Could Luke be interested in her? *Stop it. He's dating Ashley.*

"We can pencil you in," Melissa said in a weak attempt to be coy.

"Great." Some shuffling from behind them distracted him as he said, "I'll text you with the time for low tide."

With her arms full of toilet paper, Carol meandered back into the lobby. "I knew I had a secret stash for emergencies." She moved past them and set the rolls on the top of the reception desk. "This should hold us until the rest of it is delivered," she said, already on her way back to the storage room.

Melissa tugged Ellie toward the front door. "Bye. We need to run. See you later." She didn't wait for a response. As they exited, Carol said something to Luke that Melissa couldn't quite make out, but it made his demeanor change.

In a low, deep voice, that he no doubt intended only for Carol to hear, Luke hissed, "I'm not interested in Melissa."

Her heart sank, more than it should have. It wasn't anything new. Why she thought that after all these years anything would be different was beyond her. He saw her as a friend and nothing more—no matter how much she wanted to rewrite the narrative, it was always the same.

She returned her attention to Ellie as they bounded down the stairs. "Next stop, saltwater taffy!" She forced herself to sound upbeat, though she was stung from Luke's obvious rejection. Ellie freed herself from Melissa's grasp and took the stairs two at a time.

"Hold up. You need to wait for me," she called after her.

Ellie waited at the edge of the lawn for her to catch up, then said, "Mom?"

"Yes, honey."

They fell into step on the sidewalk, heading toward Main Street.

"Is Luke married?"

Startled, Melissa sought Ellie's gaze. "No, why do you ask?"

"He's nice." Ellie dragged her sandaled feet. Melissa slowed her pace to match her daughter's. "Maybe you could marry him … and then I could have a dad." Her little shoulders drooped.

"Oh, sweetie." Melissa's chest pinched tight. "I wish you had a dad, too. I wish I could give you that, but I'm not going to marry Luke."

"Why not?"

"Because he's with someone else." A couple came in the opposite direction. She steered Ellie onto the grass next to the sidewalk so they could pass. "He has a girlfriend named Ashley.

Remember, she came to dinner at Cole's house. If Luke marries anyone, it will probably be her."

Ellie wrinkled her nose. "Aww. But I like Luke."

No kidding, kid.

"Come on, enough of this talk about Luke." Melissa reached for her daughter's hand, squeezing it. She fought to sound peppy and upbeat when she said, "I can't wait to show you my favorite candy store in the entire world!"

Ellie's face lit up. "I want cotton candy and cherry!"

Bless children's short attention spans.

"Done and done."

They walked the rest of the way to the candy store and bought a brown paper bag full of saltwater taffy. They took it home and ate most of it on the back porch overlooking the ocean. Ellie drifted off to sleep for a rare nap on the porch swing. Melissa went and grabbed the romance novel she'd been meaning to finish, kicked off her sandals, and curled up on the comfy outdoor sofa. The sticky summer air filled her lungs as the steady sound of her daughter's breathing competed against the sound of the waves. She reveled in the blissful feeling of having nothing pressing.

As she read, her eyes grew heavy and eventually, she drifted off to sleep too.

CHAPTER SEVEN

The rest of Luke's day sped right on by. With extra wedding guests checking in, an understaffed kitchen, and flaky teenaged servers, he didn't have time to think about anything besides solving one almost-fiasco after the other.

So he was startled to see Ashley, still in her scrubs, breeze through the front door at three o'clock. Ashley never stopped by in the middle of the day, and Andrew's office closed at five.

"Hey," he greeted her, continuing to leaf through the day's mail. "You're off early."

Ashley smiled. "My last two patients cancelled, so I decided to stop on by on my way home. Would you be up to walk to get some dinner tonight?" She crossed the rest of the lobby and rounded the desk.

He paused when she leaned in and gave him a quick kiss. Opening the proper drawer, Luke shoved the mail inside. Tonight, he'd have to meticulously go over the bills. But it could wait.

He wrapped an arm around her shoulders. "I think that could work." Then he remembered the plan he had made with Melissa and Ellie to walk to the tide pools. He checked his watch. "I'm walking Gigi to the tide pools pretty soon. Ellie and Melissa are coming to join me. But it shouldn't take long, so I can still do dinner."

"Oh." Ashley looked taken aback. "Do you do things often with them?"

He paused. This was probably something he should've run by her, right? But in his mind, Melissa was Andrew's little sister —a friend.

"We're friends, but I wouldn't say we do things together. At least, not often. They stopped by earlier to see Gigi, but she was sleeping. I always take her for a walk in the late afternoon, and Ellie was excited to see her again, so I suggested she and Melissa come along." Luke saw how Ashley could misinterpret his plans, but hoped his explanation cleared everything up. "You are welcome to come too," he added, hoping to lessen her worries.

"I— I—" Ashley shook her head and shuffled away from him enough that he had to drop his arm from her shoulders. "I'm not sure about how I feel about you hanging out with an attractive single mom who's probably on the prowl for a new man."

"She isn't on the prowl," Luke protested.

Carol came in from the backyard, her timing impeccable as always. "Hey there, Ashley." She shut the back door behind her. Her back stiffened for a second as she clocked Ashley's tightly pressed lips. Carol snatched her to-do list from the reception desk. "I'll get started on this list, Luke." Then, to his surprise, she scurried back out the door without another word.

"Come with us to the tide pools, Ash." Luke grasped her hand and attempted to tug her toward him. "Ellie will play with Gigi, and you'll see that Melissa isn't interested in me. She told me today her date with Jake went well."

"I guess I'd rather be there too." But her body remained rigid, with her feet firmly planted. She didn't move closer. He dropped her hand when she said, "I need to go home and change. What time are you leaving?"

"Let me check the time for low tide." Luke took his phone out of his pocket. He typed into the search bar and scanned the results. "It's in an hour. Can you be back here in forty-five minutes?"

"Yeah, I'll be back."

"Great," he said, way too cheerfully.

Ashley left.

Tightness in his shoulder blades made his neck ache. He rolled it back and forth to try to loosen the tension, then shot Melissa a text with the information about the tide pools. A few seconds later, she texted back confirmation that they would be there.

For a second, he hesitated. Should he tell Melissa that Ashley was coming too? He went back and forth for a minute, but then he got distracted by the arrival of an order of decorations for an upcoming wedding.

He and Carol worked in tandem unloading the boxes into the storage room. When it filled up, they carried the remaining supplies out to the shed next to the garage where they kept surplus items. Then he headed back to the lobby.

Ashley returned. She had changed into shorts and a gray tank top, with a sweatshirt tied around her waist.

"Hey there, beautiful." He greeted Ashley with a quick peck in hopes of putting the awkward exchange from earlier behind them. "Let me put Gigi on her leash then we can head to the front yard to wait for Melissa and Ellie."

Ashley's hand slid down his abdomen. "I'm sorry about earlier. I know I overreacted. But thanks for inviting me to come."

Hope wiggled its way back into him. "No problem." Luke squeezed her around her waist then let go. "I'm glad you're here, and it will help you to feel more comfortable around Gigi."

He swiped the leash off the hook by the front desk. Once he secured Gigi to it, he interlaced his fingers with Ashley's.

On their way out, Luke looked over his shoulder and announced, "Carol, I'll be back in an hour."

Carol popped her head out of the storage room. "Have a nice time." Her gaze glided over Ashley. Then her brow furrowed. "I thought you were going on a walk with Melissa and Ellie."

Ashley tensed beside him.

"They're coming too." Gigi tugged the leash, clearly anxious for a walk. "We're going to wait for them in the front yard."

Carol pursed her lips together. He knew she was itching to say more. Over the past weeks of his relationship with Ashley, she had made it known she didn't like her. She had reminded him multiple times of his own rule: if the woman didn't like Gigi, then they wouldn't make it to a third date. It was a rule he had made years ago after a bad relationship with a woman who hated dogs, he promised himself never again. Funny how he'd made an exception for Ashley, but when they started dating, he had been overwhelmingly lonely. Ashley's company had been a welcome relief, plus he still had hope that somehow Ashley would learn to love Gigi.

Uncharacteristically stoic, Carol said, "Okay, tell them hi for me."

Luke opened the front door. "I will. See you soon."

They exited the B&B and went down to the front lawn to wait. Luke unhooked Gigi from her leash to let her run around for a bit. Gigi, overly excited to be outside, ran in circles around Ashley's ankles.

"Oh, no." Ashley jumped and scuttled, shooing her away. "Can you put it back on the leash?" Her jaw locked. "I didn't know you were taking it off her leash. I don't know how many times I have to tell you—I'm not a dog person." Her words came out bitter and harsh.

"You were the one who wanted to come," he practically hissed. Luke forced himself to take a deep breath. As frustrated as he was, there was no need to lose his temper. He waited for his heart rate to settle before he continued. "I can put her back on her leash once she's done doing her business. But I am going to take her back off the leash when we get to the tide pools." He clapped for Gigi to come back. She dashed back across the lawn toward him. When she arrived in front of him, he crouched down and scooped her up. "Gigi really would never hurt anyone. I hope you can try to like her."

Ashley pinched the bridge of her nose and said, "I don't—"

"Gigi!" shouted Ellie from the sidewalk.

They both turned in the direction of her voice. Ellie scampered across the lawn toward them. Slowly, Melissa strolled up the walkway. Her gaze danced between Ashley and Luke. For a split second, he swore her shoulders drooped a tad, but before he could be sure, she squared them and trekked the rest of the way to them.

"Hello." He lowered his arms with Gigi so Ellie could pet her. "Gigi is excited to see you again, Ellie."

Ellie stroked Gigi between her ears.

Melissa placed her hands on her daughter's shoulders. With a smile, she commented, "You really do love this dog, don't you, sweetheart."

"She loves you too." Luke found Ellie's innocent gaze. She blinked. "I know it."

"It's a dog," Ashley huffed, throwing her hands down at her sides. "How would you know if it loves someone or not?"

Luke stilled, trying to combat his mounting blood pressure. Gigi had seen him through a broken engagement and the loss of not one, but *two* parents. Ashley clearly had no clue how much love a dog could offer someone.

His chest heaved as he sighed. "I just know."

Melissa stroked Gigi too, with the same gentleness as her daughter had. "I think Gigi loves you too, Luke. I remember how much she comforted you after your mom passed." She lifted her head and met his gaze, almost timidly.

Heat flooded his core in a way he couldn't remember ever happening before. It made his lungs compress. Melissa was beautiful. Why hadn't he noticed it before?

Don't.

He pushed away the thought as quickly as it came.

"Thanks."

For a minute, he held Gigi as they petted her.

Then, after Ashley cleared her throat yet another time, he announced, "I think we should go." He lowered Gigi to the ground and hooked her leash onto her collar. "Ellie, would you like to hold her leash and walk her to the tide pools?"

"Yes!" Ellie clapped her hands together. "Please, I want to!"

"Great, I need someone who's very strong, and you look strong." He handed her the leash. "Remember to tighten the leash when we pass someone on the sidewalk, so she doesn't scare them. Once we get to the tide pools, we can take her off it to run around."

"I'll help you, Ellie," Melissa offered.

She shooed her away. "Luke said I'm strong enough to do it."

Melissa held her hands up in defeat. "Okay, then. I can't argue with that. But why don't I walk next to you?"

Luke took Ashley's hand then motioned in the direction of the tide pools. "We need to go to the right and then cut across the grassy sand dunes to get there."

Melissa tucked a few loose strands of hair behind her ears. "I remember where they are, in case we get separated."

"Right." He cleared his throat. "Of course you do. It's Ashley who hasn't been there yet."

Melissa walked alongside Ellie. Luke and Ashley wandered behind them, hand in hand, at a much slower pace. He hoped that he was showing Ashley she had nothing to worry about with Melissa. Gigi tugged on the leash and kept urging Ellie to walk faster. Soon, Melissa, Ellie, and Gigi reached the sand while Luke and Ashley were several yards behind them. Ellie handed Melissa the leash and dashed across the dry sand, yanking her sandals off and tossing them behind her as she sprinted to the water. She stopped when the water whipped around her ankles. Melissa watched her, laughing, and waited where the wet and dry sand met.

Luke and Ashley arrived next to her.

Luke stared out at the water, watching with delight. "I think Ellie loves it here," he commented.

"I know." Melissa smiled. Her eyes sparkled with the reflection of the waves and sun. "I wish we could stay at the Cape forever, but we can't. I'll have to get back to my job. But I'm grateful I can give her this summer."

"What is it you do again?" Ashley asked.

"I'm a software engineer. I mainly work with Java, doing programming, that sort of thing."

"That's right, you mentioned that." Ashley leaned into Luke's body. "Are the hours bad?"

Luke adjusted himself and wrapped an arm around her shoulders.

"Well, the hours vary, but they work for me. My boss is good about letting me finish up at home in the evening, since Ellie's daycare closes at six." Gigi tugged at her leash, wanting to play with Ellie in the water. Melissa crouched down and rubbed her space between her ears. "Do you want to go play too, girl?" She glanced up at Luke. "Can I let her off the leash? I think we're the only ones out here." Miraculously, the beach and tide pools were vacant.

"Of course." Luke unwrapped his arm from Ashley's shoulders and bent down too. He ran a hand along Gigi's back next to Melissa's. Their fingers brushed, and Melissa yanked her hand away and rapidly stood up.

Luke unhooked the leash and said, "Go play with Ellie."

Gigi dashed across the sand toward the little girl and the ocean. Ellie laughed when Gigi jumped up on her, leaving two big, sandy paw prints on her shorts. A summer breeze played with her loose blonde hair. Sunshine mixed with the tangy sea salt air as rhythmic waves crashed against the shore. Previous stresses and worries faded away. He loved this place, this moment. Then it abruptly ended.

Ashley interrupted the quiet. "Are we going to see these tide pools or what?"

Luke's jaw tensed. He rubbed a hand down his face. Why did this feel like the beginning of a fight with her? It hadn't always been this way between them, had it? Luke supposed it was possible it had, but he hadn't wanted to see it. For some reason, her impatience embarrassed him in front of Melissa.

"If you two want to go ahead, I can keep an eye on Ellie and Gigi." Melissa waved to Ellie, who was waving back at her as she jumped in and out of the waves.

"But I said I'd take Ellie to the tide pools." Luke *wanted* to take her there, to share the place he loved with them. "That was the entire point."

"I'm in no hurry," Melissa assured them. Her gaze skidded down Ashley's clearly impatient stance. "I have all day, but I know that isn't the same for you both. I'll just let Ellie play with Gigi in the water for a while. I can take her to the tide pools afterwards." She peeled her eyes from them back to the water. "Then, if you need to get back, you can."

Luke didn't like it. He'd wanted to spend this time with Melissa and Ellie, and Ashley's presence was getting in the way of that. If he was being completely honest with himself, he knew it wasn't the greatest indicator of their relationship having what it took to go the distance.

"Sounds good to me." Ashley hooked her elbow through his. "Come on, show me these tide pools."

"Fine." Luke glanced over his shoulder as Ashley tugged him away. He ached to stay, but didn't know how to refuse. "I'll be back soon."

Melissa simply nodded, her attention elsewhere. She walked a few feet further from the water and plopped herself down on the dry sand. Casually, she leaned back against her palms. He forced himself to look away and pay attention to Ashley.

The tide pools weren't far—you could see them from where Ellie and Gigi were playing in the water. They consisted of a formation of rocks on the beach where the water got trapped and created small pools during low tide. Depending on the day and what the ocean brought in, the pools contained a wide variety of fish and other sea creatures. When they arrived, several of the pools had whole schools of colorful fish in them. He didn't want Ellie to miss them with the tide coming in. In a little bit, the waves would edge past the rock formation and the tide pools would be lost under the sea until tomorrow.

"I think I need to go back and get Ellie." Longingly, he looked over his shoulder toward them. "She'll love seeing all of this."

Melissa had crossed her long, lean legs in front of her. She looked beautiful and at peace. The sunshine made her silky hair sparkle. She tossed her head back and laughed as a wet, dripping Gigi jumped onto her lap out of nowhere. She snuggled the dog against her chest, and a switch flipped inside Luke. The sight warmed his heart and caused a swooping sensation in his gut. Melissa's patience and kindness felt like a stark contrast to Ashley's more rigid personality. The two women were vastly different. Though he could enjoy Ashley's company most of the time, at the moment, he longed to be around Melissa because her calm demeanor put him at ease. Maybe it was just their years of shared memories.

Maybe it was something more.

Ashley clocked his gaze and asked, "Why can't you just enjoy this place with me?"

"Because—" Luke forced himself to look away from Melissa and focus on the tide pools in front of him. "I invited them to come."

"Fine." Ashley's mouth was a hard line. She stepped away from him. "Then go get them. But I've seen enough. I'm walking back on my own."

It was a test. A game where he didn't quite understand the rules, but knew he had already lost. Suddenly, he realized he was too tired to play.

"Okay, you can head back if you like." Luke scratched the stubble on his chin. "I'll talk to you later."

Ashley huffed. "Are we still on for dinner?" she asked with a hint of a whine that made his skin itch.

He exhaled. Had she always had these unpleasant moments? "I've got a lot going on at Bayberry House." It wasn't a lie, but a big part of him felt he just needed some space from her. Maybe if he had that, he could sort out the strange, developing feelings he had for Melissa. "A huge wedding party checked in, and I need to help Carol double-check everything for the ceremony. It's probably best if I take a raincheck."

"Figures," she muttered. "I should've seen this coming." Then she stomped away.

Luke didn't chase after her. No, he let her go. Instead, he traipsed back across the beach to Melissa. He halted in front of her seated on the sand with Gigi still in her lap.

Melissa raised a hand to block the glare of the sun. "Everything okay?" She glanced past him. "Where's Ashley?"

He plopped himself down next to her. "She saw the tide pools, then left."

Slowly, Melissa tugged her gaze from him to where Ellie was playing. "I know I'm not one to give relationship advice, seeing as I only have a failed marriage to speak of, but is everything okay between you two?" She gnawed on her bottom lip.

"Honestly?" Luke brushed the sand off his hands and cradled his knees to his chest. "I'm not so sure. I thought things were going great, but in the last week or so, I have seen a different side of her."

Melissa tapped her shoulder against his. "I'm sure you'll find a way to work it out. Andrew certainly speaks highly of her. And she'd be a fool to let you go so easily."

"I don't know about that." Luke shook his head as he reflected on everything that had happened with Ashley over the past little bit. "I think Ashley is starting to see how demanding running Bayberry House really is. Things come up last minute, sometimes I have to cancel. I don't know if going with the flow is easy for her."

"Yeah, I can see how that would be a little tricky." Melissa stared out at the ocean, where Ellie was hopping and laughing as the water danced around her ankles.

"And she doesn't like Gigi," Luke added.

Melissa winced. "That is a hard one. I'm not sure there's a way you can force someone into being a dog person."

"I'm beginning to see that," Luke muttered.

Gigi scampered from Melissa's lap to his. "But enough about me and my potential relationship problems." He ran his hand across the dog's back. "Neither you nor Ellie have ever mentioned her dad visiting. Does your ex ever see Ellie?"

"Nah." Melissa cradled her knees to her chest. "He's never seen her, not even when she was born. I couldn't tell you where he lives now or what he's up to. Honestly, I don't care. It's easier this way. I get to raise Ellie with stability and love. I think having a dad who pops in and out whenever he wants would be worse."

Luke patted Gigi then peered out at the water where Ellie played. "Well—if he ever does take the time to see her, he'll instantly fall in love with her and see how great she is."

And probably be reminded of how great her mom is, too.

Melissa smiled softly. "She is a pretty amazing kid." She stood and wiped her backside to rid it of sand. The entire front of her shirt was wet and sandy from Gigi. "Should we go see the tide pools before it's too late?" She used her hand to shade her eyes as she faced him. "Or I can take Ellie by myself if you need to get back to Bayberry House."

Gigi hopped out of his lap as he scampered to his feet. "Are you trying to get rid of me, Melissa?" He rubbed a hand behind his neck.

"No." Melissa chuckled. "I would never want to be rid of you. I like being around you. We've been friends for a long time, and it's nice being around someone who already knows you. I don't have to pretend to be someone I'm not."

"I like being around you too," managed Luke. "And I like you just the way you are."

Melissa cupped her mouth with both hands. "Ellie, come back, please. We're going to the tide pools."

Ellie splashed out of the water, darting across the sand toward them.

CHAPTER EIGHT

Melissa listened as Luke pointed out the sea urchin in the tide pool.

"You have to be extra careful around sea urchins. Their spikes are very painful." He glanced across the tide pool and winked at Melissa. "Your mom knows a little something about that."

"I can't believe you remember that," Melissa replied.

Ellie looked up at her. "Remember what?"

Melissa scrunched her nose at Luke. "When I was a little girl, I came to these tide pools with Andrew and Luke. I lost my footing and stepped on a sea urchin. My foot was covered with its spikes."

"I still remember your scream." Luke shook his head. "It scared me so much. I knew you must have been in a ton of pain."

"Did you get the spikes out?" Ellie asked.

"Yes." Melissa nodded. "But Andrew and Luke had to carry me back to the house. I had to soak my foot in hot water for an hour to loosen the spikes, and then my dad had to use pliers to pull them out. It stung worse than anything I can remember." She peered over at Luke. "I remember you brought me a bag of Hershey's kisses and told Andrew it was just for me."

Luke smiled. The sunshine made his hazel eyes sparkle. "I figured after an experience like that, you didn't need to share."

Melissa patted Ellie's back. "So, be careful by the tide pools. The rocks get slick, and you can slip."

"I'll be careful," Ellie replied sincerely.

Luke pointed out a few more sea creatures to Ellie. As the hour grew later, Melissa didn't want to keep Luke from his work at the B&B any longer.

"We should head home," Melissa said to Ellie.

While Luke and Ashley walked to the tide pools, Melissa had finalized her dinner plans with Jake for later that evening. Olivia and Andrew enthusiastically agreed to babysit Ellie.

"Ahh." Ellie dipped her hand into the tide pool. "I don't want to leave."

"I need to shower and change before I drop you off to play with Cole," Melissa explained.

"Why is this water so much warmer than the ocean?" Ellie skimmed her hand across the water. "It's the same water, right?" She squinted up at Melissa.

Luke chuckled. "You sure are sharp." He tightened his grip on Gigi's leash. "I think you get that from your mom." Then he winked at Melissa.

It felt like her heart nearly stopped. If she didn't know better, she might have thought Luke was flirting with her. But after years of being around him, she reminded herself that he was like this with everyone. His easy and carefree demeanor had made him popular with the girls back in high school.

"Thanks." Melissa mustered a smile. Her stomach swam more than she would've liked from his compliment. "Honey, the water is warmer because it's shallow in the tide pools. The sun has time to heat it up, while the ocean is big and constantly moving, so the sun can't warm it up as much."

"Really?" Ellie stood and paused for a moment. "I guess that makes sense."

"But it's time to go." Melissa held out her hand for Ellie to take. "I know Luke has a lot to do at Bayberry House, and I need to get you to Cole's."

Ellie complied, slipping her wet hand into Melissa's. They carefully scrambled across the rocks and down onto the wet sand. Luke followed beside them with Gigi on her leash.

"Where are you going tonight?" Ellie peered up at her. "Can I go too?"

Melissa wasn't about to explain she was going on a date.

"I'm going to dinner with a friend." She squeezed her daughter's hand. "Sorry, adults only. But you'll have a wonderful time playing with Cole."

They reached the dry sand, slowing them to a crawl across the uneven surface. The sun dipped lower, cooling the air. Melissa shivered in her damp shirt and shorts, which still hadn't dried from when Gigi had jumped on her. Goosebumps spread across her arms, and she forced her teeth not to chatter. She regretted not wearing a swimsuit. Cotton took forever to dry. *Lesson learned.*

Melissa had thought Ellie had dropped her curiosity of her dinner plans, but as they reached the path leading to the sidewalk, her daughter spoke again.

"Luke's an adult." Ellie's gaze flicked between Melissa and Luke. "Is he going?"

Melissa shot her gaze toward Luke. His lips twitched mischievously. Heat rushed to her cheeks despite the cool summer air.

"I've noticed Luke is an adult, but he's not going," Melissa said, hoping that would end the conversation.

"Then who is?" Ellie asked.

To her surprise, Luke came to her rescue when he asked, "Ellie, do you want to hold Gigi's leash?" Luke shifted the leash from one hand to the other, then shook his hand dramatically. "My hand is getting tired."

Ellie smiled and nodded eagerly. "I want to hold her leash!"

"Thank you," Melissa mouthed over the top of Ellie's head.

Luke smiled knowingly. *Gosh, he was easy to love.* But then she reminded herself, they were just friends. Friends helped each other out without it being anything romantic. He was with Ashley, and tonight, she had a date with Jake. She needed to give her date a real chance.

They walked in comfortable silence along the sidewalk to the B&B. Soon, they rounded the curve, and Bayberry House came into view. Melissa's gut twisted when she spotted Ashley waiting on the front porch swing. Even from a distance, she saw the scowl on Ashley's face. Melissa made a point of widening the gap between herself and Luke. She didn't need to cause Luke any more problems. As they stopped at the edge of the lawn, Melissa knew they needed to make a quick exit.

"Ellie, tell Luke thank you."

"Thanks, Luke." Ellie handed the leash to him. He took it and unhooked Gigi. Gigi raced across the lawn to relieve herself. "I hope I can see you and Gigi soon."

Luke ruffled Ellie's hair. "Anytime, kiddo." He seemed to be ignoring Ashley, who appeared to have steam coming out of her ears.

Melissa tipped her head toward the porch. "It looks like you have someone waiting for you." She gnawed at her bottom lip. "I hope we didn't get you into trouble with Ashley."

His back stiffened, but he kept his voice upbeat when he

said, "Nothing I can't handle." Then he looked toward Gigi and clapped his hands together. "Come here, girl." Gigi dashed obediently to Luke.

"Thanks, Luke." Melissa grasped Ellie's hand. "I'll see you when I see you."

Luke leaned in closer so only she could hear him. "Have a wonderful time on your *hot* date," he said playfully. "He'd be a fool not to take you off the market." Then he muttered something to himself that she didn't catch. He bent down and rubbed Gigi's fur.

Melissa rolled her eyes and whispered back, "I didn't even know I was on the market, but according to Andrew, I am." She stepped away from him, widening the gap between them.

"Ahh." Luke squinted against the sun as he glanced at her from his crouched position. "You know he loves you and wants the best for you."

"I know." Melissa stepped away with Ellie in tow. "He does want what's best for me. I hope you can smooth things over with Ashley. I'll see you later." They walked away.

When Melissa glanced back over her shoulder, she spotted Luke's shoulders drop as he climbed the stairs to the porch. Ashley's scowl no doubt was the reason for his heavy and slow steps. She almost felt sorry for him. But Melissa had a date to get to; she didn't have time to worry about Luke and his woman problems. He'd always managed to sweet-talk his way out of things. He'd be just fine.

When they arrived home, Melissa quickly directed Ellie to the bathroom where she rid her of her sandy clothes and bathed her before showering and changing herself. She put a movie on for Ellie while she changed in and out of every outfit she brought with her to the Cape. Finally, Melissa decided on a button-down blouse tucked into her nicest pair of linen pants, she hoped the date with

Jake would go well. A part of her wished she could skip to the part where she'd know if they had potential for a relationship, because she hated dating. She hated getting her hopes up for something new and different only to have them dashed.

They left so Melissa could drop Ellie off to play at her cousin's house. As she walked Ellie to the front door, she said, "I'll back for bedtime. I'm only going to be gone for a few hours."

"Okay." Ellie darted the remaining distance to the door. She opened it without knocking and disappeared inside.

"Ellie, you can't just walk in." Melissa knocked on the now-opened front door. "I'm here." Melissa would discuss with her daughter later that you couldn't enter someone's home without knocking, even if you were related.

She tentatively crossed the threshold into the house but waited in the foyer.

Olivia popped her head out of the living room and wandered toward her.

"Sorry." Melissa closed the door behind her. "Ellie let herself in. I won't let it happen again."

"No problem." Olivia walked the rest of the way to the foyer. She took in Melissa's appearance and made an "okay" sign with her hand. "Looking good. I think Jake is going to drool all over himself."

Melissa smoothed the front of her blouse. "Do you think so? I changed about ten times."

Andrew came up behind Olivia, cupping his hands on his wife's shoulders. "You look nice. I hope the date goes well. A second date without us there will be the true test. Are you meeting him there?"

"Yes." Unnecessarily, Melissa fluffed her hair. "I thought it would be easier to meet at the restaurant since I needed to drop

Ellie off. Also, I want to have the ability to make an exit if the date is a total bomb."

Melissa had been on enough bad dates to know that having your own car was essential when you were first getting to know someone.

"Nonsense. I think you're going to have a wonderful time." Olivia reached around her and opened the door. "Now," she waved Melissa out, "you get out of here before Ellie even realizes you're gone."

"Right." Melissa pivoted. "Thanks again." Then she rushed out the door.

She found the restaurant and a parking spot easily. It was a place she remembered from her childhood. The previous owners had been friends of her parents, but they had sold it and moved to Florida to retire.

After she parked, she wandered into the waiting area. Jake wasn't inside. With jittery hands, she checked her phone and realized she had arrived ten minutes early, due to her mad dash out to keep Ellie from becoming upset. With nothing else to do, she slipped onto a chair in the far corner of the waiting room. Separate groups came in, crowding the area.

Bored, she retrieved her phone from her purse and pulled up a social media app to occupy herself. Lost in thought, Melissa jolted when she heard someone call her name. When she peered up, the last people she thought she'd see were Luke and Ashley. Her stomach dropped. *Great. What were the odds?* Why did she have to keep seeing them all cuddled up together? Ashley appeared happy, her sour mood from earlier now a distant memory.

Luke ducked around a few people, directing Ashley toward her. They landed in front of her. "I thought that was you," he said.

He could've ignored her. In fact, she probably would've preferred it.

Melissa forced a smile as she looked at them. "It's me." She decided she should stand too, so she rose. A group crowded in, making her step closer to the corner of the wall and pushing Luke and Ashley forward. Their bodies packed in tightly together, and Melissa desperately wanted to be anywhere but there. She attempted to look over their shoulders to locate Jake.

"I'm waiting for Jake." When she didn't spot him, she settled back down on her heels.

Luke's lips twitched. "Ahh, the big date." He stared at her in a hypnotic way, and she forced herself to look away.

"Yep." Melissa shuffled a bit, peering past them again. *Nothing.* "I arrived a little early." She wondered why she kept talking but having Luke so close and Ashley's scrutinizing glare made her anxious. "He should be here any minute."

The host called Luke's name.

"Coming," Luke called over his shoulder. Ashley tugged him away. Before he left, he said, "You look great, Melissa. I hope you have a nice dinner." Then he disappeared into the sea of people.

Melissa watched them as they approached the waiting host. Ashley snuggled up against him by wrapping her arm around his waist. Luke mirrored her movement and wrapped his arm around her waist. They looked happy together. Clearly, whatever had transpired earlier in the day was long forgotten. She tried not to fixate on their apparent perfectness for one another as the host led them to a table in the far corner of the restaurant. But she couldn't help but notice how Luke helped Ashley into her seat. Nor could she glance away when he laughed at something she said. Melissa would never be what Luke wanted, so it was high time she stopped entertaining the idea.

A minute later, Jake arrived. He wore slacks and a button-down blue checkered shirt with a sports coat over it. Jake certainly knew how to dress, and she enjoyed the view. His lips tugged into a smile the moment he spotted her in the waiting area.

When he pulled her into a hug, he whispered into her ear, "You look beautiful." His words tickled her neck, and her nostrils flared from his cologne.

"Thanks," Melissa whispered back. His compliment eased the knot in her stomach. She released their embrace and let her eyes roam over his attractive facial features: the chiseled jawline, the perfect five o'clock shadow, and the dazzling hazel eyes. "You clean up nicely too."

Jake placed a hand on the small of Melissa's back. "Come on. I made a reservation."

They walked to the check-in desk. While Jake was sorting out the reservation with the host, Melissa's gaze wandered to Luke, but his eyes were already on her. She became flustered and darted her glance away, promising herself not to look in his direction again for the rest of the night.

Luckily, the host led them to a table on the opposite side of the restaurant, which made it more difficult for her to peer over at Luke. Melissa and Jake sat down across from one another at the small two-top. Their knees brushed under the table a few times as they settled into their places.

Melissa set the open menu on the table in front of her. "Now, what do you recommend?" She leaned closer. "I don't think I've eaten here in years, and I can't remember what was good."

Jake squeezed her shoulder. "Everything here is good, so you can't go wrong. But I like the baked salmon, or the pecan crusted mahi-mahi."

"Mm, those do sound good." Melissa's finger ran along the

menu as she read the selection of dishes. "What are you going to get?"

"I think I'm feeling salmon tonight."

She closed the menu. "I'll get the same." She set her menu next to her place setting.

Jake snapped his menu closed. "Now," he adjusted the ends of his sports coat. Then he rested his forearm next to hers on the table. Their hands were only an inch apart, and she wondered if he'd try to hold her hand. But then she questioned if she wanted him to. He continued, "Tell me about this daughter of yours I've heard so much about."

Melissa couldn't help but smile. "How much do you want to know? I can talk about her for hours."

Jake took a sip of his water, "Tell me everything. I want to know all about her." Then he shifted his hand two inches and placed it on top of hers. "Did I tell you that I was raised by a single mom?"

"Really?" Her skin warmed under his palm. "How about that?"

"I'm convinced single moms have superhero powers."

"We don't." Melissa tipped her head closer to his. "But it certainly is great that your mom made you believe that."

"She's incredible."

"I'm sure she is."

"Just like you. You're incredible too."

Geez, Jake was slick.

"You barely know me."

"I know enough to know I like you."

Jake sure knew how to wiggle his way into Melissa's heart.

The server arrived, breaking their hand-holding as they reopened their menus and placed their orders. Then the server left.

Melissa smoothed out the napkin in her lap. "What did you want to know about Ellie?"

Jake leaned in closer. "Why don't you start with what you love about her?"

She couldn't help but smile. "What don't I love about her?" Melissa knew she always lit up when she talked about her daughter. Who could blame her? Ellie was both the hardest and proudest thing she had ever done. "She's five. She's creative, curious, and kind. I love her beyond words, and anyone who even has a chance of being with me will have to know being a mom comes first."

"I wouldn't expect anything less." Jake placed his hand over hers. "I completely understand. It's what I would have wanted if my mom had dated anyone."

His words put her at ease. Maybe Jake was different? Hope wiggled its way into her heart. Even if he didn't end up being the one, it opened her up to the possibility of someone.

"Tell me more about your mom." She moved closer, making their faces hover dangerously near one another. "I know you mentioned she's in upstate New York."

"She remarried after I graduated from college and moved to a different town in upstate New York than where I grew up. I'm glad she has someone, and my stepdad is a great guy. I couldn't be happier for her." Jake looked genuine as he spoke about her. "She was alone for so long, always putting me first. I'm glad she has someone to grow old with."

Melissa smiled. "I love to hear stories like that. You already know my ex-husband left me when I was pregnant. It's only been me with Ellie the entire time. It gives me hope when I hear about other single moms finding happiness again."

"I hope that for you too," Jake remarked. "Do you mind telling me a little about Ellie's dad?" Jake took a drink of his water. "Is he in the picture at all? Do you have to share custody?"

"He's not in the picture." She couldn't even hide her disgust. "He's never even met her."

"Really?" Jake scoffed. "That's a shame, he'll regret it later. Ellie sounds awesome. He's the one who's missing out."

"I think so too."

Their food arrived and they let go of each other's hands. Over their meal, they found no shortage of things to talk about. Jake was easy to talk to, and Melissa realized how much she missed having a stimulating conversation that wasn't about work with another adult.

As she poked the salmon around with her fork, she asked, "So, what about you? Have you ever been married?"

"No, never." Jake spooned some of the rice into his mouth. Once done chewing, he continued, "I came close once, but she ended it before we ever got engaged."

"How long ago was that relationship?" She refolded the napkin in her lap.

"A few years."

"And since then—" Melissa prodded.

Jake took a sip of his drink, then set it back down. "And since then, nothing has stuck. I've dated here and there, but nobody has interested me. You might have changed all that."

Heat smeared across Melissa's cheeks. He was being forward, and normally she would appreciate it, but she wasn't even ready to think about anything but one date at a time.

They finished dinner and made their exit from the restaurant. Jake put his hand on the small of her back as he directed her through the crowded space. She wanted desperately to see if Luke and Ashley were still eating or if they had left, but she would have had to crane her neck to peer over in that direction. And she remembered the promise she made to herself not to look over there.

The overhead lamps which lined the sidewalk and parking lot flicked on, illuminating the area as it became darker with each passing minute. Melissa hadn't realized how long they had been in the restaurant.

Jake asked, "Where's your car?"

That's right, they had driven separately.

Melissa pointed at her car. "Over there."

They strode across the parking lot, holding hands. When they arrived at her car, she spotted Luke's slick black sedan nestled beside hers. They hadn't left yet, which meant their dinner was going even better than hers. She stopped at the driver's side door and dug into her purse, tugging out her keys.

Boldly, Melissa met Jake's gaze. He stepped closer, making her back gently hit the back of her vehicle. "I had a nice time." She managed to keep her voice even. "I'd like to see you again if you're feeling the same."

"Oh, I am." Jake brushed her hair over one shoulder. His hand lingered on her neck, cupping the back of it. "I'd love to take you out again. I know I took you to that lighthouse, but I know another one that looks spectacular during the day. It's only a half-hour drive from here. Would you be interested in going there with me?" He inched closer. His warm breath cascaded on her neck and down her spine.

She wondered if he was going to kiss her, but this time longer and more passionately than before. Did she even want that? Anxiety pumped through her veins, and panic set in. She wasn't ready to kiss anyone like that, even if Jake seemed like the perfect guy to end her dry spell.

"Yes." Melissa swallowed. "I'd love to go with you there."

Jake leaned in and placed the gentlest kiss on her lips. His lips left a blaze of heat that made her knees nearly buckle. The keys in her hand dug into her skin as she gripped them for balance. His hand swooped away from her neck and down past her shoulder. When his hand touched her free hand, he gave it a squeeze.

"I'll call you." He let go and stepped away. "Until then, good night, Melissa."

"Night." She waved and pressed the unlock button on her keys.

As he strode across the parking lot to his own car, Melissa slipped into her driver's seat. In a daze, she closed her door and gripped the steering wheel. Was she dating? A few weeks ago, Melissa would have laughed at the idea. But maybe things were changing; maybe finding someone wouldn't be the worst thing in the world. Being alone forever didn't sound appealing.

A knock at her window startled her. She snapped her head toward it and peered through the glass. Luke's face hovered a few inches from the glass, then he made a roll-down-the-window motion.

Melissa stuck her keys in the ignition. Music blared out of the stereo. After she turned down the volume, she pressed the window button, lowering it. Luke leaned in, resting his forearms on the open window.

"What's up, Luke?" Melissa peered over his shoulder. When she didn't spot Ashley, she settled back against her seat. "Where's Ashley?"

Luke pushed a hand through his hair. "We drove separately."

"Ahh." Melissa nodded. Then she decided to turn her car off. "So, is there something you needed?"

"I'm parked next to you," Luke stated.

"I noticed." She unflinchingly stared back at him, waiting for him to elaborate on why he found the need to knock on her window. He could've slipped into his car and driven away without her even registering he'd left.

"I saw you sitting in your car." Luke scratched his chin. Then his gaze peered around the parking lot then back at her. "And I wanted to make sure you were okay."

"I'm good." She wondered if Luke wanted to know more than just confirm she was okay. "Jake's great. I was about to leave when you knocked on my window."

"I see." Luke removed his arms from the window and straightened. "I'm glad to hear you're hitting it off with him."

"Thanks."

Luke lingered. Melissa stared.

Finally, he yanked his keys out of his pocket. "You have a nice night, Melissa. I hope you come by Bayberry House again soon to visit. Or we could go for another walk along the beach. Gigi loves playing with Ellie."

There was something in his lingering gaze that made Melissa believe he did want her to stop by again, but it didn't mean it was because he was interested in her.

"I appreciate it." Then Melissa remembered Ashley's scornful expression on his porch when they had returned from the tide pools. "But I don't want to cause any trouble between you and Ashley. I don't think she likes me being around."

Luke's mouth opened, but he hesitated.

For a second, he fiddled with his keys. "I—" he stammered. "I mean, come by anytime you want. If not, I'll see you around at Andrew and Olivia's. I'm happy to hear the date went well. I think he realizes what a catch you are."

"Thanks, Luke. That means a lot."

She watched as Luke left. Many years before, Melissa would've analyzed and reanalyzed simple words such as those, wondering if Luke meant more than he said. She needed to give up on the dream because he didn't like her like that. Luke was her brother's best friend. By default, he was stepping into the protective role, because Andrew wasn't there to do it himself. Nah, Melissa wasn't entertaining those thoughts anymore. Time to move on, even if he did look smoking hot in his khakis and button-down.

Melissa drove to Andrew and Olivia's to pick up Ellie.

After tucking her daughter into bed, Melissa took a warm cup of chamomile tea out to the back porch and settled down with a blanket on the outdoor couch. Stars twinkled against the dark sky, the full moon illuminating the sea. With the calm, soothing waves crashing on the shore, she relaxed as she enjoyed the beauty and serenity of the beach at night.

As she sipped her tea, her phone dinged. Melissa set her mug on the coffee table and grabbed her phone from the cushion next to her.

> When do I get to see you again?

Melissa grinned. He certainly didn't appear to worry about looking too eager. She hadn't been pursued in a long time. The part of her that missed being thought of delighted in the text staring back at her. She relaxed against the couch cushion, tucking her feet under herself. Her fingers zipped across the screen.

> I don't know. You tell me.

The three little dots danced at the bottom of their open text thread.

> What are you doing Saturday morning?

She gnawed on her bottom lip. If she wanted to go out with him again, she'd have to ask Andrew and Olivia to watch Ellie. It didn't sit well with her to ask again so soon, but she wasn't ready for him to meet Ellie either.

> I'll see what I can do. I'll have to find someone to watch Ellie, so pencil me in, and I'll try my best to work something out.

> I don't mind if she comes too.

She inhaled.

> Thanks for the offer, but I'm not ready for her to meet you.

> I understand. But someday? Can I meet her?

She paused for a moment, staring out at the empty beach. A part of her wondered if she'd ever be ready to introduce Ellie to someone she was dating. For something like this, she'd have to trust her instinct to know when the time was right.

> Someday in the extremely far future. I'm not bringing guys in and out of Ellie's life. It isn't fair to her. So, the answer is I have no idea when it will happen.

The dots at the bottom of the screen jumped and jived, then stopped and disappeared. Her heartbeat rose. Melissa stared at her screen, wondering if he'd respect her caution regarding Ellie. Then the dots danced again, and her phone dinged. The message appeared at the bottom of the screen.

I completely understand. I can tell you are a great mom. If a day date won't work, we can hold off on our trip to the lighthouse. I'm happy to see you whenever you have time and whatever works for your schedule. Just let me know.

Geez, he sure knew a way to her heart.

Thanks, let me figure out when we can see each other again, and I'll get back to you.

Great. Have a nice night.

With a sigh, Melissa set her phone back on the cushion next to her. She picked up her tea and sipped it until her body warmed. And there it was again—hope.

CHAPTER NINE

The crick in Luke's neck made his head throb. He forced a cleansing breath in and out of his chest. After his extremely awkward dinner with Ashley, he wondered if their relationship had been a complete facade this entire time. The glaring red flags were waving.

First, she wouldn't let it go that they had to drive separately to the restaurant. It was only because he had to run out to a hardware store two towns over to pick up some parts to fix one of the washing machines. He thought she would be happy he hadn't been late. Then Ashley had yelled at the server when they forgot to put her rice on a separate plate. Luke knew what it was like to have a thousand things going on at once—sometimes you made mistakes. It wasn't the end of the world. The final straw had been when she asked how many years dogs lived and how old Gigi was. It was like she was doing the math to figure out how much longer she'd have to put up with Gigi.

Deep down, he knew they wouldn't last if these problems kept popping up so frequently in their relationship. Being single wasn't uncharted territory for him, but he dreaded the entire process of unraveling a relationship. Did he want to end things now? He let the thought settle in his mind.

Melissa jumped to the forefront of his mind. He remembered how jealous he'd felt whenever he looked in Melissa and Jake's direction during dinner. Ashley had noticed. After that, he'd forced himself to not look over again, no matter how hard he found it. But when he'd seen them in the parking lot, cuddled up against her car, it felt like a swift kick to the gut. *But Melissa?* He'd known her his whole life. The Melissa from his childhood had run around with messy hair and sandy feet. She tagged along on his adventures with Andrew because his mom told him he had to include her. Sure, he had been protective of her, but only because she was Andrew's sister. And Andrew was like a brother to him, which made them practically family.

But she wasn't a child now.

He had noticed.

And no matter how hard he tried, he couldn't stop noticing.

Out of nowhere, Carol clapped a hand on his back. "Earth to Luke." She raised an eyebrow. "I've called your name about ten times. The workers are ready to pull the table and chairs out of the storage shed for the wedding this afternoon."

Luke shook off his thoughts of Melissa.

"I'm ready. I'll head there right now." But he didn't move, instead he stared out across the crisp grass covered with morning dew toward the majestic ocean. The setting for a wedding was spectacular. He wondered if he'd ever get married or if he even wanted to, after his broken engagement those few years back. "Do you ever think about the people who get married here? Like about how many of them make it and don't end up divorced?"

Carol whacked him on his arm. "What is up with you?" She tsked. "No, I don't think about it." She scrutinized him for a second. "That's not our job. Our job is to make their day perfect, so they think they'll defeat the odds. Life happens. Some stay together, some don't. That doesn't mean you need to sit around stewing about it."

"But ..." Luke rubbed the back of his aching neck. He'd tossed and turned all night, unable to sleep, his thoughts of Ashley and Melissa jumbled up together. "When you really think about it, only half these people will stay married. Doesn't that bother you at all?"

"No, not really." Carol put a hand on her hip. "So, half will divorce. The other half will stay married and happy until they die. What is with you? You're acting weirder than normal." Her gaze ran over him. "What's stirring up all these random questions?"

"Forget I said anything." He shook his head and stepped away. "I'll start setting up of the table and chairs. They are going in the usual places, right?"

"Yep." Carol moved to leave. "It's a big wedding, so we need every single table brought out."

"Oh, okay. I'm on it."

"And remember, I have that dance recital with my granddaughter." Carol paused and raised an eyebrow. "I must leave right after they cut the cake. You'll need to stay until the end to oversee cleanup."

"I remember." Luke smiled. "I'm not going to let you miss seeing Talia dance her little heart out."

Carol squeezed his bicep. "Thanks, boss."

Luke groaned. "You know how I hate it when you call me that."

"I know." She smirked. "That's why I do it."

Luke rolled his eyes and exited the B&B, heading to the backyard. He trekked across the yard toward the storage unit, where a few members of his normal wedding crew waited for further instructions. He directed them on the basic set up details, then helped roll the tables out of the unit. Soon, the crew arranged them in a big *U* shape around the dance floor, which they placed in the center. Gigi ran back and forth between the tables as Luke helped the crew.

Then, out of nowhere, Gigi darted toward the ocean. Usually, Gigi never left the safety of the grass without him. Luke jogged across the lawn toward the edge of the sand. A sharp glare from the sun made it impossible for him to see beyond the grass. As he neared the sand, he spotted Ellie kneeling and petting Gigi. Melissa stood beside her. Their eyes met at the exact same moment. Then she smiled, making her dazzle under the sun's golden light. The tension in his neck dissipated in an instant. Melissa looked beautiful in her black leggings, tank top, and flip-flops. His chest tightened. A warmth spread through him, making his stomach swim. But wait, this was Melissa. The same Melissa he'd known forever. Nothing had changed, right?

Wrong.

Everything had.

In that instant, he knew.

He liked Melissa. And Ellie made everything better. Just knowing this made everything a bit clearer for him. Now, he wondered what he was going to do about it.

Luke jogged the remaining distance, leaving the smooth surface of the grass for the uneven grit of the sand. He reached them, slightly out of breath.

"Hey." He leaned forward, grasping his knees with his hands. "I wondered why Gigi darted away out of nowhere. She saw you."

Ellie hugged Gigi tightly against herself. "She loves me." Then she grinned up at him, making him melt into an ooey-gooey mess. His breath slowly returned to normal and he straightened himself. "I told you." He patted Ellie on the shoulder. "I'm always right about these things."

"Ahh." Melissa's lips twitched playfully. "You caught us there."

He crouched down and hooked his finger around Gigi's collar. "I would love to have Gigi stay and play with you, but I'm setting up for a wedding. I need to get her back inside."

Ellie patted her one last time and stood. "Bye, Gigi."

"Go on back to the house, girl." Luke unhooked his finger from her collar then gently tapped her on her back end. She scampered across the sand toward the house. Luke nodded in her direction. "I need to make sure she obeys." He watched her go but knew he needed to leave to double-check.

"Yes." Melissa waved him away. "Go on, we're only out for a walk. I'm taking Ellie back to the tide pools. She loved them."

"I hope to see some sea urchins or maybe a starfish," Ellie revealed.

"I wish you luck." He kept his gaze on Gigi as she darted around the crew finishing the arranging of chairs. Then he spotted Carol snag Gigi and take her inside. Grateful for a few more minutes, Luke shifted back to face them. "You should come by tonight after the wedding. There is always way too much food left over from the catering, more than I could ever eat. I'd hate to see it go to waste."

Melissa pushed up the sunglasses slipping off her nose. "That's such a nice offer."

"But," Luke prodded. He itched to know if her evening included Jake, which made her unavailable. "Do you happen to have plans with," his gaze darted to Ellie. Clearly bored with their exchange, Ellie had kneeled and begun to dig into the sand with her bare hands. "You know who?" he whispered.

"My, my, my." Melissa scrunched her nose. Then she stepped closer to him than he ever remembered, so close he smelled the lingering scent of her citrus shampoo. It made his breath hitch. "Why are you so interested?"

"Just making conversation." He scratched his jaw, peering back at the lawn.

The crew had completed the set up. Carol bustled around the tables, laying out the crisp white tablecloths while simultaneously giving orders to those standing nearby.

"If you must know," she lowered her voice and moved even closer, which he didn't know was possible. Her body nearly brushed against his. He almost stopped breathing. In a whisper, she continued, "Jake asked me out for a day date on Saturday, but I'm not sure if I can find a way to go. I don't want to beg Olivia and Andrew to watch Ellie for me when they just watched her last night. I'm not sure what I'll do, so it might not happen."

Without reservation, Luke blurted, "I can watch her for you." The words slipped out before he even had a chance to think about them.

Ashley was going to hate this.

She stared back at him blankly. "Are you being serious?"

"Sure." Luke shrugged. "It's not a big deal. Drop her off, Ellie can play with Gigi. Carol will be around too, she has experience with kids. Between the two of us, I believe we can handle one five-year-old for a few hours."

"Ellie—" Melissa wrung her hands together. "She can be a bit of a handful. Are you sure you're up for it?"

"Absolutely." Luke peered down at Ellie. "Ellie, do you want to come over and play with Gigi on Saturday morning?"

Ellie tossed the sand in her hands back down. "Really?" She jumped to her feet. "Please Mom, can I go?"

"See?" He tipped his head toward Ellie.

"Okay." Melissa pushed up her slipped sunglasses. "I guess thanks in advance." Ellie grasped her around the thigh. Melissa patted her arm and stared directly at him. "You've no clue what you've just signed up for." It came across as a half dare, half challenge.

Some part of him wanted to prove to her he was up to the challenge.

"I think I'm going to be the best babysitter she's ever had."

"I think I'm going to regret this later," Melissa muttered. Then she peeled Ellie off her leg. "Come on." She twisted toward the direction of the tide pools, taking her daughter's hand in hers.

"Are you still coming by tonight for the free food?"

Melissa glanced over her shoulder. "Free food? Of course, I'm there. Also, Andrew, Olivia and Cole would love some too. What time?"

"The wedding party must be cleaned up by six. So, six-thirty. I'll text Andrew."

"Sorry, I think I just made it a party without running it by you first." Ellie tugged her farther away. "See you tonight."

They left and walked toward the tide pools.

He trekked back across the lawn. Every table was now covered with a white tablecloth. He went in search of Carol. After a few minutes of searching for her among the workers milling about, he spotted her chatting with the caterer. He slowed his stride and stopped beside her.

"Remember, the couple wants the crepe bar open the entire reception." Carol wagged a finger at the caterer. "I'd better not see you packing up early, or I'm docking your pay."

The caterer held up their hands. "I won't. I promise."

"The couple paid for an extra hour of food service, and I expect you to deliver," Carol reminded them.

"I remember."

"Is everything okay here?" Luke asked.

The caterer rolled their eyes. "Yeah." Then they escaped without another word.

"Of course it is." Carol straightened and rolled her shoulders back. "I'm just making sure we get what we paid for. I don't need anyone giving us a negative review based on a vendor packing up early."

"This is why I keep you around." Luke smiled. "You put out all the fires for me."

"I know." Her faint smile told him she appreciated his compliment. "The crew is placing the centerpieces on the tables. The bride and her bridesmaids checked into their honeymoon suite to get ready. Soon, we'll be ready to rock and roll."

"Terrific." Luke took in the complete setup—crisp white tablecloths with pink roses and tea lights. "I think the couple will be thrilled. It looks beautiful out here."

Carol snatched her clipboard off a nearby table. She flipped through a few of the pages. "The ceremony is at two, followed by the late lunch reception."

"Great, I'll be here the whole time. You slip out when you need to. I invited Melissa and Ellie to come by and eat some of the leftover food. I'm going to invite Andrew's family too."

"What about Ashley?" Carol's voice didn't hide her disdain.

Ashley, he'd completely forgotten to invite her. "Thanks for reminding me." He pushed his hand into his pants pocket, freeing his cell phone. "I'll invite her right now."

"I wasn't reminding you." Carol removed the pen from the top of her clipboard and jotted down a few notes without looking up. "I was only pointing out that you seem to be spending a lot of time with Melissa and her daughter lately. For a second there, I thought maybe you'd ended things with Ashley. I guess that was wishful thinking on my end."

"We're still together." Luke's jaw tightened. "You'll be the first to know if anything changes."

"Wonderful. A girl can dream." Then without another word, Carol wandered away.

Luke didn't have time to unpack Carol's disapproval. But he shot off texts to Ashley and Andrew. Then his day catapulted into troubleshooting, directing, and organizing for the wedding. But during the ceremony, as he watched the couple exchange their vows, an image of Melissa, not Ashley, popped into his mind. He pictured Melissa in white with him across from her in a tuxedo. Gigi had the rings tied around her collar, and Ellie was the flower girl. As the image filled his mind, he waited for the panic to set in, for him to brush off the idea and cast it away. Instead, he smiled.

CHAPTER TEN

Melissa rounded the corner to Bayberry House with Ellie in tow. In the evening, the crisp white paint of the B&B with its blue shutters stood out against the darkened sky. The lights from the porch and the ones that dotted the walkway were bright enough that they could see where they were going. Before they could climb the stairs, Gigi scampered down to the lawn. A second later, Luke emerged after her.

Ellie broke from Melissa's grasp and ran the remaining yards to greet Gigi, who welcomed her with a bark and a few slippery licks on the face.

"There, there, Gigi." Ellie giggled as she patted her golden fur. "I'm here now."

She knew her daughter had wanted a dog, but she hadn't expected her to bond so quickly with someone else's. If only their apartment complex in Boston allowed pets, maybe Melissa would cave.

Luke descended the steps then lingered at the bottom. "Hey." He shoved a hand into the back pocket of his pants. "It's nice to see you again."

He wore dark slacks. The sleeves of his button-down shirt

were rolled up to his elbows, revealing his muscular forearms. The porch light made the deep, chiseled slope of his jaw more pronounced. His normally messy hair was combed back. *Dang.* Her knees wobbled a tad as she inched closer. She hated how attracted she was to him, even more so today than when they'd been kids.

"Thanks for inviting us." She allowed herself to take one last look at him before darting her gaze back to her daughter chasing the dog across the grass. "Are we the first ones here?" Melissa smoothed out the top of her hair.

He peered over his shoulder back up the stairs as if he was looking for someone. When he confirmed nobody was there, he faced her again. "Ashley is inside."

"Okay." She didn't want to let on how uneasy Ashley's presence made her, so she skipped past it. "How did the wedding go? Did anyone back out last minute?"

"No, it went well." The porch light reflected in his gaze. "The couple seemed happy." They watched Ellie play a game of fetch with a stick she found. She tossed it across the grass, and Gigi darted to find it, bringing it back and setting it in front of Ellie's feet. Luke broke the quiet when he added, "I've only had one couple back out the day of their wedding. It was super uncomfortable for everyone in attendance. Right when the bride was about to say her vows, she confessed to sleeping with the groom's brother the night before. Mayhem followed, and they didn't end up getting married."

"Yikes." Melissa cringed. "How awful."

Her thoughts drifted to her own wedding. In the days leading up to it, many people had tried to warn her to not marry her ex, but she obviously hadn't listened. Instead, she'd dug in her heels and pressed forward, ignoring everyone's advice. Sometimes, she wished she could go back and rewrite the whole thing. But without that marriage she never would have had Ellie. It hadn't all been for nothing.

"I know," Luke replied.

Footsteps from behind them ended their conversation. Andrew and Olivia walked hand in hand up the sidewalk. Cole dashed in front of them, joining Ellie and Gigi.

Andrew waved and with a booming voice said, "Thanks for inviting us for free food."

"Yes, thank you." Olivia smiled. "I always appreciate a night off from cooking." They halted next to them at the edge of the steps leading to the porch.

"Anytime." Luke pushed a hand through his hair. "We'll have to make it a regular thing. Bayberry House is booked solid with weddings this summer, which means lots of leftover food."

Ashley appeared at the top of the porch steps and asked, "Can you put the dog away in its kennel so we can eat in peace?" She didn't climb down to join them.

Her voice sounded harsh, even to Melissa. She noticed how Luke's jaw clenched. He loved his dog, and she wondered why he was with someone who didn't like Gigi at all.

"I can put her in the kennel while we eat." Luke climbed the stairs as he continued, "But I'm sure the kids will want to play with her on the back lawn afterwards."

"Fine," Ashley hissed, loud enough for them to hear at the bottom of the steps. "Then I'll make sure I leave before then."

Olivia's eyes widened. Andrew and Melissa exchanged shocked glances. Ashley's prickly attitude followed her voice down the stairs, and they weren't in a hurry to join them at the top.

"Fine." Even though she couldn't see Luke's face, Melissa heard the annoyance in his voice. But he clapped his hands together. "Come on, Gigi. We need to go inside, girl."

Gigi happily bounded up the steps. He swept her into his arms.

"Ellie, we're going to eat," Melissa called across the lawn.

Cole and Ellie begrudgingly dragged their feet on the grass. Then from her place at the base of the stairs, Melissa saw Luke lean in and say something to Ashley, who shook her head and disappeared into the house without them.

They all climbed the steps, joining Luke on the porch.

"We have chicken marsala and pesto pasta along with lots of salads and rolls." He ran a hand over Gigi's fur. The dog snuggled against his chest.

"Wonderful," Melissa said.

"That sounds great," Olivia added.

When they entered the lobby of Bayberry House, a few members of the wedding party lounged in the living room off the reception area. Ashley tapped her foot as she waited for them. After Luke placed Gigi in her kennel in the storage room, he motioned with his arm for them to follow him to the kitchen.

Melissa hadn't remembered the industrial-sized kitchen, but it was massive. Shiny steel as far as the eye could see ran along the length of the space, complete with an industrial-grade dishwasher and stove. Multiple stainless-steel fridges lined one wall while another was lined with ovens. The long steel countertop contained some catering chafing dishes. Tantalizing aromas wafted out of the sealed lids. Her stomach growled.

Luke removed the lids of the chafing dishes. "Here's the chicken and pasta. There should be plenty for everyone. I have the rolls and salad out on a table outside. We can eat out there." He opened a cupboard and removed a stack of plates, placing them on the counter next to the food. "I'll take the napkins and cutlery out to the table, so you don't have to juggle carrying it." He disappeared out a back door.

Ellie stood on her tiptoes and peered into the dish

containing the chicken marsala. She pointed to a piece of chicken and said, "I want this one."

Ashley sidestepped and gestured toward Melissa. "Why don't you serve the kids first?"

Was Ashley being nice? Maybe she did have some redeeming qualities.

Melissa smiled and swiped a plate from the stack. "Thanks, Ashley. This is later than we usually eat, and I think Ellie is pretty hungry."

"I. Am. Starving," Ellie emphasized.

"I think," Melissa said, dishing out some of the chicken onto her plate, "you'll survive." Once she'd filled Ellie's plate, Melissa walked toward the exit door. "I'll have you start eating, and I'll go back for my food. Okay?"

Ellie agreed.

Melissa used her hip to push open the partially propped door. It led directly to the wraparound porch, which had a few permanent outdoor tables. Melissa glanced across the back lawn and noted everything was already put away, nobody would have guessed a wedding happened earlier. Luke waved her over from one of the tables, which was set with some pitchers of water.

He pointed to the two chairs way down at the end. "Do you mind sitting there?"

She wondered if he would sit on the opposite side with Ashley. It made sense to have Andrew and Olivia wedged in between.

"I want to sit next to Cole," Ellie said.

"Of course." Luke patted the chair next to it and said, "I'll have him sit right here."

Ellie appeared satisfied. Melissa helped her settle into her seat. She poured half a glass of water from one of the pitchers in the middle of the table. Olivia and Andrew came out with Cole, though they had their plates of food already. Once she confirmed that Ellie was fine and Cole was in the seat next to her, she made her way back into the kitchen, passing Ashley on the way. Luke came in behind Melissa, leaving them alone in the kitchen together.

"Thanks again for having us." She snatched a plate off the stack. "I'm glad Ellie is getting to know other people. We rarely go out. Most meals are just her and me huddled around the little table in our breakfast nook. This is such a welcome change in the routine."

"Do you ever get lonely?" Luke picked up a plate too.

"Oh." She pushed the serving spoon into the chafing dish of pasta, a little taken aback by his question.

"Sure, I do," she began. "Especially in the evenings after Ellie goes to bed. Most nights, I don't have much energy to socialize after a full workday. My colleagues will go meet up after work sometimes, but I have Ellie. It makes things like that not possible for me." She shuffled over to the next chafing dish. "If anything, I think it would be nice to have someone to come home to and share my day with. Have them tell me about theirs." She scooped out some chicken marsala. Luke listened, following behind her, serving himself then replacing the lid on the dish.

He nodded. "That sounds nice. I'd like that, too." He reached out just as she turned to look back at him. She saw how his fingers nearly grazed her bicep, and how he instead clasped his hand into a fist and pounded it against the side of his leg. "I'm sorry you're alone. I hope you don't have to be for much longer."

"Thanks. I don't think my situation will be changing anytime soon, but I'm fine." She lingered as Luke put the lid back on the final chafing dish. The plate warmed her hand. "All I was saying was this was a pleasant change. So, thank you."

Luke nodded then motioned for her to go first. They exited

the kitchen. She felt Ashley's dagger eyes track them the whole way from the kitchen to the table. Luke sat down next to his girlfriend while Melissa scooted past everyone to sit at the other end of the table, close to Ellie.

The kids finished eating as soon as Melissa sat down next to Olivia, with Andrew on his wife's other side. Exhausted, she didn't even argue when they scampered out of their seats, broke Gigi out of her kennel in the storage room, and raced back down the porch steps to the vast back lawn. Twinkle lights hung from the edges of the pergola. Despite the porch's overhead lighting, Melissa had to squint to make out Gigi and the kids in the near darkness. Further out, the ocean looked black, but the rhythmic sound of the waves reminded her of its presence.

Andrew was chatting with Luke and Ashley, then Olivia broke in.

"What do you two have planned for this weekend?"

To Melissa's horror, Luke's gaze landed squarely on her.

Without glancing away, he smirked and said, "Funny you should ask. I volunteered to babysit Ellie so Melissa could go on a day date with Jake on Saturday."

Olivia gasped then whacked Melissa on her arm. "You've been holding out on us! How dare you!" She rested her forearm on the table and cradled her chin, turning to look at her. "Another date with Jake. Things must be going well between you two."

"I—I—" Melissa stammered, unsure how to respond. "I mean, it's going okay."

Ashley stiffened in her seat. "I thought you would want to spend your day with me, Luke. You know Saturday is my only free day this weekend, because Sunday I'm heading to my friend's birthday party up in Chatham." She crossed her arms, brow furrowing.

"It's only for the morning." Luke wrapped his arm around

the back of her chair, either completely missing or choosing to ignore her sour demeanor. "You usually sleep in on Saturdays. I didn't think it mattered, but you're welcome to come over too."

"I wanted to spend time with you *alone*," Ashley hissed.

Luke flinched. "Then we'll go somewhere for lunch. Didn't you mention you wanted to take the bikes out for a ride along the beach path? We could do that on Saturday afternoon, alone."

Andrew and Olivia exchanged glances. Melissa stared down at her plate, wishing she were anywhere but at this table watching them argue.

"I can find someone else to watch Ellie," she offered. "That way I won't be ruining your plans."

Olivia quickly nodded. "Sure, bring her on by."

"No." Luke's jaw flexed. "It's fine. I promised to watch Ellie, and I was looking forward to hanging out with her. Ashley and I will have the rest of the day to spend together."

Then Ashley tossed her napkin down, pushing her chair away from the table. "I'm out of here." She rose abruptly and stalked back into Bayberry House.

Luke stumbled to his feet so quickly his chair crashed to the ground. He didn't bother picking it back up before he chased after her, disappearing back into the B&B.

Luke raced after Ashley, weaving through the guests lingering in the lobby then out the front door. Her speed quickened as she bounded down the front steps, so much so that he had to jog to catch up with her.

"Ashley, wait up. Let's talk about this." She didn't turn around and only stopped when she reached her car parked on the street. "Hey." He halted in front of her car, out of breath.

"Please don't leave like this. I want to talk this thing through with you."

"I think—" Ashley dug around in her purse, "that you don't care about me as much as I care about you." She yanked her keys out.

"What?" Luke ran a hand down the length of his face. "I care about you, of course I do! I just think we've been off lately. Haven't you felt that too?"

"If by 'off,' you mean you've put everything and everyone before me, then yes, I guess we're 'off.'" Ashley repositioned her purse onto her shoulder.

"I run a B&B. Things come up—emergencies that I have no control over. It's the job. I try my best to give the work to those on my staff who can step in, but a lot of times it's cheaper and faster for me to deal with it myself. I guess dating me means you'll have to be flexible about these things that come up."

"Well, I'm not flexible, and I don't understand." Ashley crossed her arms, making the keys in her hands jingle. "It's not just that. You've been putting Melissa and Ellie before me too— even *Gigi* seems to take priority over me! You care more about your stupid dog than you do about my comfort!" Her voice had steadily risen as she'd spoken, and their argument was beginning to attract the attention of passersby.

"Oh my gosh." Luke closed his eyes for a moment, trying his best to maintain his composure. "I—I don't even know how to respond to that."

This relationship was over, big time. He wondered how he had been so blind to this conclusion for so long.

"That's just it! You should be saying, 'No that's not true!'" Ashley was gesturing wildly with her hands, making Luke take a step away from her. "'I want to be with you, Ashley! I'll rehome Gigi for you!'" She slammed her arms down at her sides.

Luke was quiet for a moment. He knew what he had to do.

"Ashley, I'm really sorry, but I think we both know this isn't going to work. I can't do this anymore."

"Fine." Ashley pressed the unlock button on her key and swung open her car door. "I hope I *don't* see you around." Then she slid inside and slammed her door shut.

Luke stepped onto the sidewalk and shoved a hand into his pocket, watching her drive away.

CHAPTER ELEVEN

Melissa gnawed on her bottom lip, glancing back toward the inside of the B&B. Luke had been gone a long time, and she wondered if Ashley would be with him or not when he returned.

"Uh-oh." Olivia took a sip of water then smacked her lips together. "They've been gone too long. I think there might be trouble in paradise."

"I feel partly to blame, since part of the fight was over him watching Ellie for me," Melissa said. "He was the one who offered, but I never would have accepted if I knew it would make her so angry."

Olivia waved her off. "Don't worry. Luke knew what he agreed to do. I'm sure he'll sweet-talk himself back into her good graces." She twisted to look out at the kids then shifted back. "I am a bit surprised by how much Ashley overreacted to the whole thing, but ... maybe she doesn't like kids? Does she do okay with the kids at your practice, Andrew?"

Andrew stared straight ahead at the door to the kitchen. "Ashley is really good with our kid patients. I don't think it's that. If I didn't know better," he turned to look at them, "I'd think Ashley is threatened by you, Melissa."

She laughed nervously. "I'm not a threat, not even close. Besides, Luke is watching Ellie so that I can go out with another guy. That clearly means Ashley has nothing to worry about."

If only ...

Olivia pursed her lips. "Still." She looked like she was mulling it over. "I do think Melissa being around has shone a spotlight on some shaky points in their relationship. I never knew how inflexible Ashley is on things. I don't know if that will work with Luke's job and personality."

"You might be right," Andrew added. "Ashley is a great dental hygienist, because she's very detailed oriented, punctual, and reliable. But Luke isn't that way. He's more flexible and carefree. You'd think opposites would attract, but in this case, I think it only causes them problems."

The words had no sooner left his mouth than Luke barreled back onto the patio. "Sorry." He sat down across from Melissa in a huff.

They turned and stared at him, waiting to see if he would elaborate.

"Where's Ashley?" Andrew asked.

"We broke up." The words landed heavily in the middle of them.

"Are you okay?" Melissa asked gently.

"It's for the best." Luke reached for his half-eaten plate of food, picking up his fork. "She asked me to get rid of Gigi. And yeah—we were doomed." His hand shook as he speared a piece of chicken.

They watched him eat it. Melissa was at a loss as to how to respond or comfort him.

"It's a dog," Andrew said. "Surely, a dog can't be the reason you ended things."

Olivia lightly placed a hand on Andrew's arm and squeezed, a signal for him to stop talking. "Andrew doesn't mean that. We all love Gigi and know she means a lot to you."

"It's not only about Gigi." Luke set his fork down and took a big swig of water. "There are some other big things that weren't working between us."

Then Luke glanced across the table at Melissa. Like he'd forgotten she was even there. He paused, licked his bottom lip, and swallowed.

"Like what?" Andrew probed.

"Umm." Luke peeled his gaze from Melissa. Then he sat up straighter, squaring his shoulders. "I don't know. Just ... things."

The table went quiet. The playful shouts of Ellie and Cole echoed faintly as they chased Gigi on the lawn. Melissa desperately wanted to know what other *things* hadn't worked for them, but she didn't have the guts to ask.

"Well," Andrew began, "I only wanted to see you end up with a nice woman. I thought Ashley fit the bill, but it looks like you guys aren't a perfect fit. Work might be a little awkward for a while, but I think it will pass."

With a nod, Luke's shoulders relaxed. "Sorry, I promise to never date someone you work with again."

"Deal." Andrew smiled as he stared out at the kids playing with Gigi. Their little bodies danced with a golden ball of fur.

They finished eating without broaching the subject any further.

Then Olivia said, "Melissa, why didn't you ask Andrew and me to babysit Ellie? You know we don't mind."

Melissa rubbed her hands back and forth over her thighs. "I don't want to be a burden. I feel like the last five years have been a long stream of IOUs. I didn't want to add another one to the pile."

"That's what family is for," Andrew protested. "I'm

thrilled to hear that you and Jake are going out again, so just know Olivia and I don't mind helping watch Ellie. Usually, with you all the way in Boston—" Melissa felt Luke's eyes on her, but she didn't sneak a glance. "—we can't really help, so let us help you now. You certainly deserve to have a bit of fun this summer."

"This will be what, the second date for you two?" Olivia interjected.

Melissa stared out across the lawn at Ellie and Cole. Ellie looked alive and free, running around chasing her cousin and Gigi. The sight filled Melissa with contentment. The burden of being a single mom lifted for a moment. Coming to Cape Cod had been the perfect thing for them both so far. And Jake certainly was a pleasant surprise.

"The third," she answered, trying to sound nonchalant.

"Ooh, have you kissed?" Olivia asked, leaning in with a grin.

Melissa sucked in the air. "Geez, Olivia—I never asked you questions like that when you and Andrew were dating." Heat splashed her cheeks.

"We dated in high school. It was a long time ago." Olivia waved it off. "I live a boring mom life now, and Luke never gives us details about his dating life, which means you are one of my only sources of entertainment at the moment."

"Yeah, Melissa, tell us," Luke piped up, looking glad that they'd changed the subject. "Have you guys kissed?" His lips twitched in an almost-smile. He already knew the answer.

Melissa scrunched her nose. "I think you are forgetting how much I can tease you about. So, I'd watch it if I were you."

Luke cackled. "Like what? I'm a dating angel."

Game on.

"If I remember correctly," Melissa began, bravely tipping her chin toward him, "didn't your homecoming date junior year dump her soda in your lap and storm off during the dance?"

"I forgot about that!" Andrew keeled over laughing. "And it was orange soda. It stained the entire front of your blue tux!"

The smirk on Luke's face evaporated. He groaned. "You're remembering it right."

Melissa leaned forward, resting her elbow on the table cradling her chin with one hand. "Please remind us why you got soda dumped in your lap?"

His gaze flickered to hers. "You know why—"

"Yep." She smugly stared back at him. "She caught you making out with" —she turned to face Andrew— "what was her name? She was that blonde girl on the cheerleading squad."

Andrew furrowed his brow for a second then exchanged a glance with Olivia. "Kylee?"

"Yes, that's right, Kylee!" Olivia said.

"Yeah," Luke muttered. "You're right. I made out with Kylee when I was on a date with someone else. It wasn't my brightest moment, but I was like, sixteen. That's what you get for *trying* to be a player. 'Trying' being the key word there, because I never managed to do it very well. By college, I learned the error of my ways. I promise, I've changed."

"Sure, you have." Melissa nodded sagely. "You're a model citizen now."

His gaze narrowed teasingly. This was the mistake with taunting Luke—he knew how to win every single time. Her breath hitched. Even from over here, she smelled his cologne mixed with the scent of the sea breeze. Wickedly, he moistened his lips. The air grew thick as the roaring in her head competed against the commotion in her chest, while Luke looked ridiculously calm.

"So, nice try, you changed the subject." Luke leaned back and folded his arms. "But inquiring minds want to know: Did you kiss Jake already, or are you holding out on him? Are you making him work for it?"

"I—uh—" Melissa stammered.

Uncrossing his arms, Luke slowly picked up his glass and took a sip of his water. With the glass still hovering near his lips, he shot Olivia and Andrew a glance. "I need you to speak up for the crowd." He sipped again then placed the cup back down. He cracked his knuckles.

She rolled her eyes.

Olivia squealed. "You kissed!" She clasped her hands together. "Why didn't you tell me?"

"I didn't want to make a big thing out of it." Melissa stood abruptly. "It's getting late. I need to get Ellie to bed." She nearly tripped over her chair but managed to catch herself. She cupped her mouth and waved her other arm. "Ellie! We need to go."

Reluctantly, Ellie stopped playing and begrudgingly dragged her feet across the lawn on her way back to the porch.

Olivia checked her watch. "My, it is late." She waved at Cole. "You too, we're leaving."

Cole dashed through the grass with Gigi scampering behind him, but he quickly became distracted when he found a new stick to throw. Andrew gathered up the plates and disappeared into the kitchen while Olivia went down to the lawn to get Cole.

As Ellie approached stairs to the porch, Luke cupped Melissa's elbow. "I'm sorry." His deep voice made her stomach swim. "I was only teasing you."

Melissa straightened her back, trying not to let on how much his touch made her feel out of control. "I know. It's fine."

Luke leaned in closer. His breath tickled her neck and made her skin ignite. "Jake is a lucky guy. Because any guy would be lucky to kiss you."

A tightness tugged in her chest. Melissa peeled her gaze away to Ellie who was only a few steps away. "Any guy but you, right?" Her pulse thundered.

As soon as the words slipped from her mouth, Melissa desperately wanted to tug them back in. She didn't want Luke to know how she felt about him. If he did, then their friendship would surely be ruined. Everything would change—their banter, his interest in Ellie, all of it would be gone. No, she needed to recant her words, find some sort of witty remark to sweep this under the rug, but she came up short. Her mind went blank, and her mouth felt bone-dry.

His hand was still on her elbow. Heat laced down her body then into her toes. He finally just let go without responding at all.

Just then, she stumbled a bit as Ellie nearly tackled her, wrapping her little arms around Melissa's left leg. "I'm tired. Cole's going home too."

Luke took a wide step away from them. Then he bent down and scooped Gigi into his arms.

Her words ricocheted in her mind, making it hard for her to concentrate.

She cleared her throat and smoothed out Ellie's ruffled hair. "Okay, let's get you home."

"I'll see you in a few days, Miss Ellie." Luke snuggled Gigi against his chest.

"You will?" Ellie loosened her grip around Melissa's leg.

"Your mom has some important things to get done." He winked at Melissa, then redirected his attention to Ellie. "You and I get to hang out with Gigi all morning long."

Ellie clapped her hands together. "Yay! I'm so excited!"

"Me too, kid. Me too." He smiled, making his eyes sparkle.

CHAPTER TWELVE

A huge stack of towels toppled off the shelf, hitting Luke in the face. "Yikes!" he yelled. But thanks to his knee-jerk reaction, he managed to catch them before they fell to the ground. The save kept him from having to rewash them.

Carol popped her head into the storage room. "Everything okay?"

"No." He rubbed his jaw and shoved the towels back in with the other hand. "Why is this room so crowded?"

"I've been telling you for over a year," Carol said, stepping fully into the room and leaning her hip against the wall, "we need a second space to store the linens. One closet for cleaning supplies and toiletries, and another for linens."

"I know." He breathed out the pent-up tension in his chest and rubbed a finger between his sternum. "I'll clear out the storage closet between rooms four and five."

Ever since he'd broken up with Ashley, he'd tried his best to throw himself into the tasks that needed to be completed around Bayberry House. He thought he'd be more out of sorts with his relationship ending, but he found himself relieved, which he was taking as confirmation that they were not right for each other.

Instead, Melissa constantly ran rampant through his mind. He finally admitted to himself he was jealous of Jake. He wanted to be the one kissing her, not him. But with things going well between Jake and Melissa, he had no choice but to pack up his newly discovered feelings and tuck them away.

"I thought you were babysitting Ellie this morning." Carol crossed her arms and raised a skeptical eyebrow.

"I am." Luke flipped off the storage room light and brushed past her.

She trailed behind him. "And you think you'll have time to clear out a closet while Ellie's around?"

He shrugged. "Sure, why not?"

Ellie seemed like a good kid. He didn't have much experience around children besides Cole, but what was so hard about watching a five-year-old for a few hours?

"Oh," she laughed. "You have no idea what you signed up for. I can't wait to see this unfold."

"How hard can it be?" His voice hitched, and he suddenly questioned his offer of help.

"Hard." She swiped away the tears of laughter forming in her eyes. "I forget how little experience you've had with children, being an only child and all. Have you ever babysat a child before?"

"I know, I don't have a lot of experience." With a huff, he walked back to the reception desk, Carol following him. When he reached the desk, he wiggled the computer mouse. His stomach twisted. Maybe he did need some advice. "So, quick, what can you teach me about kids in—" he quickly checked his watch, "five minutes?"

"They get bored very easily." She leaned a hip against the reception desk. "Boredom often leads kids to do messy and dangerous things. And if you return Ellie to Melissa in worse shape than when she arrived, you have zero chance of ever dating her. I mean zero."

"I'm not trying to date her," Luke mumbled. He pulled up his emails, scanning for anything that might need his attention and to keep Carol from seeing the truth written on his face.

"Yet," Carol added.

Then, as if on cue, Melissa pushed through the front door with a canvas bag slung over her shoulder and Ellie beside her. He paused. His hand gripped the computer mouse tightly. He gulped. *Dang, Melissa looked good.* She wore her hair down in loose waves. Her light linen shorts had a floral tank top tucked into them. The outfit made her curves stand out in all the right ways. There wasn't any way to describe her other than dazzling. He wondered what it would feel like to run his fingers through those silky strands or better yet—*Wait, what?* His fingers turned white from gripping the mouse so tightly.

"You're wearing that to go on a hike?" Luke blurted.

Carol whacked his arm and coughed loudly.

Melissa's face fell, and he scolded himself. She meandered the rest of the way across the lobby, stopping at the front desk. She peered down at herself and back up at him, disappointment filling her eyes.

"Why? Does this not look good on me?" She tugged her tank top down with one hand. "I tried on about ten different things. I wanted to look like I was trying but not trying too hard, if you know what I mean. Ahh, I knew I should've stuck to my athleisure wear, but I'm going to brunch afterward."

"Who are you going to brunch with?" Ellie asked.

"Oh," Melissa's eyes widened, "just a friend. Remember, you get to stay here and play with Gigi and hang out with Luke. I'm sure you'll do lots of fun things together."

"We will," Luke said. "Gigi is resting on her bed behind the desk. Why don't you come pet her?" He waved her over.

Ellie rounded the desk without another word and kneeled next to Gigi. Her hand ran in long strokes down Gigi's fur. Carol made herself scarce, disappearing into the storage room.

Luke rubbed the back of his neck. "Sorry, my comment came out wrong." Melissa cautiously met his gaze. "I think you look beautiful. I was just worried about your choice in footwear."

She glanced down at her sandals. "But," she peered back up, "these sandals are extra comfortable. The lighthouse is on the beach, and I hate getting sand in my socks. I figured I wanted something easy to slip on and off."

The image of Melissa walking around the lighthouse with her sandals in one hand and Jake's hand in her other made him shudder. Try as he might, the thought made his jaw tighten. He wondered if they ever went out together, if she'd put as much time and effort into what she'd wear. He'd never know.

"Me too," he managed. "I hate sand in my socks. Smart choice. Jake's a lucky man."

"He sure is," she smirked.

"Attagirl. I like your confidence," Luke replied.

They stared at one another. Tension weaved between them.

"How have you been since your breakup with Ashley?" Melissa tilted her head to the side. "Do you need me to eat Hershey's kisses with you while we watch your favorite movie?"

Luke laughed. "Thanks for the offer. I'm doing fine. It was for the best to end things, and as for the Hershey's kisses ..." he pointed to the bowl on the reception desk. "I've already been indulging myself."

"Okay, I just wanted to check."

"Thanks, I appreciate it."

"Anyways." She held the bag out to him. "Here's a bag with

snacks, a swimsuit, sunscreen, and a towel in case you want to let Ellie play at the beach." Luke snagged the bag from her. Melissa shoved her hand into her front pocket, "But if you decide to take her into the ocean, I need you to promise me you won't let her in past her waist."

"Right, waist. No problem. I promise." He set the bag on the edge of the reception desk and waved her off. "Now, go. I've got this covered. I have your number if something comes up—which it won't."

"Okay." She gnawed on her bottom lip and hesitated. "Thanks again." She peeked around the desk at Ellie. "Bye sweetie, I'll be back by lunch time."

Gigi had woken up and moved to Ellie's lap. Ellie smiled brightly at Melissa. "Bye, Mom."

Melissa exhaled. "I guess I'm off. Wish me luck."

"Good luck." The words felt heavy on Luke's lips. "You won't need it though." His throat felt dry and constricted.

He knew Jake would take one look at her and completely lose his mind, fall head over heels in love with her, and kiss her senseless. Jake would see a good thing and go for it. Luke envied him.

Melissa straightened her back. "Thanks." A genuine smile spread across her lips, making him want to chase that smile repeatedly. "I'll text you when I'm headed back."

Without another word, she turned and left through the front door.

Melissa hung her arm out the window of the car. Jake had rolled them down to let the sea breeze filter through the car. She closed her eyes for a moment, tilting her head to bathe in the delectable feeling of sunlight.

"We're almost there," Jake said.

Her hair whipped in front of her face, and she tried to secure it back behind her ear. "Is this all the way at the tip of the Cape?" They'd been driving for almost an hour.

"Yeah." Jake glanced over at her then back to the road. "It's a little bit before Provincetown. I hope that's okay." He furrowed his brow.

"Yes, of course. I'm enjoying the drive. It's a nice change not to have anyone complaining in the back seat or asking for snacks," Melissa remarked.

Jake laughed. "I can get you snacks if you want, I don't mind stopping."

"Ellie is the snack queen. I swear she'd live off Goldfish crackers if I let her." She pulled her arm back inside the car and pressed it against her chest. "I prefer actual meals."

"Me too." The song on the radio ended, and a loud advertisement blasted through the speakers. Jake quickly turned it off. "Though, every time I smell popped popcorn, my mouth waters and I always want some."

Melissa smiled. "I can't go to the movies without getting popcorn."

Conversations with Jake were easy, but she was still waiting to feel some sort of spark. Melissa wanted to feel more attracted to Jake and pull toward him, but she didn't. This morning, when she kept changing clothes, the only person she wanted to impress was Luke. She had tried to tell herself it was ridiculous. Why give up an okay thing for the uncertain possibility with someone else? She didn't know the answer but hoped by the end of this date, she'd have a bit more clarity.

The lighthouse appeared on the horizon. "We're almost there. We'll have to park along the road and walk down the sandy path to reach it." A minute later, Jake pulled over to the side of the road and parked.

After climbing out of the car, they scurried down the path until it smoothed out, making it easier to walk.

As they walked to the lighthouse, Jake told her about an upcoming humanitarian trip he was taking to an impoverished country to provide medical care.

Melissa listened, then asked, "When are you leaving?"

"In about a month."

"And how long is it for?" In her mind, she imagined it being for a week—maybe two, tops.

"For a year."

Melissa halted. "You're going to be gone for a year?"

What in the world? Why was she even wasting her time going out with him? A year in her world felt like five lifetimes.

"I thought I told Andrew. I assumed you knew and were okay with it." Jake shuffled his feet and looked down. "I know the timing isn't great, but I planned this long before I agreed to go out with you. I've really enjoyed getting to know you, and I wouldn't mind hanging out with you for the next month until I leave."

"We're hanging out?" Melissa's mind reeled. "Is that what they're calling it these days?"

"I like spending time with you, but you'll be gone by the end of the summer." Jake shrugged. "I figured the timing was perfect —neither of us needed to put too much weight into this."

"Okay, I see," Melissa said.

Suddenly, the drive home seemed awfully long. Longer than she ever could've imagined.

"So, you're cool hanging out the rest of the summer, right?" Jake asked.

"Nah," Melissa replied. "I'm not. This will be our last *hangout*."

CHAPTER THIRTEEN

After Melissa left for her date, Luke paid a few bills while Ellie continued petting Gigi under the reception desk. Then, he checked out a few guests. Luke's stomach growled, and he wondered if Ellie might be getting hungry too.

Carol entered with some supplies to put into the storage room. "Did any of the guests check out already? I'm wondering which rooms I can have the cleaning crew start on."

Luke pulled up the list on his computer. "Rooms five and six are checked out." He checked the time at the bottom of the screen. "It looks like rooms seven and eight still have another hour."

"Okay, I'll tell them to start there." Carol disappeared down the hallway toward the guest rooms.

Luke crouched down to where Ellie held a sleeping Gigi in her arms. "Are you getting hungry, kiddo?"

"I'm always hungry," Ellie whispered.

"Okay," Luke whispered back. "I'm going to grab us some muffins from the kitchen. I'll be right back. Don't move or go anywhere until I return."

Ellie nodded.

Luke stood and left. He went into the kitchen and grabbed a few leftover muffins from the breakfast buffet. Just as he was about to head back to check on Ellie, one of the kitchen workers stopped him, pointing out a leaking dishwasher. Luke set the muffins down and helped the worker fix the problem.

When he returned to the lobby with the muffins, he found Carol behind the reception desk typing something into the computer. Luke set the muffins down on the desk and bent around it to tell Ellie.

Panic rose in his chest. "Where's Ellie?" Luke asked.

Carol stilled. "I thought she was with you. Gigi isn't here either."

His heart skipped a beat and he sputtered. "I left her here petting Gigi and ran into the kitchen to get us some muffins."

"I'm sure they are around here somewhere," Carol said. "Maybe she took Gigi out front to do her business."

He jogged across the lobby toward the front door, his pulse thundering in his ears as he yanked it open. Carol came up behind him and peered out at the lawn.

"She's not here." Carol squeezed his arm. "If you lost Melissa's kid, she's never going to forgive you."

He shook off her hand. "Geez, Carol. That doesn't help." They stepped back inside. "And Ellie isn't lost. I was in the kitchen for maybe five minutes. She couldn't have gone too far. I'll find her." He spoke the words he desperately wanted to believe.

"You'll find her," Carol agreed. "I can check the secret hiding place I showed her when she stopped by with Melissa."

"Okay." He rubbed his chin raw, forcing himself to stay calm and not jump to any unnecessary conclusions.

Bayberry House was huge, full of unusual places to hide. Honestly, it was a jackpot for a kid's game of hide-and-seek. But Ellie had Gigi with her, which meant they were probably off playing together somewhere. "I'll check out back first, I think that's where she would've gone with Gigi." He didn't wait for Carol's response, dashing across the lobby and out the back door. He could feel Carol on his heels, so he didn't waste time looking back.

When he didn't spot them on the lawn, he raised his hand to block out the blinding sun. Way off, Ellie played on the beach with Gigi. While she was currently on the sand, she was dangerously close to the water's edge.

"I see her!"

He bolted down the patio steps and across the lawn. His feet hit the uneven sand, making his steps wobbly and filling his shoes with sand. The sand slowed his pace down, but he picked up his knees, determined to reach Ellie before anything bad happened.

"Ellie!" Luke yelled. "You can't come out here alone."

She turned toward the direction of his voice. Gigi heard him too and scampered across the sand, leaping onto his thigh. Luke scooped her up and continued his trek to Ellie. He remembered Carol had followed him out at a slower speed. He turned back and waved at Carol who had stopped at the edge of the lawn. Luke gave her a thumbs-up. Satisfied that Ellie and Gigi were safe, Carol turned and walked back across the lawn toward the B&B.

Luke's pulse slowly returned to its normal rate. His labored breathing evened out as he reached Ellie.

"You scared me." He willed his voice to stay calm and even. He stopped in front of her tiny frame. "You can't come out here alone."

She clasped and unclasped her hands. "I wanted to play with Gigi in the waves."

"I know." He plopped down on the sand to be eye level with her. Then he patted the sand next to him. "But I'm sure your mom has told you before you can't go out to the beach alone. It's not safe."

Ellie sat down next to him, crossing her legs. "I wasn't alone." Her eyes shone with childlike innocence. "I was with Gigi."

His heart tugged in his chest. "Gigi doesn't count. She's not an adult." As if sensing the intensity of the conversation, Gigi hopped out of his arms and into Ellie's lap. "I promised your mom I would keep you safe. Next time, you need to tell me where you're going. I would've said yes if you'd asked if we could take Gigi to the beach."

"I'm sorry." Ellie cast her gaze on Gigi and snuggled against her fur. "Please don't tell my mom. I don't want to get in trouble."

"You shouldn't keep secrets from your mom. So, sorry kiddo, I'm going to have to tell her, even if it means we both get into trouble."

She scrunched up her nose. "My mom would never get mad at you. She's always talking about you, which means she probably likes you."

Luke's heart clenched. "Wait …. what?" he stammered.

Before she could respond, Gigi wiggled out of Ellie's lap and darted toward the water. Ellie scrambled to her feet, running after her. *Melissa talked about him?* He certainly liked the thought. Maybe she did have feelings for him. Then again, kids said all sorts of things, and sometimes they were far from what they meant. Still, the possibility planted itself into his mind.

He wanted to question Ellie further and get to the bottom of this bomb she dropped. But then he reminded himself—she was five. Chances were her words didn't mean anything.

He stood, brushing the sand off his clothes. "Ellie, come back. We need to get your swimsuit and sunscreen on before you play in the water."

Ellie grinned. "Okay." She dashed back to him with Gigi nipping at her heels. Out of breath, she arrived in front of him, "Can I have that muffin you promised me before I put on my swimsuit?" The girl sure knew how to melt his heart with her sweetness.

"Of course, let's go back to the house. We'll eat and then get you ready to play. I'll put on my swimsuit too and can go out in the waves with you." He ruffled her hair. "Should I grab the beach toys too?"

"Yippee!" Ellie jumped up and down. "Will you build a sandcastle with me? I've always wanted a dad to do that with me."

He paused, knowing how he responded mattered. "I'm sure that's true. Luckily, you have a pretty awesome mom. I'll bet she builds sandcastles with you."

"Mom does sometimes." She squinted against the sun. "Uncle Andrew has too."

"See? That's already two people who love you and will build sandcastles with you."

Ellie nodded. "Okay, but they aren't here. So, can you build one with me?"

"I'd love to build sandcastles with you." He smiled at her. "I thought you'd never ask."

Ellie grinned, and he knew the little girl had completely wormed her way into his heart without even trying.

Back at the house, they ate muffins while other guests helped themselves to the buffet. When they finished, he put Gigi on her dog bed. Carol promised to bring her out later once she had calmed from the excitement of the morning. She kept an eye on Ellie while Luke changed into his swimsuit. Ellie used the guest bathroom in the lobby to change herself.

Luke gathered Ellie's bag with her towel and sunscreen, then found the sand toys in the garage. For a second, he wondered if he should bring a chair and an umbrella but decided against it. Who was he kidding, he wasn't going to sit down at the beach.

He applied sunscreen liberally to Ellie, making sure every inch of her skin was covered. He sprayed himself the best he could. Then, Ellie wasted no time playing.

She tugged him out to the water. He remembered Melissa's rule and only allowed her to go out to her waist. They laughed and shrieked as they played in the waves. He held Ellie's hand, lifting her high whenever a big wave crashed against them. Luke couldn't remember a morning that had flown by so fast.

"Can we go build sandcastles now?" Ellie asked. "I'm getting tired."

"Sure thing, kiddo." Luke took her hand as they waded out of the water.

Ellie suddenly dropped his hand and sprinted ahead toward the dry sand. "Mom!" she yelled.

Luke shaded his eyes from the sun. Melissa stood near their pile of beach stuff on the edge of the dry sand. Her hair was wild and frizzy from the sea breeze, her cheeks rosy and her lips a bright red. He couldn't remember a time when she had looked more captivating. A rush of warmth flooded through him.

He wondered how long she'd been watching him play in the water with Ellie. *What time was it?* He hoped the date was a flop, and Melissa had returned early. *Did she kiss Jake again?* The questions came in fast as he made his way toward her.

Melissa kneeled and hugged Ellie's wet body without hesitation. She didn't seem the least bit worried about getting wet and messy. Their eyes caught over Ellie's shoulders, and he could've sworn she gave him a once-over. *A guy could dream.*

"How was it?" She released her daughter, snagging a towel from her canvas bag. She wrapped it around Ellie's shivering body. Then Melissa plopped down on the sand, and Ellie climbed onto her lap.

His pulse rose, almost making him forget what he needed to say. "Oh, great." He ran a hand over his messy, wet locks. "But ask Ellie, her opinion matters most."

Ellie grinned. "Luke is so fun! He held my hand in the waves and lifted me up so I wouldn't get scared. He promised to build a sandcastle with me. Can I please stay a little longer?"

Melissa laughed, then gently swooped Ellie's sloppy hair out of her eyes and gingerly tucked it behind her ears. "I think that depends on how much time Luke has. He might need to take a raincheck. I think you were playing in the waves longer than you thought." She gazed up at him still towering over them.

She set up an easy out for him.

Luke swiped his towel and ran it over his wet face and hair. "I've got time." With face and hair dry, he moved the towel down his abdomen. "I promised Ellie sandcastles, and I plan on delivering."

To his delight, Melissa traced his every move, making his blood pressure simmer. He wondered if she liked what she saw.

"So, can I?" Ellie brought Melissa's face closer to hers. "He said he'll do it. And I like playing with Luke. He's way more fun than you, Mom."

"Ouch." She dramatically placed a hand over her heart. "Ellie, don't hold back." She laughed. "Tell me how you really feel. I can be fun though." She winked up at Luke. "Just ask Luke, he's seen it. Way back when I was a teenager."

"Totally." He plopped down next to them. "Your mom used to be pretty adventurous."

"What's adven-tu-rous?"

Before he could answer, Ellie moved on.

She scampered out of Melissa's lap and scooped up the sand

toys in a heap next to them. "I still think Luke is more fun, but it's okay. He can show you how to be fun too, Mom."

"Well," Melissa's lips twitched intoxicatingly. "I'll have to ask Luke for tips."

She looked stunning. He had to glance away as heat crawled up his neck.

"I'm ready to build," Ellie chimed in.

"Give me a second to catch my breath." He cradled his arms around his knees. "You get started on it, and I'll help." Luke held up his hand. "Give me five minutes."

"Mom," Ellie dropped a toy and snatched it back up. "Start the timer!"

Melissa tugged her phone from her pocket and tapped the screen. "I'm setting it right now." She pulled up the timer. "Done." Then she shooed Ellie away. "Now go, Luke has earned a five-minute break."

They watched as Ellie dumped the sand toys near the wet sand. She snagged a bucket and raced to the water, filling it up. A gentle breeze nipped at Luke's skin, but despite that, he felt warm all over. He had to resist the urge to wrap his arm around Melissa and tug her close to his side.

Instead, he tightly gripped his hands together around his knees, wondering what any of these growing feelings for Melissa meant. One thing was certain: he was glad she had come to the Cape. Now, he needed to convince her to stay.

CHAPTER FOURTEEN

Melissa watched Ellie ferry bucket after bucket to her hole in the sand. She stretched her legs out in front of herself and crossed her ankles. The sea breeze misted them with the ocean water.

"Thanks again for watching Ellie." Melissa shifted to glance over at him. "I think she had a good time with you, since you're *so* fun," she teased.

Luke chuckled. "I've always thought I was fun, but having the opinion of a five-year-old only confirms it."

She smiled then peered back at where Ellie played. A minute passed.

"So," Luke broke the silence. "How did the date with Jake go?"

"Ahh, you know ..." she shrugged then leaned back on her hands. The gritty sand dug into her palms.

He scrunched up his nose. "That bad?" He laughed then stretched his legs out in front of him too. "Are you going to give the guy another shot?" He ran a hand through his hair, brushing the messy locks out of his eyes.

"No ..." Her voice trailed off, and she cradled her legs to her chest. "I'm not. Apparently, we were just 'hanging out,' and he failed to tell me he's off to some third-world country for the next year on some humanitarian aid thing. Something I would've loved to have known before I went out with him the first time."

"Ahh." He bumped his bare shoulder against her bare shoulder, then kept it there. Heat rippled down her arm. "You can't fault the do-gooder." He smirked at her.

She kept her gaze on Ellie. With his skin against hers, she found it hard to breathe. "I guess I can't," she managed, trying to keep her voice even and undeterred. "It's for the best. I'm headed back to Boston at the end of summer. This made it easier to end things now."

She wondered if he'd move his shoulder away, but there it was, pressed tightly against hers. Did the feeling of their skin touching do anything to him? She wanted to sneak a sideways glance, but she'd never been sly enough to pull something like that off. Instead, she forced herself to breathe in and out, trying to focus on her surroundings.

Ocean waves crashed on the shore. Seagulls squawked. Ellie giggled as the cool water nipped at her ankles. She fetched another bucket full of water. Melissa loved it here. She'd forgotten how magical this place was in the summer. Honestly, she wished she could stay here forever. But like everything else, summers ended. Fall came. The winters were cold enough to knock you over, but today at this place, Melissa felt lighter and happier than she had in years.

"So," Luke prodded. "No more Jake."

"Nope." Melissa wiped her hands off on her soggy shorts. Her tank top stuck to her skin from the wet spots Ellie's swimsuit left behind. She peeled her eyes from her daughter to him.

"Would you ever date someone like me?" The words tumbled out quickly, almost recklessly.

His question startled her. "*Like* you? Or *you*?"

"I don't know why I said, 'like me'—I chickened out there for a second." Luke gulped. "Would you ever date me?"

Her pulse galloped, making her stomach flip. "What about Ashley? You guys just broke up. It sounds like maybe you're on the prowl for a rebound."

"It wouldn't be a rebound."

Melissa wanted to believe him. How long had she waited and hoped for him to ask her out? But she'd never imagined it like this. Before she could come up with a response, her phone timer sounded, interrupting them. It was loud enough that Ellie heard it and dashed across the sand back to them.

"It's been five minutes! It's time for sandcastles!"

"You're right." She stumbled to her feet, brushing off her backside to rid it of sand. "I'll build sandcastles with you."

Ellie placed her hand on her hip. "But I said I wanted Luke to help me."

"Hey." Melissa placed a hand over her heart. "What am I, chopped liver?"

Ellie looked confused. "What's chopped liver?"

Luke laughed and got to his feet. His arm brushed against hers as he stood beside her. Her skin sang from the momentary graze. One touch, and she lost her entire sense of control.

"Chopped liver," he said, patting Ellie's shoulder, "is something you'll never want, and something I promise never to give you. Let's go build this sandcastle, but I know your mom is an expert at building the tallest ones. She was always good at it when she was your age. Her castles were the highest because they were structurally sound."

She found his gaze from behind the comfort of her sunglasses. "You remember that." Her heart tugged. She hadn't expected it to mean so much to her that he remembered that.

"Yes." He blinked. "You always were so patient and precise

at making sure everything was built correctly so it would be strong and tall."

Her cheeks warmed. Sure, Melissa had tucked away plenty of memories about him from way back then, but only because she'd had a major crush on him. Hearing Luke speak about her from the past made her way too pleased.

"I did love to make sure it was strong and perfectly shaped. The key is making sure the foundation is packed extra tight," Melissa said.

"You heard her. What do you think, Ellie?" He raised an eyebrow. "Three people is better than two, no?"

Ellie shrugged. "Fine, Mom, you can help too."

Melissa caught Luke's eye and mouthed, "Thank you."

He didn't say anything. He simply squeezed her bicep as he brushed past her over to the started pile of sand. Melissa's heart nearly exploded from the quiet intimacy of his touch. Her skin buzzed for the next ten minutes as the three of them worked in tandem to stack bucketfuls of packed sand to build a castle that was both wide and tall.

While they were building, Carol wandered over from Bayberry House with Gigi on a leash. When Gigi spotted them, she barked and tugged against her collar, crawling toward Ellie. Ellie dropped her sand bucket and raced to give Gigi a hug.

Carol unhooked the leash. "I hope I'm not interrupting." Gigi scampered out to the water with Ellie chasing her. "You looked like a pretty picture together from way back on the lawn, but Gigi needed to get out and Luke told me to bring her out before I leave for the day."

They rose to their feet. Sand stuck to Melissa's shorts, legs, and hands. She was a total mess. Part of her wished she had worn her swimsuit so she could rid herself of her soggy, sandy clothes.

"Thanks." Luke took the leash from Carol. "I appreciate you

bringing her out to me." He wrapped it around his hand a few times.

"I'm off, but Braden arrived." Carol smiled. "He'll be starting his shift and should have everything covered, so no need to rush back."

"Okay, thanks," Luke said.

Carol shot him a pointed glance Melissa couldn't decipher.

"Did Luke tell you about losing Ellie?" Carol questioned.

Melissa's jaw dropped. "Wait, what?"

Luke's eyes nearly bugged out.

A hand shot to her heart. "How long was she lost?"

Melissa promised herself she would never go anywhere ever again. Yep, she wasn't dating until Ellie was eighteen. It was settled.

"Not long." He rubbed the back of his neck. "Sorry, I wasn't trying to hide it from you. I forgot to mention it. So, thanks for reminding me."

Carol cackled. "Sorry, I have to tease Luke about it, because he had been telling me smugly how easy it is to take care of a kid, then less than a minute later, he couldn't find Ellie." She patted him on his back. "But Melissa, don't worry, he learned his lesson. Luke found her within two minutes. So, no harm, no foul, and I know he'll do a better job next time."

"Thanks," he muttered.

"I don't want the details. It's best for me not to know." Melissa exhaled. "The important thing is that she's safe now. Besides, I guess you get what you pay for."

"Isn't that the truth," Carol replied. She lingered for a moment, then said, "Anyhow, I'm off. But Luke, remember you have the entire rest of the day free. I hope you can enjoy yourself. Maybe go somewhere nice this evening."

"Okay, thanks." His jaw tightened. "I'm not sure what my plans will be."

Carol patted him on the arm and winked. "You'll figure it out. You're a smart guy." Luke blushed. Melissa couldn't remember ever seeing Luke blush. He was the poster boy for smooth and put-together. Carol turned to leave, then added, "Oh, I had Chef Tony make up some lunch for you all. I told him you'd be back soon."

Luke's back stiffened, and he shot Carol a salty look. Melissa felt awkward; she didn't need a pity lunch, and they already eaten up half of his day.

"That's so thoughtful of you, but Ellie and I need to head back home," she said.

"Why?" Ellie said out of nowhere. Sometime during their exchange, she had come up right next to her without her noticing.

Melissa plastered a crooked smile on her face. "We need to get you in the bath, plus I think we've taken up too much of Luke's time today."

"But I *want* to eat lunch with Luke!" Ellie stomped her foot. "He's nice and fun."

"Ellie," Melissa said, trying to be patient. She pinched the bridge of her nose. "I've told you—"

Luke interrupted her. "I'd love for you both to stay for lunch." He placed a hand on Melissa's shoulder.

His touch startled her, and her eyes traced his arm all the way up to his face. Her insides did a somersault. Something hovered between them that had never been there before. Desire. Could Luke really want her to stay? Maybe he did want to ask her out for real. For a second, she let herself bask in the beauty of hope, because she felt warm and steady under the grip of his palm.

Carol smirked then tossed Luke a nod. "I hope you enjoy lunch. I'll see you tomorrow." She puttered on back to the house without another word.

"Are you sure?" Melissa studied his face, looking for an indication of what he wanted. "I don't want to keep you. I'm so grateful you watched Ellie this morning. I'll have to make you dinner sometime as thank you."

"How about tonight?" Luke cleared his throat and dropped his hand. "I'm free tonight for dinner."

"Oh—" Melissa fidgeted with some loose strands of hair then pushed them behind her ear. "Fantastic. Tonight works. Come on over around six."

"Perfect." Luke smiled and turned his gaze to Ellie. "Come on, I'm starving. Aren't you?"

Ellie hopped and skipped. "I'm *so* hungry." Gigi ran a couple of circles around her ankles.

He crouched down and hooked Gigi to her leash. "Then let's eat!" He held the leash out to Ellie. "Do you want to walk Gigi back to the B&B?"

Ellie beamed, grasping the leash tightly in her little hand. "Yes!" Gigi tugged at her collar and soon she was racing from the sand to the grass with Ellie in her wake.

Leisurely, Luke and Melissa made their way behind them. The sun warmed her skin. She breathed in the salty air. And there it was again: hope.

CHAPTER FIFTEEN

Luke swiped a hand across the foggy mirror in his bathroom. He stared back at his reflection. His hands trembled, and he forced them down to his sides to rid them of the anxiety pulsating through him. *It's only Melissa. It's only dinner. With Ellie in between. This isn't a date. Although you still need to ask her out on a real one.* This could be their practice round, he reassured himself. A very non-threatening, practice date with Ellie keeping things G-rated.

Quickly, he tugged on jeans and a gray short-sleeved Henley tee. With the sand off his skin, he hoped feeling refreshed would replace the jitters inside of him. But why did he still feel out of sorts? Why did his heart pound at the thought of being near her again? The prospect equally terrified and invigorated him. And he was done with Ashley. It hadn't been long since they'd broken up, but he knew, deep down, that if he did start to date Melissa, it wouldn't be a rebound. Far from it, in fact. His relationship with Ashley paled in comparison to the possibility of something with Melissa. Hard emphasis on *possibility*; he still didn't even know if she was interested in him romantically.

His phone buzzed on the counter, Andrew's name flashing across the screen. Luke answered, putting it on speaker, "What's up?" He placed it back on the counter and retrieved his hair balm from the top drawer of his bathroom vanity.

"Hey, I have a tee time that I snagged at the country club for early evening. I wanted to see if you're free to join me."

Luke loved to golf. Normally, he would have jumped at the chance to go with Andrew. "Umm. I'd love to, but unfortunately, I have some plans this evening." No need to bring up Melissa. He wasn't hiding anything, but he didn't want to elaborate until there was something to share.

"Oh?" Andrew waited for him to elaborate. When he didn't, Andrew said, "So, what are these mysterious plans you have? If you don't mind me asking."

"Actually, I do mind." Satisfied with his hair, Luke capped the hair balm and put it back in the drawer.

"You're being very tight-lipped." Andrew laughed. "Sounds fishy. You tell me everything, what's going on?"

"True, normally I do." Luke located his cologne and spritzed his neck. He couldn't remember the last time he'd put it on. Maybe he was deeper into this thing than he thought.

"And—"

"And I don't want to tell you."

"Are you taking out Mrs. Fitz or something?"

"Our old chemistry teacher?" Luke laughed. "I haven't thought about her in years! She's probably close to sixty these days."

"If not her, then who—"

"Fine." Luke stared back at his reflection in the mirror and wondered if he'd regret this entire conversation later. "Melissa invited me over for dinner as a thank-you for watching Ellie today while she went out with Jake."

"Is that all?" Andrew tsked. "Cancel on her, she'll

understand. It's only Melissa, and it's not like it's an actual date. By the way, she isn't exactly known as a cook. She's probably going to serve you mac and cheese with hot dogs in it. Text her you can't go and come golfing with me."

"I'm not going to cancel on her." He grabbed his phone from off the counter and left the comfort of his bathroom. "Besides, Ellie seemed excited. I promised to bring Gigi with me."

"Well, that's true, I'd be a jerk to make you disappoint my niece." Andrew then spoke to someone in the background. "Hang on a second, Olivia's telling me something."

Luke couldn't make out what they were saying and only heard muffled voices. When more than a minute passed, he took the phone off speaker, putting it to his ear. "Hey." Luke retrieved his keys and wallet from the kitchen table. "I'm going to hang up now. I need to stop by the hardware store before I go to dinner."

When there was no reply, he double-checked the connection. Then right as he went to end the call, Andrew said, "I'm back. Sorry, Olivia thinks—anyways." His voice sounded weird, but Luke couldn't put his finger on it. "Have a wonderful time at dinner. We'll hit the links another time."

"Okay." He shoved his wallet into his back pocket. "You too."

Andrew said goodbye and hung up. Luke felt like his friend was acting strange, but he didn't have time to stew about it. A door to one of the rooms had a broken latch. He'd promised Carol that he would pick up the part they needed from the hardware store. Tonight, the room was vacant, but tomorrow, the B&B would be completely full.

Since Carol had left for the weekend, she also left him a list of things he needed to fix. Nothing he couldn't handle: a squeaky hinge, a broken part of the pergola, and a sprinkler on the front lawn. His day-to-day work was vastly different from his days as an attorney. Some days he missed the hustle and bustle, but lately, with Melissa around, he found the flexibility in his schedule to be very appealing.

He made the quick stop at the hardware store for the latch part. Luckily, the family-owned shop didn't mind him bringing Gigi in with him. The owner helped him find the proper hinge and reassured him it was a quick fix he could complete in less than an hour. Luke made a mental note to complete it before he went to bed.

Then Luke drove to Melissa's parents' house. After he parked in front, he gathered Gigi in his arms and trekked up the stairs to the front door. A surge of nervous energy shot through him, but then he reminded himself that it was only Melissa. He'd known her his entire life. Tonight wouldn't be any different. Or would it? Did he want it to be?

He knocked and waited. Gigi squirmed in his arms, but he held her tightly and ran a hand down her back to calm her down. The door swung open, revealing Melissa. She looked like a goddess in white. A tank top dress hugged her in all the right places and made her sun-kissed skin glow against the fabric. He thought she looked more beautiful than ever before, and he wondered why it had taken him so long to see her in this light.

His throat was dry. "Hey," he managed.

"Come on in." Melissa pulled the door open wider and motioned for him to enter. "Dinner is almost ready." He entered, and she shut the door behind him.

Tantalizing smells wafted from the kitchen down the hallway, making his stomach growl. "Smells delicious! Andrew said you couldn't cook."

"What?" A hand flew to her hip. Her jaw tightened a smidge. "Remind me to punch him next time I see him," she joked.

Luke laughed. "Can I set Gigi down?" He peered past her

and wondered when Ellie would make an appearance. "She's completely house-trained. She'll let me know if she needs to go."

"Absolutely." Melissa stepped closer and stroked the fur between Gigi's ears. Her perfume wafted off her, filling his lungs with the fruity, floral scent. His head spun, and he forced himself to concentrate on the words coming out of her mouth so he wouldn't look like a fool. "Let her wander around." She removed her hand.

Luke crouched down and let Gigi out of his arms. "Where's Ellie?" He stood back up.

"Um." Melissa bit her bottom lip. "It's only us tonight. Olivia randomly called about a half hour ago and insisted on taking Ellie to a movie with Cole. I shouldn't have answered on speaker phone, because Ellie promptly accepted the invitation." She crinkled her nose. "Sorry, you and Gigi were outbid by a kids' movie."

Gigi stayed close to his feet. "It wouldn't be the first time."

Melissa's eyes sparkled back at him. "Ahh." She wagged a finger. "I think you're lying. I think this might be the first time you've been outranked by something else."

"Well yeah, but there's a first time for everything," Luke teased.

"Apparently."

Then he stared at her, and try as he might, he couldn't think up another funny retort to flirt back. Instead, he swam in the intoxicating intrigue of her beauty, making his mind blank.

Melissa smoothed out the front of her dress. "Follow me back to the kitchen." She waved over her shoulder as she wandered down the familiar hallway. "I don't want my soup to boil over."

He trailed behind her, knowing the way like the back of his hand. A flood of memories came roaring back, although Luke hadn't been to Melissa's parents' house for a while. When he met up with Andrew, it was usually at his place or at Bayberry House. The familiarity made him miss his own parents and the carefree days of his youth.

He tried not to dwell on all he'd lost too often, because it only deepened his pain and emptiness inside. Having friends like Andrew and Olivia helped ease his loneliness. Melissa slipping back into his life had made him hopeful again and brought on a longing to find someone to share things with.

When he rounded the corner, Melissa stood behind the stove. With a long wooden spoon in her hand, she stirred the soup in the tall pot. He glanced out to the patio, the ocean in the distance. A nice table setting, complete with lit candles to keep the bugs away, made him realize he was on a date. The reality made sweat begin to glisten on his brow. He swiped at it with the back of his wrist.

He stayed on the other side of the kitchen island. "Smells good." He leaned his hip against the island and shoved his hands into his pockets. He itched to touch Melissa, imagining his fingers running across her milky skin. No, he needed to stay on this side of the island, where he was safe. "What is it?"

Smiling, she peered over her shoulder. "Minestrone soup. Sorry, I know it's summertime, but I have exactly three things I make well, and this is one of them." She shifted back to the stove and flipped off the burner. The smell of fresh bread drifted from the oven as she grabbed a hot pad and opened the door. She placed the crispy loaf of bread on the unoccupied burner. With a swift movement, Melissa closed the oven door. "I did make a loaf of sourdough too. My mom put me under strict instructions to not let her starter die while they're away."

"Ahh." Luke rubbed his jaw. "You'll have to remind me to tell her thank you. I love sourdough bread."

"I remember." She smiled. "You used to come over after

school with Andrew, and the two of you would polish off an entire loaf."

The memory of it came back to him, making him smile. "I did eat an insane amount of food back then. I was always starving after football practice. I could eat whatever I wanted, and I still had a six pack."

"A six pack that got you *all* the ladies." Melissa stirred the soup again.

He pushed off the counter, rounding it and coming up next to her. "That was then. This is now."

"I would say you've still got your swagger." Her cheeks flushed. She stepped away from him and opened a cupboard, retrieving two bowls and two plates. "You certainly still have a six pack."

His ears perked up. He loved how good it made him feel to be noticed by her.

"Oh," he stepped closer, now only a foot away, "were you looking?"

She rolled her eyes. "It's hard not to see it." She dug around in a drawer and removed a ladle. "Where else am I supposed to look when you're shirtless on the beach?" She scooped some soup into the first bowl.

"I, certainly, wouldn't mind seeing you shirtless on the beach." The words spilled out without a thought. Her eyes widened with shock as red splashed her cheeks and smeared down her neck. He stammered, "That sounded way worse—I didn't mean topless. I mean, not that I wouldn't mind seeing you in a swimsuit. But that isn't the only thing that matters, though I'm definitely attracted—okay, I'm going to stop talking now."

Melissa held out the full bowl of soup to him. "That's probably for the best. I don't want you to say things you don't mean." His hand grazed her fingers as he took the bowl from her. "Though, I do enjoy seeing you all flustered," she smirked.

"I'm not flustered."

"Mm." She ladled soup into the next bowl. "Do you mind walking the soup out to the patio while I slice the bread?"

"Sure." Luke was relieved to have something to do other than talk.

So, he liked Melissa. And she knew it, thanks to his word vomit. Now what?

Luke placed the first bowl of soup at one of the two place settings, then meandered back into the kitchen. He grabbed the next bowl and took it out. When he returned, Melissa had finished slicing the bread and was placing it in a breadbasket.

"Drinks are in the fridge." Melissa sidestepped, passing by him without their bodies touching. Over her shoulder, she said, "Do you mind grabbing us some? I'll take anything."

After he got out two cans of soda, he walked out to the patio and placed them on the table. The sun lowered on the horizon, making the water in the distance glisten. Streaks of yellow and gold brought on early dusk. The beach was mostly empty; only a few stray people walked by. Melissa settled into her seat, and he did too.

"When does Ellie get back?" Luke asked.

Gigi wandered outside, plopping down next to his feet.

Melissa fetched a slice of bread from the breadbasket, placing it on her plate. "I'm not sure." She held the basket out to him. He snatched one too. After she set the bread back down, she picked up her spoon and stirred her steamy soup a bit to cool it down. "Olivia mentioned maybe taking them to ice cream afterwards. Why? Are you disappointed she's not here?" She scrutinized his face.

"Oh." He shook his head. "No, nothing like that. Though I do enjoy Ellie's company, this is nice too." His heart raced. His movements suddenly felt awkward and abnormal. Being alone with her only made him want to spend more time with her.

"I'm glad to hear it." Her posture relaxed as she ate the spoonful of soup. "It's rare I get to spend alone time with another adult. My conversations usually revolve around Play-Doh and Barbies when Ellie is in the mix. Since coming here, I've already received so much support and reprieve from my normal day-to-day life. Let me tell you, being a single parent is exhausting." She dunked her bread into her soup.

"I'll bet it is hard to do it all on your own." Luke pushed his spoon in the soup. "But I think you've handled it with grace and class. And I think your ex is an idiot."

"Hey," Melissa said before taking another bite of bread, "something we can agree on."

"He's the one who's completely missing out," Luke added. "Ellie is an incredible kid, and you're amazing."

"Thanks." She smiled brightly, making her practically sparkle. "I appreciate it."

They ate for a few moments in contented silence.

Finally, he asked the question he'd been itching to ask. "Why did you marry him?"

Startled, her spoon nearly toppled out of her hand. She caught it then placed it beside her bowl. "Do you want the truth?" She tilted her head toward him.

"Always." He leaned closer, his forearms on the table, bringing their shoulders dangerously close to one another.

She inhaled deeply, then exhaled a sigh and stared out at the ocean. The fading light of day and the approaching darkness of night made the first stars lightly speckle the sky.

"Because ... he asked me." She turned her gaze from the ocean to Luke's face. Staring back at him was the sadness, the regret, the years of hardship and trial. He wanted to wipe it away and help right every wrong. If he was lucky, he wanted to be able to fill in the gaps with goodness and love. "He asked me, and I said yes. I figured, why not? I was already thirty. Most of my friends were married, and I didn't want to be left behind. I thought being with him would be better than being alone. I'd figured some of us don't get head-over-heels, I-love-you-more-than-anything type of love. Some of us only get just enough."

She rolled her bottom lip in between her teeth and shook her head. "I was wrong. Having just some love isn't enough. It's true that some of us don't find the perfect person, but we shouldn't settle. I've learned there is something far worse than being alone—it's being with the wrong person. And he was the completely wrong person."

His heart ached. "Will you ever try again? You know, to get married?"

She tilted her head to the side, appearing to contemplate his question. She placed her hand on the table next to where his was placed, nearly grazing his own. His fingers itched to move forward an inch to touch hers, the desire driving him crazy. He wondered if Melissa also felt this thing building between them, or if it was all one-sided. His pulse galloped. He waited for her to respond.

"I would, if I fell in love." She gazed out at the water. "I would if I found someone who could love both me and Ellie. I know it's a tall order, but it's the only way I would ever consider marrying someone."

A flash of understanding cleared his mind and strengthened his resolve.

"I asked earlier, but we were interrupted by Ellie, and I want to ask again. Would you ever consider dating me?" he blurted.

She whipped to face him. The words hovered in the tight space. His heart hammered in his chest and he could feel sweat glistening on his brow. He wondered if he'd thrown everything away, years of friendship, with those six simple words. What if she said no?

"Are you being serious?" She straightened herself while each word punctured the air. "What about Ashley? You two broke up like, ten minutes ago."

"Well—I—" he tried to backtrack.

His confidence waned. He still had time to pull back his words. This was Andrew's sister. If he messed this up, then he could lose him too. He couldn't just go out with her for fun. If it didn't work out, he'd lose everyone.

But if he took the chance, then maybe, just maybe, he'd end up with everything he ever wanted.

When he didn't respond, she nodded. "That's what I thought." Abruptly, she pushed her chair out from the table, making it scrape against the patio floor. "I made dessert. Let me go get it." Without meeting his eyes, she gathered up their empty bowls and left the patio, disappearing inside.

He sat, stunned, and stared out at the ocean. Dark sky had pushed the last bit of daylight away, the moon casting a spotlight on the water. His stomach twisted. He knew he needed to be brave. This was the moment, their before and after. He'd had these moments before, these defining points in life: before law school and after it. Before the death of his parents and after. Each moment had pushed him and changed him. Like those, this moment with Melissa couldn't be undone. If he didn't act, he knew he'd regret it forever. Determined, he stood and passed through the door back into the kitchen.

Melissa's head was buried deep inside the refrigerator.

"Melissa—" His voice shook, matching the tremor in his hands.

He strode the rest of the way into the kitchen. She peeked from behind the door of the fridge. Her hand gripped the corner of it as she pulled out a cake on a stand. Then she closed the door with her hip.

"Yeah?" She didn't make eye contact with him. Instead, she

kept her eyes glued to the cake as she placed it on the counter. Then she puttered around the kitchen, opening and closing drawers. "I'll be out in a minute. I'm just finding the right plates." She yanked another drawer open and rifled through the bunch of utensils.

He rounded the island and came up beside her. If she noticed his nearness, she faked indifference and didn't stop searching for whatever she needed to find. Finally, he placed one hand at the dip in her waist. She stilled. Then she dropped the spatula in her other hand right back into the drawer.

"Hey," Luke cleared his throat. Timidly, she met his gaze. And there he saw it: the hurt, the pain, and he wanted to make it all go away. "I apologize. I got scared back there. I'm sorry." Luke squeezed her waist. The tense muscles of her shoulders and back loosened. "I do want to take you out. Honestly, I'd like to date you. I don't care about Ashley, because she isn't half the woman you are. I enjoy talking to you and just being in your company. I really admire how you've pushed through so many hard times. And, of course, it helps that you're really cute. I'd like to see if there's something more between us than just friendship."

Melissa shook her head. She stepped around him, forcing him to drop his hand from her waist. "I think you don't like being alone, and I'm a convenient fill-in until you figure things out. I'm not doing that, because—" Her voice cracked. Melissa blinked rapidly. She promptly picked up the cake and left the kitchen.

"It's not like that," he called after her, hurrying behind her. He stopped right next to her. "Melissa," He placed a gentle hand on her shoulder and twisted her to face him. "I don't know what happened, but you came back to the Cape all grown-up and beautiful. I never saw you like that before, but I'd like to see if there could be something between us."

Melissa set the cake down on the patio table. "You don't have any clue, do you?" She used the back of her wrist to push back the strands of hair in her eyes.

"Clue about what?"

"I've been in love with you since we were kids."

Her words nearly knocked him off balance.

"This isn't a game to me. I won't let you bring me out to play just to toss me aside when you get sick of me, and end up back with Ashley. I don't deserve that, and I can't do it. I wouldn't survive that type of rejection."

"You always had a thing for me?" He scratched the scruff at his chin.

His mind raced to try to play catch-up.

Her cheeks flushed red. "Unfortunately, yes." Then she moved brushed by him, heading back into the kitchen. He trailed behind, following her inside.

"You've never suspected it?" she asked over her shoulder. "I'm surprised. I thought you always knew." Melissa strode the rest of the way into the kitchen.

When he didn't respond immediately, she groaned loudly. "I can't believe I told you that. I shouldn't have told you that. Now everything is going to be so weird between us." She reached the drawer where the spatulas were held, yanked one out, and slapped it on top of the quartz countertop.

"Melissa—"

"What?" Her jaw clenched tight, making the muscles in her neck distinct.

"Stop." Then he was beside her. He firmly placed both hands on her shoulders. She managed to look everywhere but at him. "I'm glad you told me. This isn't a joke to me. I'm sorry I was completely dense when I was a teenager. But I've always enjoyed being around you. I appreciated your friendship, but you still were Andrew's little sister to me. And it kind of made you off-limits. Please don't hold it against me, because I'm interested in you now. Give me a chance to prove I'm not an idiot anymore."

Melissa laughed. "You *were* a total idiot as a teenager. A cute one, but an idiot nonetheless."

"See, we agree on the important things." This made her grin. He pressed forward. "So, when can I take you out?"

"I don't know." Melissa gnawed on her bottom lip. "Is this some game to you?"

"No, it's not. I promise you, it's not."

Her eyes narrowed, and she scrutinized him for a moment. He smiled, hoping she could read the truth in his face.

Then after a deep exhale, she replied, "I hope I don't regret this later." She squeezed her eyes shut, then opened them to look right at him. "But does Friday night work?"

After Luke left, Melissa tried her best to give herself time to process everything that had transpired. How many years had she waited for this moment to come? And now that it was here, all she could think of was everything that could go wrong.

If they dated and it didn't work out, she'd be left with very awkward encounters with him for the rest of her life. Then she reminded herself to slow down and take each date as it came. Maybe they would go on one date, and Luke would decide they were better off as friends. She needed to prepare herself for all possible outcomes.

Melissa didn't have much time to think it through, because less than five minutes after Luke left, Ellie burst through the door on a sugar high.

"Mom! I'm back!" Ellie announced loudly as she raced down the hallway to the living room. "Did you miss me?"

Olivia entered behind her.

"Of course I did." Melissa bent down with her arms open. Ellie leaped into them. "It looks like you had a good time."

Olivia laughed. "Yeah, sorry about that. Cole passed out on the way home from ice cream, and Andrew went to put him to bed."

Melissa stood. "Okay, Missy, you need to go change into your pj's. I'll be up in a minute to help you brush your teeth before bed."

"Okay." Ellie dashed up the stairs to her room.

"So ..." Olivia wagged her eyebrows. "How did things go with Luke?"

"I have no idea what you're talking about," Melissa replied in a feeble attempt to play coy.

"Spill!" Olivia playfully whacked her on her arm. "I just watched your daughter last-minute so that Luke would have the chance to make his move. So did he?"

"Umm." Melissa wondered how much to share. "It went well."

"Come on," Olivia said, wagging a finger. "I'm going to need more details. Don't you dare hold out on me."

"Luke said he wants to take me out. Even date me." Melissa couldn't fight the smile forming on her face even if she'd wanted to.

Olivia grabbed Melissa in a hug and jumped up and down. "It's happening!"

"What's happening?" Melissa's voice came out slightly muffled from her face being squished against Olivia's shoulder.

Olivia stopped jumping and let Melissa go. Slightly out of breath, she exclaimed, "You're going to get your happily-ever-after!"

She held her hands up. "Whoa there. Back that up. I have

no idea what is going to happen. I'm not going to even let myself go there."

"Well, you should." Olivia put a hand on her hip. "Because you two are perfect for each other!"

"I appreciate your encouragement."

"This is exciting. Why aren't you more excited?"

"Oh, I am." Melissa folded her arms around herself. "I'm just nervous. What if this thing blows up in my face?"

"But what if it ends up being as great as you always imagined it would be? Wouldn't you rather spend this time being excited rather than worried?" Olivia raised an eyebrow.

She smiled. "You know this is why I love you, right?"

"I know," Olivia beamed. "Just doing my job."

Melissa pondered her words as she put Ellie to bed. Even if she and Luke would only have this one date, she could at least allow herself to feel the hope that had begun to grow within her. She decided to lean in.

CHAPTER SIXTEEN

Melissa finished her makeup and admired her reflection in the mirror. Butterflies fluttered in her stomach as she flipped off her bathroom light. Tonight was the night, a date she had imagined for far too long. As she took in the mess of her room with clothes strewn everywhere the eye could see, her phone rang. She tugged the phone from the pocket of her dress. Luke's name displayed across the screen.

After a steadying breath, she answered the phone. "Hello?"

"Hey." He sounded out of breath. "I to have cancel our date tonight."

Her heart hitched. "Oh, okay."

She hated how much his words stung and didn't know how to respond. Instead, she waited for him to give some made-up excuse. It wasn't the first time a guy had backed out on date with her. She knew it was a bad idea to get her hopes up but naively hadn't listened to the rational voice in her head. Nope, she'd dived in headfirst, trusting Luke would be gentle with her. Her feelings of devastation would be hard to match.

"There's a plumbing issue at Bayberry House. There seems to always be something, but the entire basement is backed up with sewage. It's awful—" His voice faded and became muffled. Melissa assumed he was talking to someone else.

"I understand," she replied. "Emergencies come up, especially when you own a B&B."

"You have no idea." He then spoke to someone else, "Just a second. Let's start in the corner then work our way over." His voice became louder again. "Sorry, I've got to run. The plumber is an hour away, and in the meantime, I need to contain this as best I can to keep from having to send my guests to a competitor's B&B down the street."

"That sounds—" She wanted to say terrible, but he ended the call before she could finish.

So be it. She tossed her phone onto her bed and flopped backward onto it.

At least she believed Luke's excuse.

Still, she had spent the better part of an hour picking out an outfit to wear while Ellie watched some annoying kid show. Clothes littered the ground, and she didn't have the energy to put everything away. Her hair was freshly washed and curled. She wasn't ever going to get back the time she had spent. All dolled up with nobody to impress. Maybe she needed to take Ellie out for dinner on Main Street so that she didn't waste all the effort she had put in.

A voice broke her moment of sulking. "Melissa?"

She sat up to the sound of Olivia's voice. "In here!" she bellowed.

Olivia appeared in the doorway of her room. "My, my, my." Her eyes roamed the messy room. It looked like a bomb had exploded. "I can see you had a hard time deciding what to wear." She leaned against the doorway and crossed her arms. "But I love what you have on. You picked something terrific."

"Thanks, but—" Melissa stood and bent down to wrangle a handful of clothes from the ground. "Luke just canceled. I'm sorry you drove over here for nothing." She walked to the closet and picked up a hanger.

Olivia stepped into the room, snatching some clothes off the ground before joining Melissa in the small walk-in closet. "He canceled." She took a hanger and pushed it through the sleeve of a floral top. "But it's Luke, he must have had a good excuse. He wouldn't have stood you up for no reason."

"He did." Melissa rehanged the dress, returning it to its place. "I guess there's a plumbing issue at the B&B."

"See?" Olivia grabbed a cardigan. "I'm sure he'll reschedule."

Tears threatened to spill out, and Melissa didn't glance over. Instead, she focused her entire energy on rehanging all the items she juggled in her arms.

"Maybe." Melissa sidestepped around Olivia then went back into her room, swiping some more clothes from the ground.

Olivia followed her out. Tears tickled the corners of Melissa's eyes, and she blinked rapidly to keep them at bay.

"He will reschedule." Olivia reached out and cupped Melissa's shoulder, stopping her in her tracks. "It's Luke, please don't give up hope yet."

"I think I cared too much." Melissa's voice cracked. A few tears slipped down her cheeks, and she wiped them away with the heel of her hand. Straightening her shoulders, she broke free from Olivia's grasp, reentering her closet. She waited until Olivia appeared in the doorway before she continued, "I've been in love with Luke for so long. I shouldn't have gotten my hopes up. I know it's a real excuse, but I let myself dream for a minute—and I never dream."

"Oh, honey." Olivia tilted her head. "You'll get your chance to go out with him. It's good to dream, because sometimes they come true."

"I don't know." She shoved a hanger through the armholes

of another dress and hung it on the clothing rod. "I think it might hurt too much."

Olivia paused for a second. "Well then," she clapped her hands together, making Melissa flinch. She continued, "Enough of this chatter. I think you should change into your crummiest clothes. I'll take Ellie back to my house to play with Cole, and you can go over and help Luke deal with this plumbing problem."

"I don't know." Melissa furrowed her brow. "He might not want me there."

"Nonsense." Olivia waved off her hesitation. "Who doesn't appreciate some free labor? But you need to make it clear you aren't all heartbroken over this date. Instead, show him you are willing to help. Whoever ends up with Luke will have to know he runs a B&B and that unglamorous things like this will come up."

Melissa hadn't even thought that far ahead to consider the possibility of her and Ellie living at Bayberry House. Then, she stopped her overthinking in its tracks. They hadn't even had a real date. It was way too soon to think about any long-term plans.

"True," she said, quietly.

"Okay, then it's settled." Olivia pivoted, walking back out to the bedroom. Melissa followed her out. "Also, I think you should pick up something for you guys to eat for dinner. So, you're bringing food and offering to help. What guy wouldn't love that?"

Hope wiggled its way back into her heart. Even if she couldn't go out to dinner with him, at least she could brighten his evening and spend time with him. She packed up the things Ellie needed and gave them to Olivia. They left soon after. Melissa changed into her oldest clothes and dug her mom's old galoshes out of the garage. After a quick stop at a sandwich shop, Melissa arrived unannounced at the B&B.

When she walked through the front door into the lobby, she found it swarming with guests. Carol manned the front desk, appearing to be fielding a barrage of questions about the plumbing disaster. Melissa went to the front desk and waited behind the guests in line.

Once Carol finished with one guest, she waved her over. "Are you here for Luke?"

"I came to help. Is he down in the basement?"

Carol's gaze roamed over her. "I'm glad you wore clothes you don't care about because they are going to get ruined."

"I know." She held up her to-go bag. "Can I stash this in the kitchen fridge?"

"Yes, of course." Carol waved for the next guest in line to move forward. "Follow the back stairs down to the basement. You'll smell it before you see it. Promise." Then she winked.

Without further discussion, Melissa placed the food in the fridge and made her way to the basement stairs. When she opened the door that led to the basement, the smell nearly knocked her over. She pinched her nose and stepped down the stairs. When the basement came into view, she gasped. It was so much worse than she had imagined. The entire floor was covered in nasty muck. Bile rose up her throat, and she forced herself to swallow it back down.

"You weren't kidding," she said at the bottom step.

If she stepped any lower, the sewage would cover the ankles of her galoshes.

Luke snapped his head toward the stairwell. He was covered in a white jumpsuit from head to toe, with a face mask, gloves, and goggles.

"Hey." His hands tightened around the handle of his large floor squeegee. "What are you doing here?"

"I came to help." Bravely, she stepped down into the grossest thing imaginable. She peered out at the basement floor. "And," she laughed nervously, "this is so much worse than I thought."

"I know. Glamorous, right?"

"Yep." She stayed in place in fear of splashing anything onto herself. "But I'm not afraid. Put me to work."

"Really?"

"Totally." She managed to take a step closer to him without getting any on herself. Then she pointed at his hand. "Do you have another one of those squeegee things?"

"Yes." He peered past her. "Though, first you need to put on protective clothing, face mask, gloves, and goggles. There's some on that shelf in the left corner by the furnace."

Slowly, she made her way to the dry corner where the furnace and shelf were located. She snatched some supplies from the stack. Gingerly, she removed her foot from her galoshes and wiggled her way into the suit and back into her shoes. Once the suit was on, she put on the remaining protective gear.

"Has this happened before?" Melissa left the safety of the dry corner and walked back into the sludge.

"Unfortunately, yes," Luke said. "This isn't the first time it's happened, so now I'm prepared for the cleanup. It always takes the plumbers far too long to get here. The charms of having a B&B property that's over two hundred years old. The plumbing seems to be that old too."

"Here." Luke held a floor squeegee out to her. "Just push everything into this drain in the corner. It's the only one that's not clogged."

"Gotcha."

She took the squeegee and went to work. Luke snatched another one from the dry corner and joined her. Even though she wore a protective face mask, the putrid smell was still strong, making her gag every so often. She forced herself to try and breathe through her mouth and not her nose. Being a mom, she had cleaned up some major diaper blow-outs. Ellie had once vomited directly into her ear. But those experiences were mild in comparison to this disgusting experience. The only thing that made it slightly okay was doing it for Luke.

For a few minutes, they worked in silence, pushing the backed-up sewage into the single working drain.

"I'm sorry about our date." Luke scraped his squeegee across the floor. "I didn't want to back out. I was really looking forward to it."

Melissa's ears perked up. "I know, me too." She followed behind his squeegee. "Raincheck?"

He peered back at her and smiled. "Absolutely."

Another fifteen minutes passed as they tried their best to push most of the backup into the drain. The plumber and his crew arrived shortly after, taking over. The plumber fixed the overflowing drain while his crew sanitized and bleached the concrete floor of the basement. When Luke saw everything appeared to be under control, he led her out the back door.

Dark sky surrounded them. She wondered how long they had been in the basement, but she didn't dare push up the sleeve of her white jumpsuit to check. She desperately wanted to douse herself in hot scalding water to rid herself of the stench and dirty feeling on her skin.

As Luke removed his goggles and face mask, he said, "We need to strip off out here and throw everything straight into the dumpster. Whatever you do, don't touch your face." He removed his gloves next. "We're throwing everything away."

"Okay." She rid herself of the goggles, face mask, gloves, and jumpsuit, tossing them into the dumpster while Luke held the lid open. "What about our galoshes?"

"I'll rinse them off with the hose and spray them off with

bleach." Luke left the dumpster and wandered to the side of the B&B. "You'll need to leave them here. Did you bring any other shoes with you?"

"Nope."

He turned on the hose and sprayed his galoshes off. "I'll let you borrow a pair of my slides. They'll be big, but they'll work so you don't have to return home barefoot."

"I'd appreciate it." Melissa leaned against the side of the house, watching as Luke sprayed off his boots. The muscles in his forearms bulged, and she forced herself to look away, turning her gaze to the ocean. Stars speckled the sky, and a full moon shone on the water. A light sea breeze nipped at her bare arms. "I should probably head home once you get my shoes rinsed off. I think we were down there longer than I thought."

Luke stopped spraying and twisted the nozzle to stop the water. He checked his watch. "It is later than I thought." He stepped closer to her. "I'll get your boots rinsed off in no time, then I'll run inside and grab the pairs of slides for us." But when he untwisted the top of the hose, it jammed. He fiddled with it for a second before a powerful rush of water exploded directly into her face.

"Ahh," she yelped, bringing her arms up to lessen the blow.

She jumped to the left, but he over corrected himself and ended up dousing her even more. Finally, he managed to shut the water off. Melissa stood, dripping from head to toe.

Melissa clenched her eyes shut. "I'm trying really hard not to touch my face like you told me, too." The idea of germs crawling free and undeterred across her body made her cringe. She told herself not to worry, the odds of her contracting E. coli or another deadly disease from sewage had to be a myth. *Right?*

"I'm so sorry. Don't move." Luke instructed. "I'll be right back."

She heard him scamper away, leaving her dripping in water.

Water ran down her temples and across her firmly shut eyes. She counted to ten over and over again, willing herself to remain calm. The cool night air made her shiver. Melissa heard Luke round the house. His feet crunched across the grass, growing louder and louder as he neared.

"I brought you a towel." She didn't open her eyes, but she felt his forearm slide across hers. "I'm going to pat your face dry and wrap you in this towel. Then, I'll have you go take a shower in my apartment."

"Okay." Her teeth chattered. "Sounds like a plan."

The fluffy terrycloth towel grazed her face and he gently patted it dry. His nearness spread goosebumps across her arms and down her back.

"There you go." He spoke so quietly, she had to strain to hear him. "You can open your eyes now." Slowly, she opened her eyes, and he filled her vision. "You are so beautiful." He wrapped the towel around her shoulders.

His words made her heart nearly stop. "How can you say that? I'm drenched in water and smell like poop. And beware, I've most likely contracted E. coli. So, you've been warned."

Luke chuckled. "If it helps, I smell like poop too." He wrapped his arm around her waist to support her. "Can you slip off your boots? I brought you some slides. I already have mine on."

Melissa peered down at his feet. "Let me lean into you, I think I can slip them off." She wrapped an arm around his waist and shimmied her calf out of the first boot.

He bent down and placed the slide in front of her. She slipped her foot in. They repeated the process for her other foot. Then he retrieved a small bottle of hand sanitizer from his pocket. He squirted hand sanitizer onto both of their hands, and they diligently rubbed it in.

"Come on." Luke held his hand out to her, and she didn't

hesitate to weave her fingers with his. He squeezed her hand. "You need a warm shower."

"I should call Olivia and let her know I'll be late picking up Ellie."

"Of course." The lights from the back porch flickered across his face. "Melissa, I'm glad you came. You made a very unpleasant night, pleasant."

His words made her stomach swim. She feared messing up the moment by jabbering off some nonsense. Instead, she played it safe and simply nodded. They walked hand in hand around the side of Bayberry House and up the back porch steps.

CHAPTER SEVENTEEN

Luke led Melissa up to his apartment on the third floor. Nerves made his pulse thunder behind his ears. When they arrived, he dropped her hand and tapped the code into the lock on the door. The lock flipped and unlocked.

He pushed the door open. "Come on in." He motioned for her to go first. "It's not much, but I did renovate the apartment before I moved in after my parents passed."

Cautiously, she stepped inside. "You mean you didn't want avocado green kitchen appliances?"

He smiled. "I can't believe you remember that." He shut the door behind them.

Why did he feel jittery? The space suddenly felt smaller and more intimate. His lips twitched with the urge to kiss Melissa, but he shook off the feeling.

"Of course, I remember." She inched further into his apartment. The hallway immediately opened to a living room, dining area, and kitchen. Beyond the open space were two doors, which she assumed led to bedrooms. Running her fingers along the wall, she paused and glanced back at him. "I love what you've done here. It feels so much more open."

"I know. It made a huge difference." He walked into the kitchen and leaned against the kitchen island. "There was a wall here." He pointed at the beam overhead. "It was load-bearing, so I had to put in this beam."

"Did you do the work yourself?" She moved closer, scanning every nook and cranny of the clean, open space. "If you did, I'm very impressed."

"No." He chuckled. "I should've said the contractor put in the beam. I just supervised. At the time, I was going back and forth from Boston, juggling my corporate law job. But the remodel convinced me I couldn't live in both worlds. Those few months were a nightmare, trying to balance Bayberry House and my firm. I ultimately decided for now, this is where I need to be."

She gave him a curious gaze. "Do you miss it?"

"My law job?"

She nodded.

"Sometimes a part of me itches to go back to law. But for the most part, I think this is where I belong at least right now. That might change. I'm trying to take everything day by day then see where life leads me." He pushed off the counter. "Here, let me get you a towel and some dry clothes. Then you can take a shower."

"Thanks. I am freezing."

Luke left her in the living room, heading to his bedroom. He snagged a pair of sweatpants and a crewneck sweatshirt. Melissa would probably drown in them, but at least she'd be warm on the drive home. After he pulled a towel out of the hall closet and started the shower, Luke placed the clothes and towel on the marble vanity. The bathroom had been a splurge. It had all the fancy features of a spa shower. Once the water ran hot, Luke returned to the living room.

Melissa glanced up from her phone.

"Did you let Olivia know you'd be late?" He stopped a foot from her. "How much time do you have?"

"Yeah," she set her phone on the counter. "Olivia said to take all the time I needed. Ellie and Cole fell asleep watching a movie, so Ellie's going to spend the night."

"Oh." His breath caught in his throat. "So, you don't need to hurry." He gulped.

"Nope."

A string of desire weaved between them. His fingers itched to reach for her and pull her close, sealing the night with a kiss.

"The water is ready." He doused his thoughts with words, motioning for her to follow him. "Everything's in the bathroom. I'm going to hop in the other shower because I also feel disgusting." He led her down the small hallway, stopping in front of the open bathroom door.

Steam barreled out the propped door. "I picked up some dinner. It's in the fridge downstairs." She peered inside. "We could eat afterward."

"Perfect." Luke stepped aside, making room for her to enter. "That was very thoughtful of you. I'll grab it once I'm showered and changed."

She entered the bathroom and closed the door softly behind her. He made quick work of stripping his dirty clothes, showering, and changing into a clean pair of black joggers and a hoodie. When he passed by the bathroom Melissa occupied, he could hear the water still running.

He knew he had time to fetch the food. When he entered the lobby, the disgruntled guests from earlier had left. Only Carol occupied the space behind the reception desk.

Carol glanced up from the computer. "Crisis averted?" She raised a skeptical eyebrow.

"I believe so. Melissa helped me push the backed-up sewage into the one working drain, and the plumber and his crew took over. He said they'd leave when they were done and send you the bill."

"Perfect." She clicked the mouse a few times, then closed the document on the computer screen. "I'm heading out for the night. The night manager arrived ten minutes ago and is helping light a fire in room three." She reached under the desk and grabbed her purse.

"Thanks again." Luke stepped toward the kitchen. "Have a good night."

"Is Melissa still here?" She swung her purse strap over her shoulder.

"She's showering and changing. She said she put some food for us in the kitchen fridge, so I was just grabbing it."

"Oh, really?" Carol smirked. "Imagine that. A woman who actually cares about you and does nice things for you. But you ..." Her voice trailed off, and she stepped closer to the front door.

"Spit it out." He put a hand on his hip. "Whatever you are wanting to say, say it."

"You know me, I don't want to overstep."

He scoffed. "All you do is overstep, but I can take it." He motioned "give me" with his hands. "Tell me."

"Ashley never would've come help you muck out a basement." She dug a hand into her purse, retrieving her keys. "Just remember that."

"I know."

He agreed completely and planned to do something about it.

"You know she's perfect for you, right?"

"I appreciate your enthusiasm." He chuckled.

"Just remember to give me credit when you're immensely happy after you start dating."

"Good night, Carol."

She smirked, leaving through the front door.

Smiling, he entered the kitchen and fetched the to-go bag Melissa left in the fridge.

When he returned to his apartment, Melissa had settled on his brown leather sofa. His sweatpants and sweatshirt swallowed her small frame, her damp hair pulled up into a tight bun. Her feet were tucked underneath her. Though her face didn't have a trace of makeup, he thought her countenance shone brighter than he'd ever seen.

His breath hitched. *Gosh, she was gorgeous.* He gulped.

"Hey." He closed the door behind him. "I have the food you brought." He strode to the kitchen and set it on the counter. "Thanks again for coming to the rescue in so many ways. I promise to take you out on a proper date as soon as our schedules align." His hands shook, so he clenched them into fists at his sides.

He never thought seeing her in his space would make him so nervous.

She swung her legs in front of herself and scooted off the couch. "I'm just happy to be around you." She strode over to the kitchen, stopping close to him. "But next time, less poop would be ideal."

Luke laughed. Her lips twitched in a purely intoxicating way. The air between them danced with the scent of Dove soap and his tea tree oil shampoo. If he had been bold enough, he would've leaned in four inches and grazed his lips with hers. Every part of him ached to tug her close and kiss her for the first time. Why had it taken him so long to realize what he always wanted was right under his nose all along?

Instead, he cupped her elbow. "I promise—next time, no poop. I'll even leave Gigi at home to make sure nothing even remotely close to poop happens." Immediately, at the mention of Gigi, he blurted, "Snap, I completely forgot about her." He shifted, stepping around Melissa. "I need to let her out to do her business." He rushed into the spare room where he'd left Gigi in her kennel.

After he unlatched the kennel door, she scampered through the living room toward the doggie door on the front door. Luke wandered behind her, watching her disappear.

"Do you need to follow her out?" Melissa asked.

"Nah. I know she only needs to pee. Don't ask me how I know that." He returned to the kitchen. Melissa slid into one of the barstools facing the kitchen island. "She can do that all on her own. Plus, the stairs up and down tucker her out. But if she doesn't come back in a few minutes, I'll go check on her."

"Sweet." Melissa reached and pinched the bag of food, dragging it across the slick quartz countertop toward her. "I bought sandwiches from the deli on Main Street. I hope that's okay." She gnawed on her bottom lip.

"Are you kidding me? I could kiss you right now. I'm starving." The words tumbled out before he could stop them. Then they landed smack dab between them. "I mean—" Luke stammered. He shoved a shaky hand through his hair.

"Then why don't you?" Melissa arched an eyebrow, her expression challenging, yet playful.

Luke didn't hesitate. In two steps, he closed the distance between them. His hands found her waist, and he lifted her in one smooth motion from the barstool onto the kitchen counter. Then he inched closer, standing between her legs. His hand cupped the back of her neck while his thumb brushed the curve of her jaw. She wrapped her legs around his waist.

"You don't have to ask me twice." His gaze flickered between her eyes and lips, then back again. "Are you sure about this?" A fire raged in his gut.

Melissa moistened her lips, her eyes never leaving his. Then she gave the smallest nod.

That was all he needed.

He didn't hesitate, immediately brushing his lips across hers. An addicting thrill rushed through him. The scent of his soap wafted off her skin, filling his lungs. He wrapped his other arm around her waist while her palm pressed against the middle of his chest. She used her other hand to tug at his sweatshirt strings.

His lips danced with hers. And in one moment, everything changed.

The people they were before no longer existed, not when he now knew how good she tasted, how perfectly she fit up against him. He tried to memorize the curve of her face, the silky feeling of his lips coated with her tangy lip balm, and her hair tangled up in his hand. Heat lingered from wherever her hand traveled. He never knew someone could taste this good. Now that he had her, he never wanted to let her go. This moment changed everything for him. She wedged herself into a hole in his heart he didn't know was there. She fit into his puzzle perfectly.

He tugged her closer and she sighed. Her lips parted, allowing him to deepen the kiss. This evening, as horrible as it started, would be one he'd never forget. Luke lost track of time, but eventually he forced himself to drag his lips away from hers. He kissed her lightly on the temple, wrapping his arms around her waist. She snuggled her head against his chest. His pulse quickened, and he knew she could hear the galloping thunder of his heartbeat. They held each other until the dust settled and their breathing returned to normal.

"I'm starving," Melissa croaked.

Luke loosened his grip around her waist just enough to look down at her. He laughed. "Then," he tucked some wisps of hair behind her ear. "Let's eat."

She jumped off the kitchen counter and snagged the to-go bag, and she unloaded the contents onto the counter. Luke came behind her and wrapped his arms around her. He couldn't stop touching her, but he kissed her on her cheek and let go.

"What would you like to drink?" He shuffled to the fridge. Opening it, he peered inside. "Unfortunately, I don't have much up here, but the downstairs kitchen has everything imaginable." He glanced at her over the top of the fridge door.

Melissa slid into the barstool. "No, no." She waved him off. "Water's just fine."

He fetched two glasses and filled them with ice and water. He set them down in front of them and sat on the barstool next to her. She placed a Styrofoam box in front of him, then opened her own. He peeled back the lid and spotted a sandwich, potato chips, and fruit salad inside.

They each took a few bites of their respective meals in silence.

"You know," Melissa's voice broke the quiet. He tipped his head toward her and met her gaze. "Our kiss changes everything. If this thing between us doesn't work out, it'll forever make everything extremely awkward. I should've thought about that before I let you kiss me."

"I'm glad you did," he licked the salt from his potato chip off his finger, "let me kiss you. I'll make sure things don't get weird."

He knew Melissa was one hundred percent right. Never again could Melissa just be Andrew's sister. Their kiss meant if they ended up together, great. But if they didn't, it would change the dynamic they had enjoyed for this long.

"Well," Melissa broke off a tiny piece of bread from her sandwich and popped it into her mouth, "I don't know. I leave in like two months ..." Her voice trailed off. She set her sandwich down and rubbed her hands over her thighs.

Luke pressed a finger to her lips. "Shh. I promise we'll figure something out."

She gnawed at her bottom lip. "I don't know." Her hands

rubbed faster back and forth over her thighs. "I'm not a 'throw caution to the wind, let tomorrow worry about tomorrow' type of gal."

"Melissa." He cupped her shoulder. "I'm not going to mess this up. When I said I'll figure it out, I will."

"I want to believe you."

"Then do." He kissed her on the temple.

"Okay."

They returned to eating their sandwiches again. Luke tried not to think about the uncertainty of the future. Instead, he chose to focus on the feeling of her body pressed against his, her lips dancing with his.

CHAPTER EIGHTEEN

Olivia swung open her front door. She scanned Melissa's sweatpants-clad body up and down and blurted, "You guys kissed, didn't you!" She pinched the sleeve of Luke's sweatshirt and yanked her inside.

"Shh." Melissa closed the door behind them. "I haven't figured out how to tell Andrew."

"Tell me what?" Andrew poked his head out of the living room off the front hallway. His gaze scanned her outfit. "That's Luke's." He stepped out.

Melissa shrugged. "You knew where I was headed, and you know I'm only here to pick up Ellie."

"Wait, why are you here?" Olivia's eyebrows furrowed. "I told you Ellie could spend the night. She and Cole are sleeping soundly in the TV room."

In a daze from the night's excitement, Melissa had completely forgotten about it. "Duh." She hit her forehead with the heel of her palm. "Then I guess I'll come back tomorrow morning." Swiftly, she spun around to leave.

"Not a chance." Olivia fisted a handful of the extra-large

sweatshirt and stopped her in her tracks. "Your payment for free babysitting is details."

"What details?" Andrew tried to play catch-up. He glanced from Olivia to Melissa, then back again. "What details?" His eyes narrowed and jaw locked.

Olivia smacked him in the dead center of his chest without even removing her attention from Melissa. "Luke and Melissa kissed. Try to catch up."

"You *what?*" Andrew exclaimed.

Melissa crossed her arms, drawing in on herself.

"Keep it down. You're going to wake the kids," Olivia hissed. "Besides, you should be thrilled. They kissed, which is exactly what I wanted to happen."

"But he's my best friend." Andrew raked his hands through his hair. "If this doesn't work out—"

Melissa stood still. She hated having her less-than-an-hour-ago kiss being scrutinized.

"It will," Olivia interjected.

"What if it doesn't?" Andrew challenged.

"Then it will be fine," Melissa finally said. "I'll go back to Boston at the end of the summer. If things don't work out, you'll stay here, Luke will stay here, and I'll be gone. You have my permission to stay friends with him no matter what."

"How generous of you," Andrew muttered. "You'll let me stay friends with my best friend of over thirty years."

"Yes."

"I'm calling Luke." Andrew stepped around them and headed back into the living room.

"Wait," Melissa called out. "Please don't." She followed him into the living room with Olivia on her heels.

Andrew scooped his cell phone up off the sofa.

"You don't need to get bent out of shape." Melissa leaned her back against the doorframe. Olivia hugged the wall. "Luke and I kissed, nothing more. This whole thing is brand new. I don't need you sticking your nose in it and messing it up before anything has even started."

"Okay." Andrew exhaled. "Just remember, summer always ends."

"You set me up with Jake," she countered. "And he claimed you knew he was headed to some Doctors Without Borders gig for a year."

"Yeah," he rubbed his chin between his pointer finger and thumb. "Sorry about that. I found out after I set up the date, I honestly didn't think it would matter much because the chances of you hitting it off weren't great. Most blind dates are a total bust. I was only trying to get you back out there, build up your confidence a little, whet your appetite to date again. And he seemed like the guy for the job."

"Well, you did." Melissa threw her hands down at her sides. "Congratulations, mission accomplished! Now, give me a moment to figure out whatever might or might not develop between Luke and me."

"Fine." He straightened himself.

"Fine." She rolled off the doorframe. "I'll be back tomorrow morning before Ellie wakes up."

Luke stared up at his ceiling, unable to sleep. The lingering scent of Melissa on his clothes made it impossible to think about anything but their kiss. He played it over and over on repeat in his head. He wondered if he should text and wish her a good night. How was it possible to miss her when she only left a half hour ago?

If this thing didn't pan out with Melissa, he knew he'd *really* be alone. The stakes were high. But he chose not to dwell on the possible worst-case scenarios. In his gut, he believed this was different. To settle his anxieties, he'd have to lean into that feeling and not look back.

His phone pinged on his nightstand. He snatched it up and pulled the charging cord out of the bottom. A message from Andrew flashed at the bottom of the screen. He toggled to their text chain, revealing the full message.

> So, you go off and kiss my sister. You broke up with Ashley like last week. What were you thinking? This better not be just a rebound for you. And just know, if this thing goes south, I'll either have to come over and punch you in the face or leave a bad review on the Bayberry House homepage.

Luke sat straight up. He mulled over how to respond. If he didn't properly express his real and truthful feelings for Melissa, then their relationship would be doomed. The only way to move forward with Melissa was to have her brother fully on board.

> You wouldn't dare.

> Try me. You have no idea what I'm capable of.

> You did break that kid's nose during the homecoming football game. I think you got two days suspension for it.

> Low blow, you know I was defending myself. He charged me from behind.

> Because you stole his girlfriend, who now happens to be your wife.

> Worth it.

He knew he was getting somewhere with Andrew. For a second, he paused, contemplating what to write next.

> Then you understand. Melissa is my Olivia.

The dots at the bottom of the screen danced. He waited for his response.

> It is way too early for you to go around claiming you like my sister as much as I liked Olivia back in the day.

> You punched a guy over it, and you had only kissed Olivia once.

> Point taken.

> I won't mess this up.

> I wish I believed you.

> She's different.

> This sounds remarkably familiar, like every woman you've ever dated.

> No, I mean it.

> I do too.

He let out a long breath he didn't know he was holding in. Then he cranked his neck back and forth to loosen the tension between his shoulder blades.

I won't hurt her, I promise. I don't know why it took me this long to fall for her. I can't describe it, but this is different. This is real. Please, I hope you can support me with this, with us.

Okay. But if this entire thing blows up and I need to pick sides, I have to pick hers. She's my sister.

I wouldn't expect anything less.

Promise to take care of her, she's been through a lot.

I will.

I know.

A great calm washed over him. With his phone still gripped in his hand, he flopped backward and drifted into sleep.

CHAPTER NINETEEN

Sunlight bled through the curtains into Melissa's bedroom. The long summer days meant it was early, maybe five in the morning. She knew she needed to swing by Andrew's by seven to pick up Cole and Ellie. Last night, after the whole she-kissed-Luke thing was revealed, she shot Olivia a text and told her it was time she watched the kids so Olivia could have a much-needed day off.

Melissa turned to her side and snuggled down deeper into her covers. Her mind whirled from memories of the kiss from last night. Then the thoughts of returning to Boston at the end of summer soured her mood. What had she thought would happen? Summer flings were fun, but they always ended. Even if she were to date Luke in the future, it didn't change the fact she was a single mom who had to support herself and Ellie. She didn't have the luxury to be able to quit her job.

For a few minutes, Melissa tried her best to fall back asleep, but to no avail. Instead of wasting a morning alone, she peeled back the covers and climbed out of bed. An early-morning walk on the beach called her name. After she dressed and tightened the laces of her running shoes, she headed out, weaving around the side of her parents' house. The beach trail out to the ocean was worn smooth from years of use. Eventually, after crossing the uneven dry sand, her feet hit the hard-packed wet sand.

Without thinking, she found herself walking to the tide pools—the ones she'd gone to with Ashley, Luke, and Ellie. *Yikes. Ashley.* The name popping into her psyche did all sorts of things to her middle. What if she was only a quick distraction for Luke? Maybe she'd just end up being a detour on his way back to Ashley. But the few times she'd questioned Luke about her, he reassured her he wasn't ever going back to Ashley. Luke promised she was in the rearview. And Melissa knew that if she wanted them to have a chance together, she had to believe him.

So, she chose to not mention Ashley again. Even now, she surprised herself by how bold she had been when she challenged Luke to kiss her. It hadn't been how she imagined their first kiss going, but she had never wanted something more than she wanted that kiss. The tension had been palpable, and she knew she would've regretted it if she didn't voice how she felt, even if Luke hadn't returned her feelings. Luckily, he had. But doubt still whizzed through her, and she hoped the kiss meant as much to him as it did to her.

Early dawn light danced across the water. She breathed in the balmy salt air and told herself not to worry, or she'd find herself in a full tailspin. Sand stuck to the bottom of her shoes, but she walked and walked. Twenty minutes later, she arrived at the tide pools. She crouched down and peered into one pool full of sea urchins and starfish. A bark from behind captured her attention, and she glanced over her shoulder. A millisecond later, Gigi leaped onto her chest, making her fall backwards onto her backside.

She laughed as Gigi licked her face and water soaked her black biker shorts. Sand clung to her. Luke dashed across the sand then stopped beside her out of breath.

"I'm so sorry." He caught his breath then clapped his hands together. "Gigi," he called.

Melissa laughed. Gigi hopped out of her lap and circled Luke's ankles. She brushed at her shorts and thighs, trying to get the sand off.

"You can't get mad at her," she remarked as Luke held his hand out to her to help her to her feet. She took it and rose. "It's not often I get greeted so enthusiastically. You better be careful, or Gigi might leave you for me and Ellie." Melissa attempted again to rid her soggy shorts of the sand. When she determined it was fruitless, she dropped her hands to her side.

"You're probably right." He bent down, scratching Gigi around her neck. Then he reattached her leash to her collar. "But she doesn't have a choice. She's stuck with me." He straightened himself, letting the leash hang loose from his hand. Gigi sat back on her hindlegs.

"You make that sound like a horrible thing." She squinted against the bright sunlight. Her lips itched to taste him again. "I, for one, would love to be stuck with you."

The reflection of the sun sparkled in his gaze. He grinned, making her heart tug. "Thanks." He blinked for a second, a flush creeping up his neck. Neither of them spoke as the familiar web of electric tension wove them together.

Melissa turned back to face the ocean and asked, "Could you not sleep either?"

"Nope." He tightened Gigi's leash as she tugged at it. "Are you headed back?"

"I can be." She checked her watch and confirmed she had time before she needed to pick up Ellie and Cole. "Do you want to walk me back to my house?"

"I'd love to." Then he held his hand out to her.

Did they hold hands now? Were they together, together? Her mind ran rampant with scenarios fifty paces ahead of where they stood. Her heart hammered. Sweat pooled at her back. She wondered if one kiss had changed everything. A surge of hope filled her heart.

She scrunched up her nose. "My hand is all sandy." Then she held it up for him to see and tried to wipe it off on the side of her shorts.

"I don't care." He grabbed her hand, lacing his fingers with hers before she could question it further.

Heat splashed her cheeks. "Okay."

He gave her hand a reassuring squeeze. The gesture settled the worries mounting inside of her.

They headed in the direction of her house. "What's your plan for the day?" he asked.

"I'm picking up Cole and Ellie in a little bit. I told Olivia I'd keep him for the day so she could have a break." She tilted her head to the side and studied the curve of his jaw and slope of his nose. *Dang, she'd kissed that.* "Olivia deserves it after all the babysitting she's done for me. What about you? Do you have a busy day?"

"Yes and no." He dragged his feet, slowing their pace. "As long as nothing hits the fan, it should be a calm day. No weddings. After last night with the sewage pipe breaking and backing up, I'm bracing myself for some other catastrophic thing to happen next."

Their feet crunched as they walked along the wet sand, keeping far enough away from the water.

Luke continued, "I've started to wonder how long I'm meant to hack it as a B&B owner. When my parents passed, I needed to get out of the city. I needed a break from my day-to-day life as an attorney. And I didn't really have a choice, because everything was falling apart, so I quit my job and headed here without understanding what I was getting myself into. I thought the B&B life would be for me—after all, I had lived here my entire childhood and seen my parents run the place. But I had no clue how little of it I would enjoy."

"What parts don't you enjoy?" she asked.

"The days are long and boring. I don't like the stress of constantly spending my days fixing things, setting up weddings, making sure the food orders go through for the kitchen and events. When maids don't show up to clean, then I'm doing that too. Carol helps a ton, but if I ever wanted to step away, I would need to find someone to live at the property and take over all the tasks I do, which is not an easy find. I never thought I'd say this, but I have the itch to practice law again, which is something I never thought would happen. When I quit, I'd been burnt out from the long hours and demanding clients. I was a ball of stress. But now that I have had a bit of a break, I'm starting to crave the faster-paced life it gave me."

"Could you practice law here? Maybe you can have the best of both worlds."

"Perhaps, but I don't know if that's what I want."

She wondered what he did want. Would he want to move back to Boston? Her heart soared at the thought, but then she told herself to not put any stock into the thought.

They walked until they reached the path that weaved around the back of Melissa's parents' house. He shuffled behind her until they reached the front porch. She paused on the bottom step. How did one say goodbye to a guy she'd only kissed once but had loved her entire life?

"Thanks for walking me back." To keep her hands busy, she crouched down to pet Gigi between her ears. "It was a pleasant surprise to run into you."

"Anytime." He wrapped Gigi's leash a few times around his hand. She rose back up to her feet. He met her eyes and asked, "When can I see you again?"

She smiled. "I'm with Ellie and Cole all day, but Ellie goes to bed early, around seven. Do want to come over and hang out with me after she's asleep?"

"Perfect." He leaned in and gave her a quick peck. "I'll bring dinner this time. I'm looking forward to it. See you tonight."

She said goodbye, watching him grow further and further away. Once he completely left her field of vision, she traipsed up the porch steps.

Luke liked her back, *finally*.

The day passed at an annoyingly slow pace. Her anticipation of seeing Luke again and maybe kissing him another time made her practically batty, but motherhood called.

After she picked up the kids, she took them on a bike ride along the beach. They stopped and ate lunch on Main Street, then biked back. Then she loaded herself up with a beach chair and umbrella and took them down to the beach to play.

They only returned when the kids complained about being tired and hungry again. Melissa bathed them and made them cozy in their pj's to watch a movie. By the time Andrew and Olivia arrived, both kids had fallen asleep on the couch.

Andrew scooped his son up, and Cole didn't even stir. They kept their voices low to keep from waking either of the sleeping kids.

Over the top of Cole's head, Andrew asked, "So, when are you and Luke seeing each other again?"

"Tonight."

She hoped he wouldn't ask follow-up questions. She didn't care to answer any.

Olivia placed a hand on Andrew's bicep. "That's great to hear," she whispered. "I hope you have a wonderful time. Thanks for watching Cole for us."

"Are you sure about this?" Andrew raised an eyebrow. "Luke? This could be messy if things go south."

"I know what I'm getting myself into," Melissa answered defensively.

"Okay." He shook his head and shuffled down the hallway toward the front door. "I'll try to trust you on this."

They followed behind him. "Thanks."

When they reached the door, Olivia hugged her. "I want details tomorrow. Like, 'he moved slowly toward me with a look of desire in his eyes.'"

"Olivia," Andrew hissed. "My ears are bleeding over here."

Melissa laughed.

"Oh hush." Olivia whacked him on the arm. "I need details. You can't deny me a little bit of romantic entertainment."

"I promise to give you the juiciest narrative tomorrow."

"Yes!" Olivia beamed. "Call me."

Andrew shook his head as he crossed through the door threshold to the outside. Melissa waited until their car pulled away from the curb to walk back inside.

CHAPTER TWENTY

Luke opened a piece of mail. He had a large stack he needed to open and sort. "Did you remember to ask Chef Tony to make me two dinners to go?" Once he determined it was trash, he tossed it.

Carol shot him an unamused glance. "Do you remember who you're dealing with?"

"You're right." He slid a letter opener under the seal of his next envelope. In one quick flick, he cut across the top and tugged out the letter. "Sorry, I'm a bit nervous. I want to make sure everything is ready when I leave in a few minutes to take the meal over to Melissa's. But I'm sure you told Chef Tony who I'm trying to impress."

Chef Tony had been with them since his parents opened the B&B. He liked the hours and creative freedom to cook what he wanted. Every year, Chef Tony told Luke it would be his last, but luckily Luke always talked him into staying. He knew when Chef Tony finally retired, it would be difficult to find a replacement because he was like family.

"Oh, I filled him in on all the details. He's excited for you both." She clicked her mouse and closed the B&B's calendar.

"That's why he took the liberty of changing your order. Chef Tony prepared lamb chops with lemon risotto. You need to be bringing your A-game, and pasta isn't going to cut it."

Luke laughed as he put the local advertisements into the recycling. "I can see I need help, so thank you. I knew I could put your conspiring with Chef Tony to good use."

"You're welcome." She grabbed her purse from under the desk. "I also told him to add the triple chocolate cake for dessert."

"Okay, yum!"

She slung her purse over her shoulder. "I need to head out. Sam is arriving from out of town, and I promised him I'd come home in time to get dinner with him."

"How is Sam doing?"

Luke felt like he knew all of Carol's kids well, even if they didn't know much about him. Over the years, they had stopped by Bayberry House or even helped serve at weddings when they were shorthanded. Sam was a few years older than Luke, and he'd always looked up to him.

"He's fine." Carol said. She paused and tapped her bottom lip with her pointer finger. "His property management company is doing exceptionally well. It seems like every time I turn around, more and more businesses have signed with him."

He tossed the sealed envelope onto the pile of mail. "How long has he been running his property management company?"

"About five years now." She straightened and readjusted her purse. "He sold the landscaping business he started and used the money to start this new business."

"I might want to talk to him about his company's services."

"Really?" Carol asked, raising an eyebrow. "Are you thinking of bringing on help?"

"It might be more than help."

Carol halted. "What do you mean? You're not thinking of selling, are you?"

"No, not selling. But maybe hiring a full-time, on-site manager. Someone who could take over my role." He paused. "I'm beginning to itch for a change. I might want to go back to law. I don't know." His thoughts whirled.

Where in the world did those thoughts come from?

Melissa.

At the end of the summer, Melissa was moving back to Boston. Maybe he'd want to go too. The only way he could ever leave was if he knew Bayberry House was in the hands of a property manager he trusted. He'd known Sam his entire life and knew he was hardworking and trustworthy.

"I see." Carol nodded. "You keep me posted if you decide to move forward with this. I'm sure Sam would be interested. Plus, I refuse to work for anyone who doesn't value me. You and I both know I'm not in this gig for the money. I do it because I love it."

"I know, and I appreciate it."

She twisted on her heels to leave. "I'm out of here. Have fun with Melissa." Then she winked over her shoulder. "Just remember who was right from the very beginning."

"I know, I know. You were." He waved her away. "Now get out of here, and tell Sam hi for me."

Carol nodded and left.

He headed into the kitchen to pick up their to-go meal. After he made sure the night manager had everything in order, he drove the few blocks to Melissa's. His pulse quickened as he replayed last night, it had changed everything. He planned on moving heaven and earth to give them a real shot at being together. *But how?* That was the million-dollar question. If he figured out the B&B, going back into law was certainly in the realm of possibilities.

He climbed out of his car with the food. Melissa had instructed him not to ring the doorbell for fear of waking Ellie. Instead, she wanted him to simply enter the house when he arrived. Slowly, he climbed the porch steps, but before he could even open the door, it swung open.

"Hey." Melissa smiled at him.

"Hey back."

The porch light reflected in her eyes. Her hair hung loose in beach waves, and her summer dress highlighted her figure. His breath hitched as he took her in, memorizing every inch of her.

"I saw your headlights when you pulled up," she said, waving him in. "Come on in." She cocked her head to the side and asked, "No Gigi tonight?"

"No, not tonight. Gigi is snuggled soundly under the check-in desk."

"Ahh. Bummer." His heart pinched. Melissa really might be his dream girl.

They lingered at the threshold.

"You can bring Ellie by tomorrow to play with her." There he went, already opening a door to see her again. For a split second, he hesitated. Did he greedily go in for another kiss? Or would that be too forward? Where did she stand on physical affection? Go for it or take it slow? His mind reeled, but he managed to stop his spiraling thoughts. Instead, he closed the distance.

"You look beautiful, by the way." He leaned in and kissed her cheek. Then he passed through the door she held open. "Did Ellie go down okay?"

"She's out." She closed the door and motioned for him to follow. "Let's eat out on the patio, then we won't have to worry about keeping our voices down."

He followed her out. "I hope you like lamb chops."

They reached the outside patio, and he put the bag of food on the table.

"Oh my, those are fancy." She flat palmed the table with one hand. "I can't say that I've ever had a lamb chop. Pork chops, sure, but never lamb."

"Then you're in for a treat." He unloaded the contents of the bag. "It's Bayberry House's most popular dinner dish, especially for weddings with a higher price point."

"Wow, you're pulling out all the stops tonight. Thanks, that means a lot."

She settled into one of the patio chairs and lit the candle on the table to repel the bugs. He sat too and put a to-go box in front of each of them along with the cutlery and sodas. A starry sky provided an intimate backdrop. The waves crashed on the shore, and the balmy salt air tickled his nostrils.

They flipped open their boxes.

"Go ahead," Luke urged. "Take a bite."

"I'm sure I'll love it. I didn't have to cook it, which almost guarantees that I'll enjoy every bite." She picked up her knife and fork, cutting into the lamb chop. "I hate to admit, but Ellie and I survive on rotisserie chicken and bagged salad." She took a bite and slowly chewed.

Luke waited to see her reaction.

"Mm." Her eyes widened. "A girl could get used to this." She cut off another piece.

He smiled. "I knew you'd like it." Satisfied, he cut into his own meal.

"So," Melissa cut into her meat again. "Are you ready to tell me why you've never married?" She pushed a piece of lamb into her mouth.

Luke laughed. "I guess you're jumping in feet first and going straight for the hard stuff."

"You know me." She popped the top of her soda can and

took a long sip. "I don't beat around the bush. So, why haven't you ever gotten married? Did you never recover after that broken engagement?"

"I've recovered." He stilled, staring out at the empty beach. "Honestly, I'm glad it didn't work out. We fought way more than we should have, and we never agreed on anything. I've realized loving someone shouldn't be that hard. Marriage shouldn't start out as a struggle, right?"

"Oh, I know. I was the person who wasn't smart enough to end my engagement before I got married."

"Sorry," he winced. "I guess I'm lucky? Anyways, since then I've dated off and on."

"Sure." She cut off another piece of her lamb. "Like with Ashley."

Right, Ashley. He hadn't thought about her since they'd broken up, which only proved how being with Melissa was right. Ashley and he had obviously been completely wrong for each other. The ease and comfort he felt with Melissa paled in comparison to anything he ever shared with Ashley.

"Yeah, but I now see I forced it with her way longer than I should've. Even if you hadn't come into the picture, I wouldn't have ended up with her."

She gnawed her bottom lip. "What about us? Are you forcing things with me?"

"Absolutely not." He set his silverware down, taking her hand. "No, I'm not forcing anything. My feelings for you, though new, are one hundred percent real. If anything, this has felt like the most natural thing in the world." He squeezed her hand, interlacing their fingers.

"I like you, Luke." Her voice was small and fragile. It nearly did him in. If he could, he would erase all her prior hurt. She continued, "I've always liked you. Please don't play with my heart."

Luke lifted her hand to his lips and kissed the back of her wrist. "I won't, I promise."

"What happens when I go back to Boston?"

"I have no idea." Luke kissed her wrist again. "But please don't give up on me. I'll figure something out."

She exhaled, her shoulders drooping. "That's what Grant always said, that he'd 'figure it out.'" Her back stiffened. "Those words bring me no comfort." Her bottom lip quivered.

He stood, scraping his chair across the patio floor until he sat across from her, knee to knee. His hand cradled her face, and she tilted her cheek into his palm.

"I'm not your ex," he said boldly. "When I say I'll figure it out, I will. You have to trust me on this."

"I want to."

"Remember when we were kids, and we rode our bikes all the way across town to get saltwater taffy? You popped a tire on the way back." She nodded. "We had to leave your bike on the side of the road. I told you to hop on the handlebars of my bike. You didn't want to, but I promised you I would keep you safe." He paused.

"I can't believe you remember that," she murmured.

He continued, "You finally got on, even though you were scared. You trusted me then. Can you trust me again?"

They stared at one another. An array of emotions danced across her face—hurt, fear, and then an almost indistinguishable flicker of hope.

"I'll choose to trust you," she whispered.

"See?" He leaned in until his lips hovered an inch from hers. "Now that wasn't so hard, was it?"

Her lips curled against his palm. "I guess not."

She kissed his palm. He moved his hand and traced the length of her chin until he cupped her neck. Slowly and deliberately, he brushed his lips against hers in a soft, simple whisper. It was a promise of trust, a kiss to convey how much he cared for her, a kiss to show he'd be there for her—unlike the person who had failed her before.

Tenderly, he deepened the kiss. His tongue traced her bottom lip, making her lips part. Soon, his tongue whirled with hers. This time he wanted to savor it. He forgot about the pain of his past, and he hoped she did too. His mind erased the bad memories of previous relationships, broken promises, and years of heartache and longing. This kiss with her erased it all. In that moment, he felt reborn. New. Different. Changed.

Eventually, Luke tugged his lips away from hers. He brushed her loosened hair around her temple and kissed her there. Then he repositioned his chair and wrapped his arm around her shoulders. They sat side by side, enjoying the view. Melissa leaned her head against his. The moment felt so perfect, so right. He wondered what it would be like to share a life with her, one with Ellie—and, of course, Gigi too. Even as he dreamed, he knew it would be far more beautiful than anything he could have conjured up on his own.

The wait had been worth it.

They watched as a canopy of stars lit up the night sky, the moon reflecting on the water. A calm sea breeze made the air salty and sweet. He basked in the thrill of the evening.

Ellie's voice startled them when she said, "I'm not tired anymore."

Melissa flinched, and Luke dropped his arm from around her shoulders. Both looked over their shoulders at Ellie.

Melissa patted her lap. "Then come climb up on my lap for a minute."

Ellie didn't hesitate. She rounded their chairs, climbing into Melissa's lap and burying her head against her chest. Melissa rubbed her back in long even strokes. "I worried about you falling asleep too early."

"What is—" Ellie popped her head off Melissa's chest, "Luke doing here?"

Melissa flashed him a *what-do-we-do?* look.

He smiled and winked at her. "I came to bring you and your mom chocolate cake of course. But when I arrived, you had already fallen asleep."

Ellie beamed. "Really? I love chocolate cake. Is Gigi here?" She bounced off Melissa's lap. "Where is the cake?"

"Gigi fell asleep early too, but your mom can bring you by tomorrow to say hi to her." He stood and dragged his chair back to the proper place around the table.

"One slice and then it's back to bed, Missy," Melissa instructed, her lips twitching.

"I promise." Ellie climbed into an empty seat next to Melissa. "Mom never lets me eat chocolate cake in the middle of the night. You must have special powers."

"The secret is out." He waggled his eyebrows. "Do you promised not to tell?"

"I won't." Ellie rested her forearms on the table. "Where's the cake?"

"Ellie," Melissa scolded. "You need to be patient."

He chuckled, snagging the brown bag on the table. "It's right here." He fetched the two pieces of chocolate cake in their own containers, handing one to Ellie and the other to Melissa.

"Thanks." Melissa scooted her chair closer and peered inside the empty bag. "I can share with Ellie." She held out her container to him.

"No, no." Ellie brought her container closer to her chest, clutching it protectively. "Luke said he brought this just for me."

"Okay." She pursed her lips together. She peeled back the top of the container and looked over at him. "Do you mind sharing with me?"

"I don't mind, but do you have a problem with germs? I can cut it in half and put it on separate plates."

"I live with a five-year-old who drinks out of my cups and eats food off my plate. I can handle sharing a piece of cake, especially when we've already kis—" She slapped a hand over mouth.

"Since you've already what?" Ellie dug her fork into the cake and shoved a big bite into her mouth. Chocolate smeared across her lips.

"I can handle sharing a piece of cake with Luke because I'm not that hungry," Melissa replied.

"Good, because I'm hungry and I'm eating this all by myself." Ellie stuffed another bite of cake into her mouth like she hadn't already eaten dinner.

Melissa went back inside and fetched an extra fork. When she returned, she settled back in her seat then positioned her cake closer to Luke. They picked up their forks and each took a bite. Ellie gobbled hers up in no time, and soon chocolate frosting coated her lips and cheeks.

When she finished, Ellie leaned back in her seat and pressed a hand against her stomach. "My tummy hurts."

"It's probably because you finished an entire humongous slice of cake."

Ellie groaned. "I know, but it tasted so good."

Luke chuckled and set his fork down. "I get it. When I was a kid, I used to get my entire bag of Halloween candy in like two days, until one year I ate so much I spent the entire night throwing up. That cured me for life."

Melissa ran a hand over Ellie's head. "I think you should remember how your body feels right now so you don't eat this much again."

"I'll remember." Ellie curled up in a ball on the chair cushion.

"Maybe you should take a bath. You're half-covered in chocolate, and it will help your tummy." Melissa picked up the empty food containers and shoved them into the brown paper bag.

Luke jumped up and helped clean up the remaining items from dinner.

Melissa ran a hand down Ellie's back, who remained in a tight ball. "I should probably call it a night." She found his gaze and tilted her head toward Ellie. "It's going to take me a while to get her settled back in bed."

"No problem." He gathered up the bag of trash to dispose of on his way out. "But will you guys come by tomorrow?" He couldn't hide his eagerness if he tried.

Ellie perked up from her curled up position. "Yes! I want to see Gigi. Can you go to the beach with us again? I like building sandcastles and playing in the waves with you. You are a lot more fun than Mom."

Melissa laughed and scrunched up her nose. "Okay, that's enough. Time to take a bath and go back to bed. The fun is now over." She held her hand out to Ellie.

Ellie reluctantly took it and rose to her feet, dragging her little body into the house. Once out of sight, Melissa said, "I'd love to see you tomorrow too if you can manage to carve out a little time."

"I'll make time." He kissed her on the cheek. "I could probably head to the beach in the late afternoon."

"Okay, that sounds nice. Thanks again for dinner."

Luke ran a hand down the length of her arm and squeezed her hand. "I'll see you both tomorrow."

Then Luke let himself out while Melissa disappeared into the bathroom to help prepare Ellie for bed. With a permanent smile glued to his face, he drove the few blocks back to Bayberry House, already looking forward to seeing her tomorrow.

CHAPTER TWENTY-ONE

The next few weeks passed in a delightful haze. Each morning, Melissa and Ellie walked to Bayberry House, where Luke would join Melissa on the back porch to watch Ellie play with Gigi on the lawn. After they parted ways, Melissa filled the days with bike rides, walks along the beach, visits to tide pools, and trips to lighthouses. Some days, Olivia joined them with Cole; other days, she gave Olivia a break and watched the two kids play together at the beach.

By early evening, Luke would find them at the beach. He built sandcastles with them, played in the water, and sometimes brought his kite to fly with Ellie. They never put a label on their relationship, but in Melissa's mind, they were dating and exclusive. She believed Luke felt the same.

Melissa refused to dwell on summer ending. She couldn't, not when after all these years of being alone, she finally had everything she ever wanted. Sure, fall was fast approaching, but she chose to live freely in her own little fairy tale for as long as possible.

Unfortunately, all fairy tales ended eventually.

One morning, a few weeks after their turning-point kiss,

Melissa walked along the beach with Ellie toward Bayberry House. Ellie had woken up at sunrise. Instead of wasting the morning away, she knew Luke would be out for his morning run. After she got Ellie dressed, they headed out along the route he usually ran along the beach. As they neared the B&B, she spotted Luke in the distance, on the edge of the lawn where it spilled into the sand.

He wasn't alone.

Even though they were far away, she knew the person beside him was Ashley.

She froze and wondered what to do. It wasn't like she didn't trust Luke, she did. But Ashley still had a thing for him. Andrew had told her how Ashley talked incessantly about how wrong she'd been in letting their relationship end. Finally, he had broken it to her gently that Luke was dating Melissa, suggesting she should put her efforts elsewhere and move on.

From where she stood, it looked like Ashley wasn't going down without a fight.

Ellie tugged on her hand. "I see Luke." She pointed with her free hand toward them. Then she peered up at her, "Shouldn't we go over there?"

"I see him." She mulled over what to do. If they left now, they could leave without Luke or Ashley seeing them. But she didn't feel like running away was the answer.

"He's with that lady." Ellie grimaced. "The one who hates Gigi."

Melissa laughed. "I can't believe you remember that."

"What are we waiting for?" Ellie attempted to tug her forward. "I want to see Luke and Gigi."

Then to Melissa's great horror, Ashley leaned in closer. Their bodies looked intimately close to one another. Her heart pounded. *Why wasn't he moving away from her?* Then Ashley cupped his elbow. They were dangerously close, close enough for them to kiss.

Her pulse quickened. "Oh my." She watched for a split second as Ashley leaned in.

No. No. No.

Melissa forced herself to look away before she witnessed the kiss. She pivoted sharply, yanking Ellie to follow her back to their house.

They walked, but Ellie dragged her feet while peering over her shoulder. "The mean lady just kissed Luke," she said flatly.

"Um." Melissa peered back toward them. They weren't kissing anymore. Luke made some wild hand gestures, and Ashley gripped his arm. He appeared to be trying to shake her off, but Melissa wasn't positive. Perhaps it was only wishful thinking on her part. "You saw that too?" She gnawed her bottom lip and picked up their pace, putting more and more distance between them.

"Yep." Ellie peered up at her innocently. "I thought Luke liked you."

"So did I." Her pulse thundered in her ears.

"Can you kiss lots of different people you like?" Ellie asked.

"Sometimes." Sweat tickled her brow. "I mean, it happens."

Her stomach twisted as her mind flipped through every interaction she had with Luke over the past weeks. Not putting a label on their relationship meant she had no claim to him. Maybe her feelings for him were stronger than the ones he had for her.

Melissa gritted her teeth. "Come on. It looks like Luke is busy this morning." She tugged Ellie back in the direction of their house, away from Luke and Ashley. "I'll make us some pancakes for breakfast." Her shoulders drooped.

"But I wanted to play with Gigi," Ellie whined.

"Enough," she said, trying to keep her voice low. "Like I said, Luke is busy."

She trudged back to the house while her mind replayed wild scenarios of Ashley and Luke kissing. By the time she arrived, her blood boiled. She turned off her phone, knowing Luke would call when they didn't show up, but she needed to clear her head before she spoke to him.

With her ex-husband, she had looked past all the red flags. He had been unfaithful to her, and she had ignored the signs. She questioned her ability to think through everything without clearing her head first. She knew Luke wasn't her ex-husband, but she also wondered if her judgement of men wasn't sound. Maybe she didn't know how to pick them?

After a breakfast of pancakes and orange juice for Ellie, she couldn't eat with her stomach in knots, an idea popped into her mind. She took out her phone and called Olivia.

Olivia picked up after two rings. "Hey, what's up?"

"Hey, there." Melissa sped forward without even taking a breath. "I know this is very last minute, but Ellie got up early. I thought of taking her to Martha's Vineyard for the day. I know we talked about going together at the beginning of summer, and I figured we need to just do it or it's never going to happen. Would you and Cole like to come? We'd need to leave in about thirty minutes to catch the ferry."

"This summer has flown by," Olivia responded. "I think I can get us ready in time. We're in."

"Perfect."

This could work. She'd go away for the day and clear her mind. This would give her time to think everything through before she made any rash decisions. Then she would come back and face whatever storm was coming her way. "I figured we could walk around and eat lunch, maybe hit the beach for a bit then take the evening ferry back. What do you think?"

"Andrew's working late tonight, so that works for us."

Melissa let out a long breath. "Great. We'll pick you up in twenty minutes and head to the ferry." She hung up.

Then in a flurry, she snatched a canvas bag and shoved their swimsuits, towels, sunscreen, water bottles, and a few snacks into it.

Before she knew it, they had picked up Olivia and Cole, parked, and loaded onto the ferry.

After they found their seats, the kids peered out the window as they waited for the ferry to leave the dock. Melissa still hadn't turned on her phone, but curiosity got the best of her. As the ferry tugged away from the dock, she turned her phone back on.

It binged.

Then binged again.

And again. The loud noise practically made the air vibrate.

Olivia arched an eyebrow. "Group text?"

Her sporadic heartbeat made her cheeks flush. "Something like that," she muttered.

A long string of messages from Luke filled her screen.

Are you and Ellie on your way? You're usually here by now.

I hope this means you are getting some much-needed rest.

I know for a fact Ellie never sleeps past seven. Are you not stopping by this morning?

Is everything okay? Is one of you sick? If so, let me know, and I can bring some soup.

> I don't know where you are or why you aren't texting me back, but please text me when you get these. I'm starting to get worried. Should I be worried?

Melissa dropped her phone back into her lap and closed her eyes for a moment, trying to settle the pounding in her head.

"Mom," Ellie peeled her face from the window and peered over at her, "how long is the boat ride?"

She cleared her throat. "It's short, only about forty-five minutes." She dug into her bag and retrieved two packs of fruit snacks. Holding them up, she asked, "Do you and Cole want some?"

Ellie snagged the packs out of her hand. "Thanks." She handed one to Cole.

Soon, the cousins ripped them open and each popped a fruit snack into their mouths.

Olivia placed a hand on Melissa's knee. "Is everything okay?" She cocked an eyebrow. "You seem a bit distracted."

Tears tickled the corners of her eyes, threatening to spill over. She blinked rapidly and glanced out the window at the ocean. "No." She shook her head. "I'm not okay."

A long silence stretched between them. She knew if she spoke, she'd cry, and she hated to cry.

"I'm assuming something happened with Luke?"

She nodded. Then she stared down at the phone in her lap. What should she text him back? Did he even deserve a response? Surely, he couldn't hide what happened between him and Ashley. Or maybe Melissa never really knew him. Maybe she'd been blind to his flaws because she always had stars in her eyes.

Olivia shifted into the seat next to her, wrapping an arm around her shoulders. "I'm sure you'll figure it out. You two are perfect for each other. I've never seen either of you this happy.

Andrew was just saying last night he wished he'd known you'd liked Luke, because he would've set you up ages ago. He may have been skeptical at first, but not anymore."

"Luke might not want me."

The words hurt so bad.

"Nonsense," Olivia said, squeezing her shoulders. Then she removed her arm and held her hand out to the kids to collect their empty fruit snack wrappers. They handed them over before returning to watch the world go by out the window. "He wants you. I know it."

Her bottom lip quivered. "I saw Ashley kiss him on the beach this morning."

Olivia gasped and dug her nails into Melissa's forearm. "She did? I don't believe it."

"Believe it." Melissa stared down at her hands in her lap, refusing to look over at Olivia. "We were out on an early morning walk, earlier than our normal time. I saw them chatting in front of the back lawn of the B&B. They didn't see us. At first, I just thought they appeared to be standing close to each other. But then Ashley leaned in to kiss him. I quickly looked away, but Ellie saw them kiss."

"Maybe Ashley did kiss him, but that doesn't mean Luke wanted her to. Did you at least see if he pushed her away?"

"No." Melissa shook her head and stared out the window. "But I was fooled once. I turned a blind eye to Grant and his mysterious behavior. I'm not doing it again, even if it is Luke."

"I'm sure there's an explanation."

"Doubtful." Melissa's lower lip quivered. She blinked rapidly to avoid the tears from spilling out and down her cheeks. "I really thought I was smarter this time. I took my time. I didn't rush into getting remarried like so many women do. No, I waited. I didn't even date because Ellie always comes first. I found a way to move forward without a man. I don't know why I was so careless." She exhaled.

"You weren't careless, and I still think there's more to this story. Ashley has been wanting to get Luke back, but just because she kissed him doesn't mean he wanted her to. Trust him to explain."

Melissa shrugged. "He's probably getting back with Ashley as we speak."

"Well, what did he say when you confronted him?"

"Nothing, because I haven't." She handed her phone to Olivia and let her read the string of messages from Luke. The kids had started climbing back and forth between each other's chairs in a made-up game of musical chairs.

Olivia finished reading the messages and handed the phone back. "So, what are you going to text him?"

"I have no idea—maybe simply 'I saw you kiss Ashley. I hope you two are happy together.'"

"I mean it's short and to the point, but I still think you should give him a chance to explain himself. Don't throw this entire relationship away until you hear his side of things."

Olivia urged Cole to climb back down off the chair and sit properly in his seat. Melissa dug back into her bag and pried a pringles can out of the bottom. She ripped off the top seal and handed it to Ellie. Ellie happily took it and settled next to Cole. Cole dug in and snatched some, and they munched on the chips.

For a minute she mulled over what to text Luke. Finally, she typed out a text.

> I'm on my way to Martha's Vineyard for the day with Ellie, Cole, and Olivia. I took Ellie on a walk this morning and saw you and Ashley kissing. As you can imagine, I'm hurt and feel betrayed. I probably should have better defined our relationship. I thought we were dating, but I realize now maybe we weren't exclusive in your mind. I'll call you when I'm ready to talk about this.

She hit send and waited for the message to be delivered. Once she confirmed Luke had read it, she promptly turned off her phone and shoved it back into her bag.

Olivia eyed her. "You're not going to see what he writes back?"

"Nope." Melissa scanned the ferry. "I'm not in the head space to read whatever he says. I'm waiting until we get back home tonight. Then I'll deal with it. So, you need to stick close to me. I don't want to have to turn on my phone."

"Okay. If that's how you want to play it." She patted Melissa's knee. "Then I'm stuck to you like glue."

The first outline of Martha's Vineyard appeared in the distance. Melissa leaned back in her seat and her heart broke into pieces.

CHAPTER TWENTY-TWO

Luke paced the floor of his apartment. The black screen of his phone taunted him from its place on the counter. Since Melissa's text message, he'd spiraled into a ball of anxiety. He wanted to scream, because he hadn't kissed Ashley. Yes, Ashley tried to kiss him, but he swore he ducked out of the way in time. It definitely didn't look good for him, but if only Melissa would give him a chance to explain, he could clear it all up. He wanted so badly to be with her, not Ashley.

Seeing Ashley on the beach this morning had been pure coincidence. They'd chatted for a few minutes. Ashley had inched closer to him than he preferred, and he probably should've moved back more assertively. He did a few times, but she kept inching her body back to his. They probably only spoke for a total of three minutes. Then, out of nowhere, she declared her love for him and before he knew it, she was leaning in and trying to kiss him. He ducked out of the way before her lips landed on his, and she ended up getting his cheek. But no doubt it looked like they'd kissed. Ugh. This wasn't good. He knew Melissa's ex-husband had cheated on her, and he was at a loss as to how he could convince her she had nothing to worry about with him. Luke would never cheat on Melissa.

He swiped his phone off the counter and double-checked the text thread. Nothing. Nada. Zilch. All he could do was wait. He had a long list of things to do around Bayberry House, and he hoped they could distract him until Melissa returned.

Luke left his apartment and went down to the lobby. Gigi ran over to him from behind the check-in desk. She circled Luke's ankles. He patted her between her ears then tapped her on her rear end. She promptly trotted on back to her doggie bed and laid back down.

Carol peered up from the computer at the front desk. "Good morning." She clicked something with her mouse then snatched up a pile of opened bills. "These need to be paid by the end of the week."

"Good morning to you too." He snagged the stack of bills from her. "I'll do this right now." Slowly, he leafed through the bills and checked the amounts due. A tally of costs lined up in his brain. "I have that meeting with Sam in about an hour."

Carol smiled. "That's right. He mentioned it last night when he came over for dinner."

A long pause followed.

Luke believed Carol didn't want to put too much stock into their meeting. It was, after all, only exploratory. He wanted to discuss with Sam some options for the management of Bayberry House.

Last week, he'd contacted a headhunter. They'd been sending out his résumé to law offices in Boston. He hadn't told Melissa, because he didn't want to promise something and not deliver. Now, he wondered if he needed to pump the brakes on these plans of his, especially if things with Melissa weren't— nope, Luke wasn't going there. He'd fix this, even if he had to force her to hear him out.

He fidgeted with the bills in his hands. "I'm going to pay these. Then there's a sprinkler on the back lawn that I need to replace. Just find me or text me when Sam arrives."

"Will do."

A customer entered the lobby and approached the check-in desk. Luke made his exit and tried his best to keep his mind off Melissa.

After he paid the bills and fixed the broken sprinkler, his phone dinged. He fished it out of his pocket, hoping it was a message from her. Instead, a text from Carol let him know that Sam had arrived.

Luke washed his hands and returned to the lobby where Sam waited. "Hey, Sam." He held his hand out to greet him.

Sam adjusted the binder he was holding and shook his hand. "Hey, thanks for contacting me. I'm glad we can finally sit down to go over everything."

"Me too." He directed his gaze at Carol, who was organizing some paperwork for an upcoming wedding event contract. "I think we'll meet out on the back patio."

"Great," she smiled. "Do you want me to bring out some drinks for you guys?"

"That would be wonderful." Luke motioned toward the back door. "Come this way."

They wandered to the empty patio. They sat at a table to the far right in case guests came out. When they were settled into their seats, Sam placed his binder on the table.

"So, tell me a little bit about your current situation." Sam removed a pen from his pocket and clicked it.

"Sure. Thanks for meeting with me." Luke folded his hands on top of the table. "As you know, I took over Bayberry House when my parents passed. At the time, I needed a respite from my job. I was completely overwhelmed with getting my parents' estate in order, and I knew at the time I needed to drop everything to ensure the B&B didn't fail. But I'm itching to return to law, maybe move back to Boston. I need someone to manage it. They could move into the apartment I'm currently occupying to live on-site. Carol mentioned you might be able to help me figure out what to do."

"I'm glad you called." Sam scooted his chair closer to the table. "I took the liberty of mapping a few options for you. I believe together, we can come up with a plan that puts the proper management in place for you to pursue your other interests and still allows Bayberry House to be profitable."

A weight Luke didn't know he'd been carrying around lifted from his shoulders. "I like the sound of that."

Sam flipped open the binder then turned it, so the first page faced Luke. "Here is a list of your options." His finger trailed along as Sam explained each viable option. "When my mom mentioned you wanting someone to manage the B&B, I got excited because I know the place and I would make sure it was properly maintained and managed."

"What's the cost?"

"Well," Sam turned to the next page in his binder. "There's some different price points."

Luke dragged the binder closer and read over the different costs. Each outlined which services were included at each price point, and they seemed reasonable. "Would I be able to contact some of your current clients? I'd like to hear how their experiences have been."

"Absolutely." Sam flipped through the binder until he landed at the back. It listed some of his clients and their contact information. "I'll leave this information with you. Please think about it and get back to me when you've come to a decision."

"Thank you. I will."

Luke led Sam back inside to the lobby.

Carol cringed when she spotted them heading their way. "I never got you those drinks. I'm sorry about that."

Sam wrapped an arm around her shoulders. "Mom, it's fine. It was a short meeting."

"I was stuck on a call with a wedding client." Carol shook her head. "She wanted to go over *every* line item for the catering bill."

"Did you sort it out?" Luke inquired.

"Of course," Carol stated matter-of-factly.

"I wouldn't except anything less." Sam dropped his arm from her shoulders. "I guess I'll head out."

"Why don't you two have Chef Tony make something up and you two have lunch together before you go?"

"Great idea." Carol grinned. Then, almost as an afterthought, she said, "Where's Melissa this morning? Did I miss her when she dropped by?"

"No." He exhaled and rubbed at the back of his neck. Gigi emerged from the back of the check in desk. He bent down and swept her up into his arms to cradle her against his abdomen. "She went to Martha's Vineyard for the day. She'll be back this evening."

There was zero chance he planned on telling Carol about the entire misunderstanding.

"How lovely." Carol looped her arm around Sam's elbow. "Let's go eat, my son."

They disappeared into the kitchen.

He let Gigi out on the front lawn and retrieved his phone from his pocket. He checked the text thread with Melissa. It remained unread. He shoved it back into his pocket. With nothing else to do but wait, he brought Gigi back inside and returned to his long laundry list of tasks.

But the day passed by slowly. His mind replayed the interaction with Ashley on the beach. She caught him completely off guard when she showed up out of the blue. Apparently, she regretted the way they'd ended things, and she begged him to forgive her. But the feelings he had developed for Melissa were miles deeper than how he'd ever felt about Ashley. He knew he loved Melissa. He had tried to gently explain this as nicely as possible, but instead she went in for an unwarranted kiss. Now he had to try and convince Melissa that what she saw wasn't anything. But he knew with everything in her past, he was going to be fighting an uphill battle.

By seven o'clock, with his list completed, he paced the inside of his apartment. With each minute that ticked by, his anxiety went up a notch.

"Forget this," he said out loud to himself.

He double checked the ferry times. Then he swiped Gigi into his arms and headed out of the B&B to his car. He drove over to Melissa's and parked in front to wait. If she wouldn't talk to him, he'd have to respect it. But he hoped she'd at least listen to him long enough that he could explain the misunderstanding.

A few minutes after he arrived, Melissa pulled into her driveway. Her headlights shone against the garage. Luke hopped out of his car, leaving Gigi inside with the windows down. She barked, but he commanded her to be quiet. Luckily, she slunk back into her seat.

He hovered at the end of the driveway. Melissa climbed out and rounded the car. "Why are you here?" She didn't look him in the eye but popped her truck. Her back was rigid as she yanked a bag out of the back and placed it on the driveway.

"I'm here because I want to try and explain what happened."

He moved closer to her, but she sidestepped around him. Swiping up the bag, she trotted across the lawn and up the front steps. He followed. She dumped the bag in front of the door then whipped past him without even acknowledging his existence. This was bad. So bad, and he could only hope she'd hear him out.

"I told you I would call you when I was ready to talk." Melissa took the stairs down back to her car. "I'm not in the headspace tonight to hear your excuses." Her voice cracked. She stopped in front of the open trunk.

"I know what you thought you saw, but I didn't kiss Ashley." Gently, Luke touched her arm. "She tried to kiss me, but I swear I didn't kiss her back."

Her eyes snapped to his. "I know what I saw." She narrowed her gaze. "You two looked awfully cozy on the beach this morning, even from far away."

"I'm sure it looked bad." He inhaled then exhaled out a ragged breath. He dropped his hand and rubbed it at the back of his neck. "I know it probably did."

"So." Melissa jutted her chin. "I'm assuming she wants to get back together with you. Why else would she kiss you?"

"You're right." He put his hand in his pocket. "Ashley does want to get back together, and she did try to kiss me. But—"

"Unbelievable." Melissa snatched up some sandy towels and slammed the trunk closed. "Like I said—" she brushed past him and spoke over her shoulder, "—best of luck to the both of you." She trudged up the porch steps and tossed the dirty towels on top of her bag.

He only made it up half the steps before she veered past him, heading back to her car. "Wait. Would you please give me a moment to explain?"

Melissa opened the back passenger side door. Half her body disappeared inside. He came up next to the car and glanced inside to see Ellie fast asleep. "I get it." She gathered up Ellie, gently positioning her against her chest. Her arms full, she closed the door with her hip. "I can't talk right now. I'm going to have to wake Ellie up to bathe her before I put her in bed. She'll be cranky and irritable, and frankly, I am too. Let's leave this until morning. Maybe by then I'll have cooled off."

"I didn't kiss Ashley back." He raked his hard with his fingers. "And I don't want to be with her—I want to be with you!"

"Shh," Melissa hissed. But it was too late. Ellie stirred and started to whine. "See? I can't do this right now."

"Then let me help you put her to sleep."

"No." She brushed Ellie's hair out of her eyes and tried to soothe her. "Summer is almost over. I'm going to go back to Boston early. My work called about a few projects that came up, and they offered me extra pay to return a week early." Ellie started to wail. Melissa pushed past him. "I don't know, Luke—" She climbed the stairs, Ellie's crying vibrating between them. He trailed along beside her. "How was this going to work, anyway? Maybe you should be with Ashley. She lives here, and I don't."

"When did you decide to leave a week early?" Luke asked.

This couldn't be happening. Though she stood right in front of him, it was like a brick wall had been built between them.

"I decided an hour ago. They left a message for me when I had my phone turned off, I checked my messages after I dropped Olivia and Cole home. I just called them back before I drove here."

"Okay." Luke rubbed his jaw. Melissa had to leave early. Their summer was ending sooner than he'd anticipated. They would be separated for a short time. But as soon as he figured things out with the B&B and found a job in Boston, he'd move to be near her and Ellie. This only moved up his timeline a bit; it wasn't the end of the world. He'd stop at nothing for them to be together, because he'd . . . he'd fallen in love with her. "I see why you need to return early. I can handle that, but I still want us to try and make this work. I promise I'll find a way for us to be together."

Ellie continued to cry. Melissa opened the front door and put her down on the couch inside. She then went back out and gathered up her belongings and tossed them in the foyer.

"What is there to figure out? I'm leaving. You'll live here. I'll live there. I was living in a dream world, forgetting that in real life we have things to worry about like rent and bills. I let myself believe the fantasy, and now I'm not sure if any of it was even real."

"It is real. Please, you have to believe me," he pleaded.

Melissa placed a hand on Luke's chest and directed him backward a step. "I don't know anymore. I'm—confused."

"Confused?"

"Why do you just keep repeating everything I'm saying?"

A crying Ellie came and wrapped her arms around Melissa's legs. She patted her back. "Are you sure you want this?" She nudged her head toward Ellie. "It isn't all sunshine and rainbows."

"I do. I want it." He boldly met her gaze and held it.

"No, you don't. No rational guy would." Melissa reached for the door. Luke sidestepped out of the way. "Goodbye." Then she shut it.

He stared back at the closed door. Stunned, he didn't move for at least two minutes. How had everything fallen apart in less than a day? Why did she refuse to hear him out?

Because she's scared.

He was too.

CHAPTER TWENTY-THREE

A tremor worked its way through her body, making Melissa shake. Tears stung at the corners of her eyes. And Ellie wailed. She scooped her up in her arms and whispered into her ear.

"It's okay. I'm here." Ellie adjusted herself so her head rested against Melissa's shoulder. "You're only tired. I'll get you rinsed off and into bed in no time."

"Okay." Her cries subsided. She hiccupped as they moved up the stairs to the bathroom. "I wanted Luke to stay. Why did you make him leave?"

Her arms tightened around Ellie. She entered the bathroom and set her down on the closed toilet seat. "Luke couldn't stay." Melissa started the bathwater, pushing up the lever so the water would fill the tub.

"But I wanted him to stay."

She sat down on the edge of the filling tub. "I know." She motioned for her to come closer. Ellie jumped off the toilet seat and stepped in front of her. She helped her disrobe and climb into the warm water.

"Tell him to come back." Ellie picked up the bottle of bubble bath and squeezed some under the running water.

"It's late. We're all tired. Tomorrow we have to pack everything up to go home."

Bubbles began to fill up the tub. With the water high enough, Melissa turned off the tap and sat down on the toilet.

Ellie gathered up some bubbles and popped them between her hands. "Will Luke come home with us to Boston?"

Startled, Melissa almost fell off the toilet seat. "No—no, he'll stay here."

"When will I see him again? I like him." Ellie picked up a toy whale and dunked it under the bubbles. "Wait, I know! What if he could be my dad?"

"Oh, honey," Melissa tried her best to keep her voice even.

Ellie brought the whale out of the water and spun it in the air. "So, can he?" She dipped the whale back down into the water.

"Can he what?" Melissa rubbed her hands back and forth over the top of her thighs.

"Be my dad."

"I wish it was that easy." She rose and kneeled in front of the tub. "I don't know." She grabbed the shampoo and squeezed some into her hands. "Dunk yourself so I can wash your hair."

Ellie shifted back and dunked her head under the water. When she came back up, Melissa rubbed the shampoo into her hair.

"I want Luke to be my dad."

"I know." She finished scrubbing Ellie's hair and rinsed it out with a cup of water. "You've made that very clear."

A whirl of doubt whizzed through her. How careless she had been with bringing Luke into their lives. There was something about this place, the Cape, that made her rational and logical self completely forget about the consequences of real life. She hated that they would be leaving the Cape with more baggage than when they came.

With Ellie's hair and body washed, Melissa pushed the lever to drain the bathwater. "Okay, Missy it's time for bed." She swiped a clean towel out of the linen closet in the corner of the bathroom, holding it out for her.

With the towel wrapped tightly around her little body, she said, "I love it here." She brushed her sopping hair out of her eyes.

Melissa opened a drawer and retrieved the hairbrush, motioning with a finger for her to come closer. "I do too." She gathered Ellie's hair into one hand and brushed through the strands with the other. "But this is a vacation. It isn't real life. In a few weeks, you'll start kindergarten, and I have to go back to work."

"Will Luke visit us?" Her voice was full of hope.

It nearly broke Melissa. Their eyes locked in the mirror. "I'm not sure, but I'd be lying if I didn't say I want him to." She finished brushing and began to braid Ellie's hair.

"Then just tell him you want him to come."

"Come where?" She secured the end of the braid with a hairband.

"To Boston."

"Ahh." With one hand, she plucked the brush off the counter and placed it back into the drawer. "I don't know if that's possible. We'll see."

"If you don't ask him, then I will."

"Okay." She directed her out of the bathroom with two firm hands on her tiny shoulders. "Time for bed."

Later that evening, after Ellie fell back asleep, Melissa took a cup of tea out to the back patio. The dark sky was nearly starless tonight and only half a moon reflected on the water. She knew she needed to hear Luke out. If he said that Ashley had tried to kiss him, but he didn't kiss her back, then she wanted desperately to believe him. But Grant had cheated on her.

There had been signs, little clues here and there, but she had been too naïve and blind to see what was right in front of her. Despite her past, though, her gut told her that this was different. Luke was different.

Even so, it didn't solve the problem that she was headed back to Boston and Luke's life was here. Maybe it was better this way. She had had her fun, her summer fling. But summers always ended and vacations didn't last forever. Duty called.

———

How could he get Melissa to let him explain? She had completely shut him out.

He sat stiffly on his couch with Gigi curled up next to him. Then he called his last hope, Andrew. After a few rings, he picked it up.

"What?" Andrew asked flatly.

"Well, hello to you too." Luke propped his legs up on his coffee table and crossed his ankles.

"Olivia spent the entire day with Melissa, so don't act like she didn't tell me all about you kissing Ashley."

He gulped. "I didn't kiss her." His jaw tightened.

"That's not what Olivia says. She says that Melissa saw you kissing Ashley."

"Do you hear yourself? You know me. I would never do that to your sister." Luke pinched the bridge of his nose. "Correction. Ashley tried to kiss me, and I ducked out of the way. I did not want her to kiss me in any shape or form. Do you really think I'd do that? I'm not that guy."

"I don't know." Andrew exhaled loudly on the other end of the phone. "Olivia came home, guns blazing, telling me what a piece of trash you were. And if you did kiss Ashley, then I'd have to agree with her. But—you are my best friend, and I've known you long enough to know you aren't a cheater. So, let's say I do believe you. Melissa still hates you. How do you plan to fix this?"

Abruptly, he stood and paced his living room. Gigi hopped off the couch and followed him back and forth. "Why do you think I called you?" He rubbed the back of his neck. "You're my last hope. Tell me what to do."

He heard some muffled noises on the other end, then Andrew yelled, "Olivia, I need your help." Andrew spoke to him again. "I'm going to ask her for advice, give me a second. I'm putting you on hold."

The phone went quiet. He decided to take Gigi out to do her business on the front lawn. With the phone still glued to his ear, he led her outside. Gigi pranced down the steps while Luke sat in one of the porch chairs. He double-checked the connection and saw that Andrew still had him on hold.

Another few minutes passed, then Olivia said, "Andrew is putting Cole to bed. I told him I'd talk to you."

He straightened his back. "Great, can you help me?"

"Summer is ending, Luke. Melissa has gone into protection mode. Let's say I believe you, and you didn't kiss Ashley—"

"I didn't," Luke interjected.

"Fine, you didn't kiss her. But now what? Melissa knows summer is over, and she's going back to Boston. I think she's thinking about the long game here. She's probably convincing herself that it's best to break up now, because she's leaving. And don't even begin to think long-distance with a single mom is going to work; it's not."

"I'm working on it." He ran a hand through his hair. Gigi finished and trekked back up the steps. He patted his lap, and she jumped up onto him.

"Quote 'Working on it' isn't going to be enough. You better have a plan, and you better lay it out to her. If not, sorry—this is over. There is no way Melissa is headed back to Boston with any loose strings."

"I have a few interviews in Boston next week."

"You do?"

"Yes, I've been working with a headhunter." He stroked Gigi between her ears. She settled further against his chest. "I'm also working on finding a company to manage Bayberry House."

"Why haven't you told Melissa any of this?"

"Because I'm an idiot," he muttered.

"Clearly."

Why hadn't he been truthful with Melissa about his plans from the very beginning? Deep down he knew why, but he didn't have the courage to voice it out loud. What if he told Melissa about all these plans and she rejected him? Where did that leave him?

"I'll tell her," Luke replied.

"You'd better."

"But how do I get her to listen?"

Olivia laughed. "If you can figure that out, please let me know. I haven't gotten her to listen to me about anything."

"Awesome."

"You're a smart guy."

"I have my moments."

"You'll come up with something," Olivia said.

"Thanks."

"Anytime."

He ended the call. Gigi fell asleep in his lap. For a long time, he watched as people walked by on their way to Main Street.

He loved Melissa.

He loved Ellie, too.

He couldn't turn back now, even if everything blew up in his face. His only way out of this was through it. Once he had his plan mapped out in his mind, Luke carried Gigi back inside.

CHAPTER TWENTY-FOUR

Melissa tossed the dirty towels and swimsuits into the wash, then cranked the dial. Her shoulders drooped as she went through the quiet house, flipping off lights as she headed to her bedroom. Ellie slept soundly in her room. Their day at Martha's Vineyard had tuckered them both out in many ways. Though Melissa's exhaustion had more to do with her heart than her body.

Her phone in her pocket buzzed, then buzzed again. She tugged it free, expecting the messages to be from Luke, not Olivia.

> Luke called Andrew, and I ended up talking to him.

> I think this was all a big misunderstanding.

Melissa groaned, entering her bedroom and plopping down on her bed. Her fingers zipped across the screen, typing a response.

> Regardless, I'm leaving. And I have a thousand things to do to make that happen.

The three little dots danced at the bottom of her screen. Then her phone buzzed with a message.

> He has a plan. Hear him out.

> No.

There went the dots again, dancing for a long time. She leaned back against the pillows resting against her headboard. Finally, the message appeared.

> Come on now. Don't be stubborn. YOU'VE LOVED HIM YOUR ENTIRE LIFE. If you don't at least listen to him and let him explain, I'll have no choice but to drive over there and hold you hostage until you do.

> You wouldn't dare.

> I have a five-year-old who never sits still! You've no idea what I'm capable of.

With that message, Melissa chuckled to herself. The tension in her shoulders loosened. Maybe all hope wasn't lost.

> Oh, this I've got to see.

> Try me. I'm ready to come. I've gotten my second wind.

> Geez, okay. I'll listen to his so-called plan.

> Great. Now I can use my second wind to deep-clean my bathroom instead.

Melissa tossed her phone onto her bed and covered her eyes with her arm.

Luke wasn't her ex, not even close. Their summer together had been magical. Maybe it didn't have to end. The least she could do was give him a chance to explain. Her mind told her no, but her heart told her yes. She patted the top of the bed, locating her phone.

Then she pulled up the text thread with Luke. Her fingers zipped across the screen.

> Come by tomorrow morning before Ellie wakes up. We can talk then.

Her sweaty palms slipped as she grasped the phone against her chest. Even though the windows were closed, she could hear the calm waves outside. A second later, her phone binged.

> Thank you. I'll be there.

> Don't knock. Just meet me on the patio at 6:30.

> See you then.

Melissa buried herself under the covers and tried to fall asleep. Somewhere in the early hours of the morning, she finally dozed off. When the first rays of sunshine slipped through the curtains, she woke, disoriented. She flipped to her side and read the clock on her nightstand: 6:38. She smoothed her ruffled hair and rubbed her eyes to wake up fully. Then she forced herself to peel back the covers to meet Luke. After she secured her robe around her body, she wandered through the silent house to the patio.

When she pushed open the sliding glass door, Luke glanced over his shoulder from where he sat on the outdoor sofa. Their eyes locked. A familiar tingle swept down her spine. He looked as terrible as she felt.

"Hey." He stood and stepped closer to her.

She closed the door behind her. "Hey." She tugged down her sleeves, wrapping her arms around herself.

His gaze didn't leave her face.

One word—hey. That's all it took.

She marveled at how quickly his presence made her forgive him.

But this was Luke.

Her Luke.

After her mind had cleared last night, she reminded herself their relationship was far different than the one she had with her ex. Luke was steady and reliable. He took the time to get to know Ellie. Somehow, he managed to remember the little details of her life that made her happy. Grant had walked out without ever really trying. But here was Luke, trying. Here he was, showing up. The road ahead, even if it was treacherous, didn't scare him—and that calmed her greatly.

For a second, Luke hesitated, then he shuffled closer and planted a kiss on her cheek. His hand squeezed her arm. "Do you want to sit?" he asked, motioning to the sofa.

"Sure."

He cupped her elbow as she scooted around him and took a seat on the sofa. The morning dew nipped at her skin and made her shiver. She tightened her robe, regretting not grabbing a hoodie. Luke eventually lowered himself beside her. He stole a look at her, but she kept her gaze on the ocean and the sunrise.

The sky grew lighter. She was going to miss this place and what she had here with Luke and Ellie.

"I'm headed back home." She kept her gaze on the ocean. Her terrycloth robe cradled her arms that were folded against her chest. "I've enjoyed our time together."

"Stop."

His commanding tone made her freeze. She loosened her arms and gripped the couch cushion on both sides of her. With a slight head tilt, she met his gaze and waited.

He swallowed, his Adam's apple bobbing up and down. Melissa remembered all over again how his morning scruff rubbed against her cheek, or how much she loved his hair tangled in her fingertips.

Dang, she wanted him. And she didn't care what it looked like. Some of Luke was better than none.

"I've been applying for jobs in Boston. I have a few interviews lined up." He leaned forward and rested his forearms on his thighs, clasping his hands together. "I'm trying to find someone to run Bayberry House for me. I've met with Carol's son, Sam, who runs a property management company. He's helping me find someone to manage the B&B and live on-site full time. I'm ready for a change, but most importantly I want us to be together."

"Boston isn't the Cape." Her fingertips dug into the couch fabric. "I'll be back to work and Ellie will start school. We can't just play all day. Life is hard and stressful. It's nothing like our time here this summer. What if you regret your choice to go back to Boston?"

"I won't." He shifted closer and placed a hand on her shoulder. Her skin warmed from his touch. "I want you. And I know that means following you. You have Ellie, I would never expect you to uproot her."

"You want me?" She felt her cheeks flush. "What about Ashley? If you stayed here, you could just date her."

"I don't want Ashley. She tried to kiss me. I didn't kiss her back. There's nothing to worry about." He moved his hand from her shoulder and wrapped his arm around her. She melted against him, leaning her head against it. "I love you."

Melissa flinched. "You love me?" She peered up at him. Her gaze scrutinized every inch of his face. "Are you sure?"

The words, the ones she had dreamed of hearing for so many years, sounded unreal and foreign coming from his mouth. She loved him, she always had, but she only ever wished for him to say them back.

Luke cupped her cheek with his hand. "Yes." His thumb ran the length of her jaw. "I'm positive. I love you and want us to be together. I want to be Ellie's dad. I want to wake up next to you on the good days and on the bad. I know a life with you and Ellie will be beautiful and wonderful."

"Luke—" She closed her eyes for a moment and reveled in the feeling of his hand against her cheek. She let the words 'I love you' seep into her entire being.

"It's okay—" His voice sounded gruff. "If you don't feel ready to say it back, I only wanted you to know my feelings."

She opened her eyes, meeting his gaze. "No, that's not ..."

"I'm still moving to Boston. I'll wait for you to be ready."

"Luke!" She squeezed his thigh, raising an eyebrow. "Are you kidding me? I've loved you for as long as I've breathed. I was waiting for you to be ready."

He laughed. "So, you love me?"

"Yes, I love you." Melissa cupped his face with her palms. "I love you," she repeated.

Then, his lips collided with hers, his stubble rubbing against her cheek in the best way. Her hand tangled up into his hair, gently massaging his scalp. He deepened the kiss, and she parted her lips. His minty breath made the air spicy. She breathed in his scent, memorizing the slope of his jaw and the roughness of his thumb on her cheek. Her pulse quickened, and her heart soared. She promised herself never to forget this moment.

The sliding door creaked, alerting them to Ellie's presence.

Reluctantly, Melissa tugged her lips from his and smoothed out her ruffled hair. Both their lips buzzed from the kiss.

Ellie popped her head through the door. "There you are! I woke up and nobody was inside." She walked the remaining distance to them. "Luke, you came back!"

Luke smiled. "I did. You couldn't keep me away."

Melissa held out her arms and Ellie climbed up onto her lap, snuggling against her chest. Melissa's robe loosened, and Ellie dipped her arms inside for a little warmth. "I would never leave you." She kissed the top of Ellie's head.

Luke wrapped his arm around Melissa's shoulders, and she rested her head against him. They sat there for a while, just the three of them, watching waves crash on the shore, people walking by on the empty beach, and the seagulls swooping down for yesterday's leftovers.

Come to the Cape. The words vibrated in her mind. Her mom had been right, and she had so much to share with her parents when they came back from their trip. They'd barely spoken with the spotty cruise ship Wi-Fi.

"I don't want to go home." Ellie said, tilting her chin up toward Melissa. "I'll miss everyone too much."

"I'm moving to Boston too," Luke remarked. "I hope I can still see you."

Her eyes widened with delight. "You are? Does this mean you are going to be my dad?"

Luke chuckled. "Well—"

Melissa's cheeks burned. "A lot of things need to happen before then."

"Why?" Ellie pouted. "I want him to be my dad."

She touched her forehead to Ellie's. "I know, but Luke and I are only dating. We'd have to get married for him to be your dad."

"Okay." Ellie rolled her eyes. "Then get married."

Luke chuckled. "Has anyone ever told you that you'd make a great matchmaker?" He ran a hand over Ellie's hair, smoothing it out.

Ellie twisted to peer up at him. "What's a matchmaker?"

"Someone who—" interjected Melissa, "never mind, it's not important. The important thing is this isn't goodbye to Luke forever. We'll see him again in Boston."

"Fine." Ellie shrugged. "I guess Boston won't be too bad if you're coming back too." Then she climbed out of Melissa's lap and into Luke's. She wrapped her little arms around his neck, and Luke hugged her back.

He kissed the top of her head, then glanced over at Melissa and said, "I love you." Then he picked up Melissa's hand and kissed her knuckles.

"I love you too, Luke," Ellie piped in.

Luke chuckled and ruffled her hair. "I'm glad to hear it."

Melissa smiled. Their eyes locked as Ellie glanced between them.

Then she mouthed back, "I love you, too."

Then Luke wrapped his other arm around her shoulders while he held onto Ellie. Together, they watched as the beach filled up with early risers claiming their spots before it became too crowded.

"I'm hungry," Ellie declared.

Melissa laughed. "You always are." She scooted to the edge of the couch. "Come on, I can make breakfast. I'll make waffles, Luke's favorite." She smiled at him. "I'll even let you put Hershey's kisses on top and let them melt until into a pile of ooey-gooey goodness."

"That's the only way I like them," Ellie replied.

"Me too, kid," Luke smiled. "Me too."

EPILOGUE

Six months later, Luke waited outside Ellie's school. The winter wind nipped at his skin, and he popped the collar of his black peacoat to fight against the relentless chill. He'd taken off a half day from his new job at a law firm in downtown Boston. After he picked up Ellie, he planned on spoiling her by taking her ice skating at the Boston Common Frog Pond. It was located only a few blocks from Ellie and Melissa's apartment. Luke's apartment was only one train stop off the Red Line from them.

Melissa couldn't get the day off, but she planned to meet up with them for dinner. He was more than happy to step in to help make Ellie's birthday special. After he signed a contract with Sam's management company to take over the responsibilities of the day-to-day operations of the B&B, he had moved back to Boston. Then a few weeks later, he had returned to law.

Some days he missed Bayberry House, but he also loved working in the field of his choice. Melissa settled back into her job too which meant they had to be strategic about making time for one another.

Children trickled out of the brick building, scattering as they found their parents. Ellie spotted him and bounded down the steps with a construction paper art project in one hand.

"Luke!" She shouted, sprinting toward him once she hit the bottom step.

He crouched down and held his arms out to her. "Happy Birthday, birthday girl." She wrapped her tiny hands around his neck, and he hugged her tightly. "I can't believe you're six."

They broke their embrace.

From his pocket, he pulled out a Hershey's kiss. "This is for you."

She beamed and snatched it out of his hand. "Here, I made this for you." She held out the construction paper.

His hand flew to his chest, and he took it from her. "For me?" He smiled brightly as he studied what he believed to be a rainbow made from construction paper. She unrolled the foil wrapper from the Hershey's kiss and popped the chocolate into her mouth. "It's beautiful. I'll put it on my fridge."

"I knew you would like it." She handed him the foil wrapper.

He shoved the wrapper into his pocket with his free hand. "Can I put this masterpiece in your backpack, so it doesn't get lost?"

"Sure." She spun halfway so he could unzip it and put the paper inside. "Do you think I look older and taller now that I'm six?"

"A thousand percent."

He clearly answered correctly, because she beamed back at him. "I know. I think so too. Six is way older than five."

"For sure." Luke guided her around the crowded sidewalk of the other parents and children, leading her toward the subway.

"Axel in my class is still only five."

"You don't say—"

"I'm older than him, and he hates it." Her teeth chattered.

Luke stopped and crouched in front of her. "Here," he said, starting to button her jacket, "let's button your jacket. Where is your scarf and hat?" He continued up the jacket until he reached the top.

"They are in my backpack in the front pocket. I took them off at recess because I got too hot."

He motioned for her to turn around again. After he unzipped her backpack, he retrieved her scarf and hat. "Well, we are going ice skating." He placed the wool cap on her head. "You'll need these. It's even colder on the ice." He wrapped the scarf around her neck.

"But it's so itchy," she complained, scrunching her nose.

"Uh-oh." He loosened the scarf and readjusted the hat. "Is that better?"

She nodded. "Much better."

He zipped her backpack up. They walked to the subway, taking the Red Line to Boston Common. Before he knew it, they were skating around the rink on the Boston Common Frog Pond.

Ellie held onto his hand. He skated close to the wall in case he needed it for support.

"What do you hope to get for your birthday this year?" Luke asked.

He knew Melissa had purchased a huge wooden dollhouse for her. He had spent several nights putting it together. The plan was for Melissa to move it into Ellie's room before they got home tonight so Ellie could see it when she walked in.

"Lots of things." Ellie rattled off a few items on her wish list. Luke nodded along, half-listening to her laundry list of things. Luckily, a dollhouse was on it. Then he heard her say, "But most of all, I hope you can be my dad for real."

"Oh," he grabbed onto the wall, bringing them to a stop. "You know I want that too."

"Then why aren't you, already?"

"Here," he said, leading them to the exit, "let's take a little break." They left the ice and hobbled over to a bench to rest. After they sat, he continued, "Ellie, in order for me to be your dad, your mom and I would have to get married."

With wide eyes, she said, "I know. So get married already."

"I know. I want that too."

"My mom wants to marry you. I heard her talking on the phone with Aunt Olivia about it."

Luke smiled. He and Melissa had discussed it at length. He knew they'd get married, it was just a matter of when. A month after moving to Boston, he'd gone and purchased a ring. But then he chickened out and decided he needed to pump the brakes and not scare her away. Especially, when they needed to adjust to everyday life together.

"Don't worry. It's coming."

Ellie clapped her hands together. "Can I wear a pretty dress too?"

"You bet, kiddo."

He heard his name and shifted his head toward the sound. Melissa waved, headed toward them from the other side of the frozen pond.

They waved back.

"Ellie."

"Yeah?"

"I love you and your mom so much."

Ellie hopped off the bench. Melissa rounded the corner, nearing them. "I know, silly," Ellie said. Then she scampered the remaining yards in her ice skates and leapt into her mom's arms.

Melissa spun her around and Luke stared in awe. His heart

melted in his chest. How had he managed to find not one but two beautiful people to be in his life?

She kissed Ellie on the cheek. "How's my birthday girl doing? Did you like ice skating?" Then, she glanced up and winked at Luke.

"It was great."

"I'm glad to hear it." Gingerly, she set Ellie back down on the ground. Then she leaned in and gave him a quick peck. "Are you ready to eat dinner?"

"Sure," Luke replied. "Where are we going again?"

"Regina's Pizza," Ellie said happily.

"Yum. My favorite." He smiled. "How did you know?"

They removed their skates, retrieving their shoes and belongings. As they walked through Boston Common to leave, Melissa and Luke each held one of Ellie's hands. He couldn't remember a time when he felt this at peace.

From over the top of Ellie's head, he caught Melissa's gaze. "Marry me." The words slipped before he could overthink them.

Melissa's jaw dropped and she stopped. Ellie did too and looked between Luke and Melissa.

"Are you being serious right now?" Melissa asked.

Boldly, he held her gaze. "Of course, I would never joke about something like that."

Ellie squeezed both of their hands and jumped up and down excitedly. "Say yes! Say yes!"

"Do you even have a ring?" Melissa peered down at Ellie, then back over at Luke.

Luke tucked his hand into the pocket of his coat and pulled out a small box. "I've had this since the first month I moved here. I've just been waiting for the right moment."

"Really?" Her eyes sparkled.

Luke nodded, then bent down and opened the ring box.

Melissa gasped. Her hands flew to her mouth, covering it. "Luke!"

"Ooooh, it's so sparkly," Ellie exclaimed.

"Melissa, I love you." Luke locked eyes with Melissa. "I love Ellie too. I promise to love both of you for the rest of my life. You make everything better. Will you marry me?"

Tears tickled the corners of her eyes. "Yes! A hundred times, yes." She swiped at her tears as they spilled over. "I love you more than anything."

Luke grinned as he rose and slid the ring onto her finger.

After the ring was secure on her finger, Melissa cradled his face in her hands. "I can't wait to marry you." She kissed him sweetly.

"Me too, Melon." He laughed. "Thanks for waiting for me to figure everything out."

"It was worth the wait." She kissed him on the cheek. "You were worth the wait."

Ellie wiggled her way between them and hugged their knees. Luke lifted Ellie into his arms and kissed her on the cheek. "Thanks for sharing your mom with me."

"You're welcome," Ellie said, beaming.

Then Luke retrieved a whole handful of Hershey's kisses from his coat pocket. "These are for you." He placed them in Ellie's hands. "So you can remember today too."

"Yum, my favorite!" Some of the Hershey's kisses dropped out of her hands and landed on the ground. Ellie leapt out of his arms and gathered them up. "And mom can't even get mad when I eat them all."

Melissa laughed. "Why won't I get mad?"

"Because they're from Luke." Ellie shoved some into each of her pockets but left one out to unwrap. "And you always let me eat as many Hershey's kisses as I want." She put one into her mouth.

"I usually only give you one at a time," Melissa remarked.

"But today is special," Ellie said.

Melissa caught Luke's gaze. He smiled back at her and winked.

"It is special," Luke piped up, "very special indeed."

MEET THE AUTHOR

Emi Hilton is a California native who was born at March Air Force Base, to an Officer in the US Army Combat Engineer Battalion father and an English Professor mother. Emi followed in her mother's footsteps and graduated from Brigham Young University in English. While in college, she took a year and a half break from her studies to serve as a full-time missionary for her church in the Canary Islands. Emi writes sweet contemporary romance novels. Her novels, Memories in Morro Bay, Bluebird Sky and Picking Pismo were nominated for Whitney Awards. Her novel, Picking Pismo, won the Christlit Book Award. When Emi isn't writing, she enjoys training for marathons, fishing off local piers with her husband and three sons, or visiting her other love, Spain.

www.5princebooks.com
Come to the Cape *Emi Hilton*
Time To Byrne *S.E. Reichert*
Having the Vampier's Baby *Courtney Davis*
Bookish *Bernadette Marie*
Dare You to Choose Truth *Lauren Lipp*
Enlightenment *Nicole Kelley*
All the Little Moments *Savannah Reed*
The Rocking of the Ocean *Barbara Matteson*
New to Newport *Emi Hilton*
Trusting the Alpha *Courtney Davis*
Enlightenment *Nicole Kelley*
Sweet Summertide *Sarah Dressler*
All the Little Moments *Savannah Reed*
No Words After I Love You *S.E. Reichert*
Demons and Tea Leaves *Courtney Davis*
Shadow of the Throne *Russell Archey*
Shadow Among the Stars *Courtney Davis*
The Pack *E.C. Saulness*

www.ingramcontent.com/pod-product-compliance
Lightning Source LLC
Chambersburg PA
CBHW032209030726
47494CB00020B/931